RETURN TO CARTERVILLE

RETURN TO CARTERVILLE

A CARTERVILLE MYSTERY

ROBERT J. MCCARTER

LITTLE HUMMINGBIRD PUBLISHING

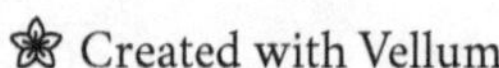 Created with Vellum

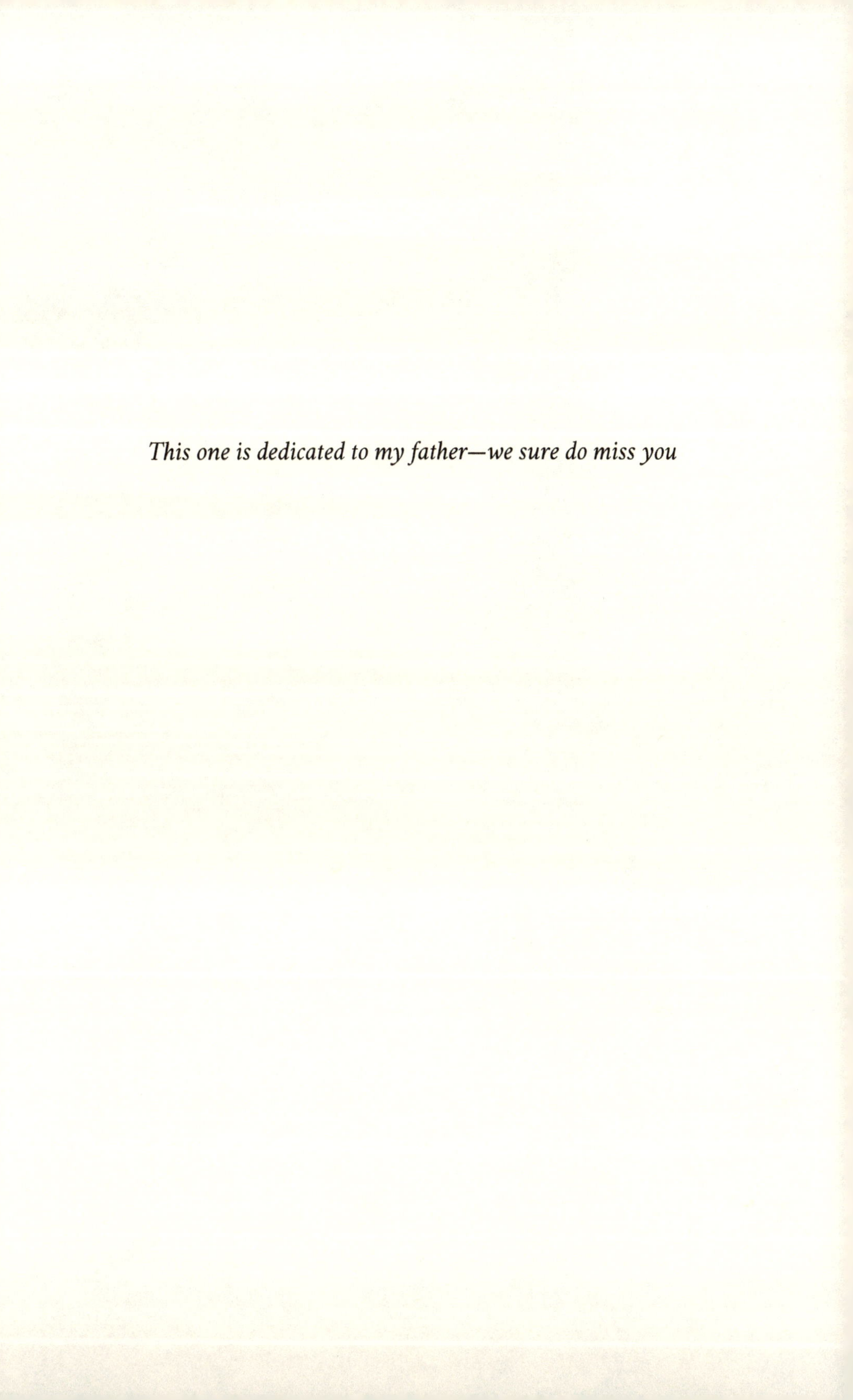

This one is dedicated to my father—we sure do miss you

CARTERVILLE MYSTERIES

Each Carterville Mystery is stand-alone, but things do change in Carterville. The chronological order of the books are:

- **Out of a Christmas Sky**
- **Destroyer of Carterville**
- **The Blood of Carterville**
- **Faces of Carterville**
- **Return to Carterville**

Note: The events of this story take place immediately after *Faces of Carterville* and nine months after *The Blood of Carterville*.

Unlike *Out of a Christmas Sky*, *Destroyer of Carterville*, and *The Blood of Carterville*, this book contains many explicit spoilers for those books as well as *Faces of Carterville*.

PROLOGUE

PEOPLE THINK OF ARIZONA LIKE ONE BIG DESERT, LIKE ALL OF IT looks like Phoenix or Tucson, or maybe if they know a little bit more about it, like the Grand Canyon. This vast expanse of desert filled with cacti, sandstone structures, with a couple of cities sprawled across it.

This, of course, is not true. Arizona is dry, although much of it is not technically a desert, and it is a big state, but there are mountains and forests, even some rivers and lakes here and there.

There are places in Arizona where you can quickly go from the mountains to the high desert, from trees to cacti, in just a few minutes. There's the wonder of the Grand Canyon, the cool expanse of the White Mountains, the 12,633-foot-tall Humphrey's Peak, the Colorado River that defines much of the western edge of the state. There's dozens of old mines and the towns built around them with the dramatic history of places like Tombstone, and the stunning turquoise waters of Havasupai.

Arizona isn't just one thing. And that goes for its people, those that were born here or those that feel this land in their bones and have adopted it as their own.

And that goes for me, too.

My name is Henry Carter, and even though I wear a cowboy hat and a badge, even though I am an Arizona boy through and through, even though I have been the elected chief of police of Carterville, Arizona—a town that my ancestor founded—and even though those things say a lot about me, that's not all that I am.

Don't get me wrong. Your history informs you. Your job shapes you. Where you live changes you. But just like Arizona is not just a vast desert with a few sprawling cities, I'm not just a divorced middle-aged white guy with a gun and a badge.

And if you've heard of Carterville, it's not just a small, historic mountain town with a bunch of people with strange powers granted when a meteor struck and tunneled into the mines below our homes eight years ago.

Carterville is a small town with many of those small-town characteristics, like a gossip network that seems to travel faster than the speed of light, and folks do have powers, but only those that were there when the meteor struck, and those powers only work if you are within about five miles of the center of town.

The town and its people are more informed by the hard work and rich history of this old mining town than by the powers that have been around for a few years.

The truth is both my gun and my badge are gone. I was

maneuvered out of Carterville and my own power was used against me so that I can never return.

Literally. I can't go back to Carterville.

When writing these stories in the past, whenever I could, I've been coy about what really happened to oust me from my job as chief of police of Carterville. At least when it comes to the "who." The "why" is still a bit of a mystery. I don't know much more than I was dubbed a "Destroyer of Carterville" by one of Carterville's rare superpowered individuals and my exit was engineered to "save" Carterville.

But what does any of that really mean?

I hid the "who" in some of my writings because I love a good mystery and I hate spoilers, but there is no telling this story without talking about the "who."

Carterville is an old mining town in Northern Arizona draped on a large hill which in turn sits on the slopes of the San Francisco Peaks. Carterville, as of this writing, has a population of 282 with 195 of those people with some kind of power.

Despite my carefully engineered exit, where my power was used against me, I am going to attempt to return to Carterville. All my other stories about the place have been written after the fact, all after I had been forced to leave, all with some of the clarity that hindsight brings, written to try to help me understand what the hell happened.

I can't say I was successful on that count. I do know what happened, that is clear, but I don't really know why, but at least I do have some more perspective on the people and the events.

This time, though, I am going to write this as I go along, as it is happening, as a diary, if you will.

It may be a tad cliché, but I'm one of those cops that carry around a little notebook in their back pocket to take notes. Because it works for me. It helps me process things through a different part of my brain. It helps me remember.

And that is what I'm trying to do here with this. So, fair warning to readers, provided this ever sees the light of day, this may not be structured quite how you would like and there is no way I can be coy about who removed me from Carterville and what her power is.

Consider this your spoiler warning. There will be many spoilers in these pages, big spoilers to all the other stories of Carterville I have written. I can't help it this time. If I am to return, I have to really look at the past and how I got here.

Okay. You have been warned. Here we go.

PART 1
FUTURE THINKING

ONE

SUNDAY, JUNE 14. FOUR CORNERS MONUMENT

PATTY WALSH WAS STILL WITH ME EVEN THOUGH I LEFT HER IN Pagosa Springs, Colorado, yesterday. I could smell her scent, clean and slightly flowery. I could see the sadness in her green eyes as we said goodbye. I could almost still feel her embrace, which was a lot fiercer than I thought it would be.

I went there to help her through what she thought might be a haunting. And it was, in part, but it was not ghosts that haunted her, but the past. The same past that haunts me.

I met Patty right after she arrived in Carterville and she left right after I did. The trauma of that night, when my enemies panicked and tried to kill us both, was too much for her to stay.

I understand why she can't go back, but I still wish she could. That we both could. That our long flirtation could finally blossom into something. But she can't go back and I have to. Or, at least, I have to try.

Thoughts of Patty were incongruous as I watched a family of four laughing as they straddled the Four Corners Monument and literally existed in four states at once. It's like they were playing a strange game of Twister with the mom, dad, and two kids trying to touch all four states at once while someone else, maybe Grandma, took a picture.

There were smiles and laughter as the family ticks something off their Southwest tourist bucket list.

Four Corners is the spot where the borders of Colorado, New Mexico, Arizona, and Utah all come together. It's a strange anomaly, the square edges of all four states joining like that.

We're in the middle of the desert on the Navajo Reservation. There's a nice paved plaza with a round marble disk about six or eight feet in diameter where the states met. Engraved along the edge of the granite were two words per state. It read, "HERE MEET, IN FREEDOM, UNDER GOD, FOUR STATES." The "UNDER GOD" part is in Arizona where I'm going and "HERE MEET" in Colorado where I am coming from.

The place has been upgraded since the last time I was here, with four rows of booths lining the four edges of the plaza where merchants show their wares, mostly Navajo jewelry. Instead of hastily constructed wood shelters, the booths were made of local sandstone and topped with a red metal roof.

It's been about two decades since I was here last, when I brought my own son and my wife-at-the-time so we could play the Four Corners style of Twister and be in four states at once.

I don't remember the plaza that well, but it was a lot less

than this, a much smaller square of cement with a metal marker in the middle and the states' names etched in cement.

The metal marker was there, in the middle of the marble disk, but everything around it has transformed. It's more of a fancy rest stop that costs $8 to enter now.

Going through Four Corners and Monument Valley is the quickest way from Southern Colorado to Northern Arizona, but I usually don't stop.

It's a fun concept, being in four states at once, but it's the kind of tourist trap where the novelty fades quickly. Here you need about ten seconds on that granite disk to say you did it, whereas you could spend a lifetime at the Grand Canyon and not see everything.

Four Corners is a strictly human concept made up of arbitrary borders that we drew, whereas the Grand Canyon is a product of nature and time.

Maybe I stopped here because this is a metaphor for me, somehow, as I start my journey back to Carterville. Maybe I am occupying four different "states," or I am of four different minds, or there are four different factions battling it out for Carterville, or something like that.

I don't usually try to read the tea leaves of circumstance like that. I'm more of a "shit happens" kind of guy and don't normally attempt to assign meaning to every little thing, but today I felt compelled to come here and I have the time for contemplation.

I've had a lot of that lately and am still getting used to it.

The entrance to the monument is in New Mexico, and I was camping in Colorado last night and I have been careful as I walked in to not step foot in Arizona. Yet.

Maybe this was symbolic. Maybe I should step over from Colorado to Arizona as a ceremonial step back to my home.

The first family left and a couple took their place, each doing a Twister pose of some sort while the other took a picture.

I slowly walked the booths on the New Mexico side, smiling at the wrinkled Navajo grandmothers with their moccasins, pleated velvet skirts, and light, cotton shirts. This being a major tourist trap, they had pulled out the stops and have on their famous turquoise and silver jewelry, including some impressive squash blossom necklaces.

I thought of Isabella Ortega, the young woman that used to be one of my officers in Carterville but is now the acting chief of police. She's a quarter Navajo and speaks the language fluently, which would change my experience here if she was with me, turning me from a white tourist into someone of interest.

I talk to her, often, as she wrestles with the complexities of Carterville and its chaotic swirl of powers. About nine months ago, when I was leaving, we sat on my deck watching the sun go down over the desert and she practically begged me to come back, but I couldn't see a way then and I can now.

That turned my mind back to Patty. I felt her presence and my heart longed to be near her again. I was quite sure this ache I was feeling wouldn't go away soon, but I longed to be back home more.

Patty was the key here. She's the reason I can step over the border back to Arizona with any hope of getting back to Carterville. Her Carterville power was one of empathy. She could feel what other people wanted and that means she knows Winston "Smitty" Smith much better than I do. She knows what he wants, and, by extension, what he fears.

Smitty is the one that executed my exit from Carterville, extracting a promise from me that I would never return. He had found out what my power was. The media now calls me the "Promise Keeper" because mine is the power of promises kept. If someone makes a promise to me or I to someone else, while in the zone of influence of Carterville, it will be kept.

Which means that as soon as I try to return to Carterville, as soon as I cross into the zone of influence, I will be compelled to leave. And this is not some mild compulsion—it's like the scratch you just have to itch multiplied about a hundred times.

In the darkness of her lakeside home in Pagosa Springs, Colorado, after the last mystery had been solved, Patty told me what Smitty feared. She told me how to return to Carterville.

To do so, I have to convince Smitty to release me from my promise. It's the only way my power will let me back. But to do that, I have to, basically, con him into thinking he needs me. The problem being I am a cop, not a conman. I have built my life around honesty.

I feel more than a little conflicted about this, which is why I think I took the turn and came here.

I smiled at the two women at the booth I was at. One was a well-tanned and wrinkled Navajo woman, the most wrin-kled one I had seen today. Her skin, which has been darkened by the sun, looked like the desert where rain erodes it. Contrasting nicely with her black shirt was an epic squash blossom necklace that must have weighed several pounds.

If you've never seen one, they vary quite a bit, but they are large with turquoise embedded in silver with the bottom being an elaborate inverted crescent.

This woman's necklace was traditional and, in my understanding, marked her as an elder of note.

Sitting next to her was a girl, maybe ten, probably her granddaughter, in shorts and a Sponge Bob T-shirt, her legs swinging on the plastic folding chair she was sitting on.

"Ya-ta-hey," I said to the elder, tipping my cowboy hat and trying to not mangle the pronunciation too much. Yá'át'ééh is used as a greeting but its literal meaning is something along the lines of "it is good."

The grandmother smiled and said, "Yá'át'ééh." The deep lines around her eyes furrowing deeper and it seemed like she appreciated the effort but thankfully didn't say anything more in Navajo. The girl barely glanced at me.

I picked up a bolo tie. It had an irregularly shaped chunk of turquoise shot with what looked like copper. There wasn't much silver to it, just enough to hold the stone fashioned to look like the braided cord the bolo was attached to.

I'm not much for jewelry. I was happy to wear my wedding ring when I was married, but that's been a long time, and I have finally embraced the fitness tracker my sister gave me after a heart scare a few years ago, but there was something about this piece that called to me.

The grandmother started speaking in Navajo and I wanted to just close my eyes and let it wash over me. I don't know how to describe the language—it has these harsh guttural sounds while still sounding musical, giving it a kind of mystical quality.

I know it's just a language, one I have been fascinated with my entire life, but have never bothered to learn. We took so much from the Native Americans that it would somehow feel wrong to me to learn their language.

But maybe that's just me.

The girl seemed to wake up, and when the older woman stopped speaking and nodded to her, the girl stopped swinging her legs and looked at me. "You are him," she said.

"Excuse me?" I asked.

"The Promise Keeper," the old woman said, her voice dry and raspy, her accent thick, and then she spoke to her granddaughter briefly in Navajo.

"She says," the girl began, her brow furrowing, "'I had begun to think this day would never come. She said you would come, the young white girl with hair the color of wheat in fall, but I did not believe it. Her eyes were haunted but I thought she was too young to speak to the Kachina on Sacred Mountain. Now I know I was wrong.'"

I just stood there, my jaw hanging open. I did get recognized, there had been enough publicity around Carterville and some of the high-profile crimes I dealt with, but it was a shock to be recognized here, and the way she spoke made me want to run away, head back to Colorado and never come back.

Because there could only be one young white girl she was speaking of. One that could see the future. And even though Smitty had executed my departure from Carterville, maybe even thought it was his idea, it was this person that actually engineered it.

And her reference to Kachina and Sacred Mountain was clearly about Carterville and our powers. The San Francisco Peaks is one of the four mountains sacred to the Navajo, and

Carterville sits on its slopes. I don't feel qualified to represent their beliefs, but Kachina are powerful spirit beings that live on the mountain, and from this Navajo's perspective they must be where our powers come from.

The grandmother started speaking to the girl in Navajo again, and as much as I wanted to run away, I couldn't.

TWO

SUNDAY, JUNE 14. FOUR CORNERS
MONUMENT

IT'S TIME FOR THOSE SPOILERS I PROMISED. IT'S TIME TO TALK about how I got here and why Smitty is not my real problem in returning to Carterville.

If you've read my other stories, this is just your "previously on" catchup where the spoilers will be coming at you fast and furious. If you haven't read those other stories… well, it's rather complicated and hard to condense since we are talking about humans with all their complexities here, but I will try.

When Patty and I were talking about it in the dark in her home, it seemed so clear and so easy. Just freak Smitty out enough so that he feels like he needs me to protect him again, and then I'm back.

But a price was paid for our exit, several people died, and a number went to jail. One of those was Smitty, and one of the others is known as the Fortune Teller.

Seems like a stupid name to me and doesn't even begin to explain her power, but it is what it is.

Her name is Brooke Jennings and she can see the future and, more than that, she can see many possible futures depending on choices she imagines.

Brooke is currently in jail in Florence, Arizona, and she knowingly created the future that landed her there. With all her power, all her ability, she believed in something enough so that she manipulated events to achieve that goal and the best she could see for herself was a nice, long stint in prison.

This says a lot about the level of her conviction. She believed she was saving Carterville... she believed it was worth going to jail for... and she believed she was saving Carterville from Smitty and me. At least, that's what she told us.

She also manipulated things so that three people died, my on-again-off-again girlfriend Annie Smith began to hate me, and she drove a wedge between Smitty and me so serious that he engineered my exit with Annie's help.

That all sounds a little silly in only a few paragraphs. I spent many hundreds of pages and three different books telling the real story, but that is the outline of it. I am up against someone who saw the future and sacrificed a normal life to get me out of Carterville.

And I don't have so much of an ego as to think that without Brooke's influence that things between Smitty and me wouldn't have gotten as bad as it did—our bad blood goes way back, long before powers—or that the toxic nature of our relationship wasn't bad for Carterville. It's just that Smitty with his healing superpower will make it back to Carterville soon, and that terrifies me.

The rumors are that the governor is thinking of commuting Smitty's sentence. His wife, who he is devoted to, is sick. A reoccurrence of colon cancer giving Smitty one hell of a hand to play since he can heal her.

For all those years since the meteor hit, since we all got our powers, I have been resisting Smitty's influence, his need to turn Carterville into *his* town, into a town that serves him. What will happen to Carterville if Smitty returns and I don't?

I am not one for hate. It's an emotion that will rot you quick, turn you into something you cannot recognize, but I have to admit that I hate Smitty. Not just because he tried to kill me and Patty, but because he cares only for himself, only feels his own pain, not that of others, and will use anyone and anything to get what he wants.

Hate isn't my only motivation, but it certainly is some of the fuel driving me forth. But standing there with the Navajo elder under the hot desert sun, realizing that Brooke had seen things this far ahead, I had to wonder if I wouldn't be better off just giving up and going back to Patty instead of going up against Brooke and Smitty.

My heart thudded in my chest, and I sucked in a gulp of air while I looked at her expressive brown eyes embedded in the Navajo elder's wrinkled face and I knew. I knew that I would be better off if I put down the bolo tie and left. If I went back to Pagosa Springs, Colorado, and told Patty that she was the future I longed for the most. If I let go of all of that and embraced a new future that wasn't encumbered by the past and by the town that bears my name.

I would be better off, but, in my heart, I knew that despite everything Brooke did and said, that Carterville would not be better off with just Smitty there.

It was clear to me. If I turned around, didn't walk across the border into Arizona, I would have a simpler, happier life, and if I walked across the border into Arizona, I would face the fight of my life, one I probably couldn't win.

No doubt there, but my heart told me that no matter the odds that I had to fight for Carterville, that the town that my ancestors had lived and died for was worth it.

That moment was filled with equal parts fear and conviction and my heart told me I had to go back.

I don't know if you know this, but sometimes our hearts don't know what the hell they are talking about.

THREE

SUNDAY, JUNE 14. FOUR CORNERS MONUMENT

The Navajo elder was speaking rapidly, her words rushed but suffused with a musical rhythm, like she was saying a prayer she had spoken many times. It felt like a ritual and, even to a cynic like me, it felt sacred.

I don't remember doing it, but I had taken off my cheap aviator sunglasses and my cowboy hat, like I was in the church made out of local volcanic rock on the top of Carter Hill. It was that kind of moment.

The girl's brown eyes were wide with wonder as she translated the elder's words.

I'm writing this the evening after it happened and I don't remember everything, like what happened there wasn't for the page, wasn't for ears other than mine.

Given my job, I have spent a lot of time thinking about power. The supernatural kind those of us in Carterville gained when the meteor hit, and the regular everyday kind of power we all have.

But this was something different. It may have not been caused by the same source as the Carterville powers, but it was definitely capital "P" Power that this Navajo matriarch was wielding.

How do I know? The mark of true power is that it doesn't matter a bit what you believe, it affects you nonetheless. Take gravity, for example. Believe as hard as you like that you are immune to the power of gravity, and your feet are still held to the ground by it. Gravity can be counteracted, yes, by technology and by other powers—a few in Carterville can (or could)—but that doesn't change it. It's still there. It's still undeniable no matter what you want to believe.

And that's what was happening here.

I was born and raised in Northern Arizona. I had seen the Kachina dances and ceremonies. I had been touched by the beauty of it, even aware of the sacredness of it. I respected it, but I had no idea of its true power.

I had been subject to the power of man, the power of nature, the power of Carterville, and I knew what all of those felt like. Standing in the hot sun on the New Mexico side of the Four Corners Monument in front of this wrinkled Navajo woman, I felt real power and I couldn't deny it.

I will do my best to record what she said—sadly, I never learned her name—but realize that her words were Navajo, translated by the girl, and what is recorded here are a mere shadow of what happened.

———

EVEN THOUGH THE NAVAJO ELDER WAS SEATED, EVEN THOUGH

the girl was translating what she said, it felt like she was standing tall right in front of me and speaking directly to me.

The musical power of her words in her language mingled with the English translation making it seem like I could understand her every word.

The old woman's eyes were intense and fierce, the brown of a desert haboob on the horizon about to bring wind and sand and chaos. My heart clanged in my chest and sweat trickled down my neck as she spoke.

"What happened to all of you on Sacred Mountain is the work of Coyote the trickster. You deny nature, you ignore spirit, and yet Coyote brought down the meteor and gifted you with the power of the Kachina. Except it is a curse for you, is it not, Promise Keeper?"

The elder's eyes were intense in her wrinkled face, bright as if lit by some inner light. There was age in her voice that sounded like rustling cornstalks in fall but also a power that made it sound youthful.

"It has often seemed like a curse," I said, my cheeks flushing red in shame as I tried to look at what happened in Carterville from her perspective. The meteor had transformed our town. We didn't know what had happened at first, it took several chaotic and confusing months to understand, but the reactions to it varied wildly. I'm sure Smitty thought it a gift, with what he could do.

"And even then, you wonder why when you leave Sacred Mountain your powers stay behind," the Navajo grandmother said through the girl.

I nodded.

She smiled and her teeth were stained, perhaps from tea

or tobacco, and even though her wrinkles deepened, she somehow seemed young.

"That is pure Coyote. And that is his wisdom. What would have happened if just a few were truly granted powers, like those you have on Sacred Mountain? If they took their power into the world. In their innocence, in their lust, in their weakness, what would they do to the world that they can only now do on Sacred Mountain?"

I really didn't have to imagine. Smitty would be trying to rule the world, or the country of his choice, at least. Mary Reilly might have let her power to command truly go to her head and become a menace. Annie Smith with her power of sleep could have been used for all kinds of nefarious things.

This was mythology she was telling me about. While I felt the power of her, the power of it, it didn't seem like it really mattered. The idea that we in Carterville were being messed with was not a new one. The limiting of our powers to that area was embraced by many as a saving grace in all of this. The Carterville powers were, for the most part, a Carterville problem.

"But you don't believe," the grandmother said directly to me, her accent once again thick. "In Coyote. In your own power. In yourself."

I took a small step back. There was truth in her words, and they stung. "I believe in my town," I said quietly as my cheeks flushed hot.

The grandmother cocked her head and stared at me and then nodded once. "Aoo'," she said. It sounded kind of like "oh," but I had been around Ortega enough to recognize the Navajo word for "yes."

She spoke in Navajo to the girl next to her, a brief sentence. "And that is what has saved you so far," she said.

I nodded because I believed it. In my job I see that those with a purpose outside themselves are still human, still make mistakes, still break laws, but by and large they are happier and more productive. They are more balanced, even with powers.

"But it is important that you learn to love those that have wronged you, Promise Keeper," the elder said through the girl. "Each wrong dealt to you, dealt to your town, you must let them go to see clearly. You must not drown in the hate that comes so easily to the weak. You must rise above, you must let Coyote help you find the way."

I nodded again. Her advice made sense. Hate will eat you up from the inside and, I have to admit that I hated Smitty, and while what I felt towards Brooke was considerably more complicated, there was hate there too. But I had no idea what a Navajo trickster could do to help me.

Not knowing what to say to that, I asked the question I needed to ask. "What of the girl that told you I would come," I said, gesturing with the bolo tie. "When was this? What did she say?"

The grandmother chuckled and it was a sound thick with schadenfreude. She started speaking in Navajo again and the girl translated.

"You must understand. Power is given, but not without purpose. Coyote means to teach with the power granted as he has already done. Some have died because of their power. Some have been jailed. Coyote has whispered in your ear long enough, Promise Keeper, that you started your scribbling so all may learn these lessons. This young one, though, she thinks she is a seer because of the power granted her. But a true seer must earn their power to see clearly, to guide their tribe, to be worthy. That is the lesson you all must learn. We must all learn."

The elder paused while the girl's words caught up, her eyes locked with mine like she was looking into me, into my soul, trying to see if I was worthy and I had to wonder if she wasn't the kind of seer she had just spoken of.

She continued speaking through the girl.

"But you want specifics. She came to me three years ago. We were near Flagstaff at the overlook to Oak Creek Canyon. She was so young, but her eyes, the color of storm clouds, were haunted. She gave me money for that piece you hold. She told me to save it for one that would be known as the Promise Keeper. She told me that I must remember her message, that I must extract a promise from you, and deliver her message."

A small smile cracked the woman's face again and she laughed, and I just stood there blinking. It wasn't her laughter, that didn't seem cruel but more of an appropriate expression given the madness of all of this. It was what she told me that froze me.

Three years? This was before Lila Chang's murder. This was before Brooke set anything in motion to expel me from my town.

My heart leapt into a gallop, and I started sweating. How arrogant am I to think I can return? How egotistical am I to think Carterville needs me when Brooke Jennings can see the future and make sure it happens? She saw this future and did something about it before she even started the wheels turning that ousted me.

"What… what is her message?" I finally managed to stammer.

The grandmother shook her head, a mischievous look on her face. "Promise first," she said directly to me.

I just stared at her. This was what I had feared. This is why I had kept my power a secret and told everyone, even those closest to me, that I didn't receive a power when the meteor hit. I knew how easily the power could be misused, could be turned against me. And even though we weren't in Carterville, and I had no power, I had no idea if a promise made here would hold once I returned to Carterville… if I could return.

She leaned forward across the table filled with Navajo jewelry. Her arthritic, swollen-jointed hands were relaxed on the white tablecloth looking so much like the desert just like her face did. She spoke three short sentences in Navajo and the girl translated.

"Coyote may be a trickster but he is not cruel. Coyote may test you but he will make you stronger. Promise me you will find a place for Coyote in your heart and keep him close."

I can't really explain that moment, but it was like the tourists were gone and the land had been returned to its natural state. The grandmother in her velvet turquoise skirt, black shirt, and regal squash blossom necklace was sitting on a rock in front of me and the only other sound besides her aged voice was the wind sighing over the desert.

I felt compelled to turn the bolo tie over. On the back, etched into the silver, was a coyote, sitting with its head raised, the round moon outlined behind its head.

I looked at the Navajo woman and she gave me a small nod. I put the bolo tie on, nodded, and said, "I promise."

I didn't know what it meant yet. I didn't understand. But I felt her power and it seemed to me that, in spirit, she was correct. The energy of Coyote the trickster was behind what happened to Carterville. We were being messed with on some fundamental level.

It still felt like we were alone in the desert and the grandmother spoke again. The girl might have been translating, but in that moment, it was still the two of us alone in the vastness of the desert.

Her eyes hardened and her voice sounded old and raspy. "The young one said to tell you, 'I am waiting for you. You know where I am. Come see me.'"

She then started laughing again, the illusion broken, and I was back at the Four Corners Monument standing across from her booth, the sound of her laughter bouncing around the plaza, loud enough so that I felt the stare of some tourists on my back as their chatter stopped for a moment.

I touched the stone of the bolo tie now resting against my chest. It was a little cool to the touch and it felt like it belonged.

I paid for the bolo tie. The Navajo elder told me that I didn't need to, that the girl had paid, but I did not want to feel like I owed Brooke Jennings anything.

When I turned from the booth, one group of tourists left and the granite disk of the monument was empty. I walked over, my strides long and confident, and crossed over from New Mexico into Arizona, a grim smile of determination on my face.

FOUR

MONDAY, JUNE 15. OUTSIDE OF FLAGSTAFF, ARIZONA

I don't know what happened yesterday. I truly don't.

After I left the Four Corners Monument, I drove into Arizona a little ways, and pulled off the road.

The land was similar to the monument, dry, pale desert, with a few weeds here and there, mostly close to the road, and very little vegetation otherwise.

That land rolled away all around me as cars buzzed by. There were low mountains on the horizon and sandstone outcroppings close by.

I slid over to the passenger's side seat, pulled my laptop out, and wrote the previous chapters.

Today I am camping in the Coconino National Forest south of Flagstaff. My route took me through a chunk of desert I used to stare out at from Carterville every day. I drove right past the turn off 89 to Carterville, but I just couldn't make the turn towards the town of my birth. I kept driving and found a place among the pines just south of Flagstaff.

It was a strange move. I could have stayed with Bo Larson not far from Carterville, or with my niece in Flagstaff, or with any number of friends, but I couldn't do that either. I lived in Northern Arizona almost my entire life and here I am alone in the forest.

I just read what I wrote, and even though it was yesterday, I don't understand what happened. What did I really experience with that Navajo grandmother and how much of it was in my head? I feel doubt today that was not part of my words yesterday. I need to focus on what I know is true.

I am going to try to put this simply, listing the facts, lining this up in some way that, hopefully, makes sense.

1. I experienced something yesterday with the Navajo elder and the child. It felt like capital-P Power, real power to me, and the perspective she offered was intriguing, but after just leaving Patty and with all the contemplation I've been doing, was any of that real? Was it all in my mind?

2. Clearly not all of it. Brooke Jennings saw me at the Four Corners Monument and acted years ago to get me a message there. That means she saw everything that led to me being there, including everything that happened in Carterville.

3. Her message to me was clear. She's in jail and she wants me to visit her.

4. If she can see that far ahead, she has surely seen what I am going to do next. Given how she operates, she will either encourage my action if it leads to the future she wants or deflect it if it doesn't.

5. Brooke is not in Carterville and our powers only work there. I do not know how far she can see ahead, but I imagine

the further ahead the future she is envisioning, the harder it must be. Maybe it's like a weather forecast, the further in the future, the less accurate it is.

6. Most of #5 is just wishful thinking. I do not understand her power, so I do not understand what is possible.

All of this leaves me with only one thing to do. Go visit Brooke.

Where I'm camped, I'm not far from I-17 and could hop on it and head down to Florence, Arizona. It's just afternoon as I write this, and it's about a three-hour-drive away. I could make it today, easily.

But I can't do it. I keep fingering the copper-laced chunk of turquoise I have on. I feel strangely attached to this bolo tie. I wore it to sleep last night.

The elder said, "Promise me you will find a place for Coyote in your heart and keep him close" and I promised her I would. Is this just me being a human keeping a promise? Is this years in Carterville and knowing that I keep my promises no matter what? Is this me just trying to hang on to an unexpected moment of beauty and mystery? Is this me avoiding Brooke?

That last part, for sure.

There are few things in this world that scare me. I can count them on one hand. Losing my sister, my only sibling is one. Alzheimer's is another. Life without good coffee is, almost seriously, another one. But Brooke Jennings is on the top of that list.

If you haven't read my other memoirs, maybe you don't understand what Brooke can do, so let me try to put it clearly. She can see the future and then see how her imagined actions will change that future. When she finds the future she wants, she takes those imagined actions and creates that future.

How the hell is a middle-aged, out-of-work, cut-off-from-his-power cop supposed to compete with that?

Not that my power could have helped me with Brooke. Unless…

Oh my. Now that's a thought. I dare not even write it down yet. I need to think. I need to take a walk.

FIVE

TUESDAY, JUNE 16. THE ARIZONA STATE
PRISON, FLORENCE, AZ

I wasn't dressed as a cop and that really bothered me as I followed the prison guard down the drab grey hallway. I hadn't been a cop for a while and that bothered me even more.

Somehow, it highlighted how my jeans fit, which is to say, poorly. Even with the weight I've lost since I left Carterville, the damn things don't fit me as well as they used to. I always have to have a belt on anymore and keeping my blue button-down shirt properly tucked in seems harder too. The fact that middle-age changes the shape of your body seems totally obvious, but I sure didn't think about it much until it happened.

And, yes, there is no doubt that my mind is focused on my clothing so I don't think about where I am and where the guard is taking me.

Our footfalls echoed ominously as we walked. "She won't come to the visiting area," the guard said. I don't remember his name. He was young with short red hair and a round face. "Normally you'd be SOL, but seeing as you're who you are…"

I suppressed a groan. Carterville's reputation had grown in the last few years. A lot. Thanks to Karen Winslow and the town council. Thanks to garish media coverage, annoying nicknames for us, a murder, and multiple people going to jail.

We weren't in a cell block, and I really had no idea what part of the prison this was. There were doors in the windowless hallway, all with locks, and buzzing fluorescent lights above us. The air was stale and had that vaguely greasy smell of institutional food.

I was getting more and more nervous the deeper we went into the prison. It didn't feel safe in here. It didn't feel right. I heard the distant murmur of voices, so we couldn't be that far away from a cell block.

I wanted to turn and run. I was cursing the circumstances that brought me here in the first place. I fingered the turquoise of my new bolo tie and part of me wished that I hadn't stopped at the Four Corners Monument, that I hadn't experienced what I had, that I didn't have a Navajo's perspective on what was happening in Carterville.

The Navajo perspective…

I stopped short as my mind raced and the guard continued, his steps echoing around me.

I had never understood why Isabella Ortega had wanted to come to work in Carterville. She had no powers and never would, but she's part Navajo. Her grandmother, specifically, was Navajo. She understood the language and the culture. The idea that Coyote was messing with us in Carterville couldn't be foreign to her, but she had never mentioned it.

Could that be the reason she came to Carterville?

"Everything all right there, Mr. Carter?" the guard asked. The quirky grimace on his face made it perfectly clear that if everything wasn't all right that he understood why.

I nodded as I turned it over in my mind. I had met Isabella Ortega during the Lila Chang murder case when we had called in help from the Coconino County Sheriff's office. She was one of the deputies and had proved to be competent and efficient.

At the end of that mess, when I was forced to fire my other officer at the time, Ortega made it clear that she liked Carterville and wanted to come back. I had worked with her enough to get a good sense of her and offered her the job.

She took it and I never understood why.

Of course, I knew that the Navajo and Hopi considered the San Francisco Peaks to be sacred. Of course, I knew that they had opinions about what had happened in Carterville, just like everyone else. I had just never come face-to-face with them like that before.

"Do you need to sit down?" the guard asked, taking a step towards me.

I felt cold and clammy despite being in this warm, stuffy hallway. "No, I'm fine," I lied.

He nodded, turned, and started walking down the hallway, but just a few more steps and stopped in front of a doorway and stood awkwardly away from it, almost on the other side of the hallway.

What I wanted to do, what I needed to do, was have a long talk with Ortega. I needed to understand how she came to be in Carterville that Christmas Day when we were looking for Lila Chang's murderer. I needed to know why she was so interested in Carterville.

Trust is an odd thing. It's so strong and yet it is so easily broken. When you trust, it seems hard like steel—once it's broken it seems as insubstantial as steam and you wonder how you ever built anything on it.

I still stood there, as the guard stared at me, and was convinced, completely convinced, that Brooke was the reason Ortega ended up in Carterville. That somewhere along the line, maybe long ago, maybe out of sight, she had manipulated things so the young woman would become a police officer in Carterville. In fact, she was now the acting chief of police in my absence.

I trusted her. I had come to think of her as a daughter, but the steel of that trust was feeling, suddenly, very insubstantial.

I needed to talk to Ortega, but I was here and I didn't think I'd have the courage to come back, so I shook off all those thoughts and walked down the hallway, my eyes following the guard's to the bland metal door.

I felt the kind of fear I hadn't felt often as an adult. Like the thing that had haunted my dreams, that had infected me with thoughts I couldn't let go, doubts that were eating me up from the inside, wasn't just a dream, but was real. And I knew that what I feared was on the other side of the door and she was a monster luring me in so she could consume me.

"She's in there," the guard said, nodding at the door. He had a strange look on his face, like he was scared of what was in the room. "It's unlocked. I'll be out here." His young face puckered into a sour expression, and he added, "She's expecting you."

I had heard rumors floating around the law enforcement circle about the creepy young woman at the Arizona State

Prison, in Florence. I didn't need to ask her name—it was obvious who the woman was.

My stomach twisted and stinging sweat beaded on my forehead. This was the monster's lair. This was the one place I shouldn't go. But I felt this weight pressing down on me like fate itself was a presence and it demanded that I go through that door.

I didn't know what was going to happen, but I did know that I would be changed when I came back out.

I nodded at the guard, grabbed the cool metal handle, took a deep breath, and pulled the door open.

SIX

TUESDAY, JUNE 16. THE ARIZONA STATE PRISON, FLORENCE, AZ

Humans have expectations. They are often wrong, but somehow it seems we need them to function in this unpredictable world. I was at the Arizona State Prison here to visit an inmate so I, of course, had some strong expectations as to what I would encounter behind that metal door, but it wasn't what I expected. At all.

Brooke Jennings was slouched in an easy chair in the corner of the room. She wore a burgundy-colored jumpsuit, which you would expect for a woman in this prison, but that was the only thing that was expected.

This was a narrow room, not much bigger than my office back in Carterville, with flat grey walls and harsh fluorescent lights. But Brooke was sitting in a beat-up brown recliner knitting what looked like a dark blue beanie. To her right was a small table with a basket on it filled with yarn. To her left was another table with a bag of Cheetos and a glass that looked to be filled with iced tea complete with a lemon wedge.

"Take it all in, Chief," she said with more than a hint of humor in her voice. "I'll be ready to talk as soon as you find your tongue."

Brooke had glasses on, like when she was a child in Carterville but unlike when she was last there doing her Svengali thing. Her shoulder-length blonde hair was half brown roots now, but her grey eyes were still sharp.

I didn't look at her for long, I really didn't want to meet those eyes. There was more in the room and my eyes flicked away to that. A small round table in the middle of the room with two metal chairs. The wall opposite her chair had a TV hanging on it. CNN was on and the volume was muted.

It wasn't fancy, not one bit of it, but for a prisoner in this jail, it was like walking into a luxury hotel. She had so much. The door wasn't even locked and she wasn't restrained in any way.

On the table was a carafe and a white ceramic coffee mug, the rim chipped. The smell of the coffee was beating back the greasy food smell of the place, and after the four-hour drive, I was desperate for it.

"Go ahead," she said, nodding, still knitting, the clacking of the needles strangely comforting. "It's a long drive back, but you'll make much better time if you just suck it up and drive back through Phoenix."

I just stared and blinked at her. She knew I was coming. She knew I avoided Phoenix and took the long way. She knew why I was here.

But how could she? Carterville powers don't work outside of Carterville. Had she seen things this far out?

My feelings were odd and conflicted. I was shocked she knew so much and yet it seemed obvious and normal for Brooke to be pulling strings.

I almost turned around and left right then and there. The trauma of that few days in Carterville and chasing her down —if that's what you can call it—came back. I felt the heavy, oppressive feeling of fate weighing me down again. My heart thumped hard in my chest, and I was having trouble catching a breath.

Powers don't work outside of Carterville. They just don't. The meteor buried deep in the mine was the source of our powers. It had to be.

After the explosion in the mine, her seemingly final test for me, after the truth about Brooke and what she had been doing came out, there had been renewed interest in the mine. The current owners had sent people. They had explored the mine, but the explosion, which had been a lot more than we had seen, collapsed a large portion of the old mine.

Getting through would have been a major effort and a major expense taking months if not years. They left after only a few days.

The explosion was one of the questions on my mind, but not an important one. It was obvious that the explosion had served multiple purposes, that keeping people out of the mine was part of her plan.

I took my cowboy hat off, sat in one of the metal chairs, and stared at the carafe.

"It's not poisoned," she said, "if that is what you are thinking. There were many futures that ended with you dead long before now. If that was what I wanted, it would have been easily done." She ended in a little chuckle, like a girl that had a secret she was dying to tell.

I poured the coffee, just half a cup, and the scent of it filled the small room. The coffee was hot. I wrapped my hands around the warming mug and looked back at Brooke.

Without the makeup she had been wearing in Carterville and with her round face and glasses on, she looked young. Too young to be here. Too young to have done what she did.

"So ask away, Chief," she said with a shy smile. Her gaze met my eyes briefly but then flicked to my new bolo tie.

"Don't you know what I want to ask?" I said.

She shrugged. "Maybe I want to hear it."

I hate games like this. Why can't people just say what they mean? But I was here, so I might as well ask the only question that made sense, given who I was talking to.

"Why am I here?" I asked.

She smiled and nodded, gesturing towards me with her knitting. "The scarring's not too bad," she said. "It makes you look tougher. It fits you."

I suppressed the urge to touch my face and the three scars from the scratches Patty Walsh delivered on that terrible night. I've already written about that, so I won't say much more here, except to say that Brooke was much more responsible for them than Patty.

This was Brooke's way of exerting her dominance, reminding me that she was responsible for not just my scars, not just my exile from Carterville, but so much more, including the chunk of turquoise I was wearing.

"I got your message," I said, keeping my voice mild, bored even. "Why am I here?"

She sighed and rolled her eyes. "It's so boring here, Henry," she said, and I found her using my first name to be wrong on so many levels. "I was hoping for a little interesting conversation at least. You're the closest thing I have to an old friend in this awful place. Indulge me a little. Please."

It was always games with Brooke. Games I didn't understand. Games I didn't want to play.

I gritted my teeth and nodded. That realization I had up in the forest was on my mind. I had figured out a way to beat Brooke. But I'm not going to write it down yet, this thing isn't over, but I will say that it was on my mind, and dancing with Brooke right now might help, as distasteful as it might be.

"You know, I can't look in the mirror without remembering what I was forced to do to Patty," I said. "Without remembering my hands around the throat of someone I love. So 'not too bad' wouldn't be the term I'd used for my scars."

Brooke smiled and nodded. "There we go," she said. "Now he's awake."

I blinked, looked away, and took a sip of the coffee. It was terrible coffee, but hot and caffeinated and I needed something to bolster me up.

"I am hoping," she said, "that not far from now you will come to appreciate those scars, come to see the necessity of all that happened, come to—"

"Lila Chang's death was not *necessary*," I said, cutting her off, my voice no longer calm. "And neither was William Reilly's."

"Let it out, Henry," she said, with a nod, a grim expression on her face.

"I still don't understand what you are after," I said, and I didn't sound bored anymore. I wasn't speaking carefully—my words were just rushing out. "Why you maneuvered things so that people died, so that Lila was murdered. I could have saved her if I had just been a little more present that night, if I hadn't been fighting with Annie and had really paid attention to her. And William? If Smitty and I hadn't been in the middle of the hell you directly created, he would have survived. What the hell did you accomplish that was worth all that pain and destruction?"

I was breathing hard and sweating again. I realized I was clenching my jaw, and I unlocked it with a force of will and growled, "Why the hell am I here?"

Brooke slowly put her knitting aside and sat up straight in the recliner which made her look rather uncomfortable. "William was an old man with a good life and died of a heart attack," she said, her voice even but sharp as a knife. "If he had been anywhere else, he wouldn't have had a chance, so forgive me if I don't cry a river of tears over his quick and clean death."

I opened my mouth to speak, probably yell, but she continued and cut me off.

"Lila's death, on the other hand," she said, her shoulders sagging. "I feel that one. Every day. I didn't really know her, I only met her a few times, but the whole town loved her and there were other futures for her. If I'm being honest with you, Henry, that's the one thing I regret, and she's the real reason I deserve to be here."

I slouched back in my chair as if I had just run a race, feeling drained and exhausted. Did Brooke Jennings just express regret? But this was Brooke, she was always doing what it took to create the future she wanted, so it wasn't like I could really believe her.

She leaned back and a manic smile lit up her face. "And let's face it, Henry, you and Annie needed to be done for good. That was not a healthy relationship. Not at all. I did you a favor."

I sat there for a moment blinking. From regret to cruelty without missing a beat. Now this was Brooke.

I thought of Annie when I got here. She wasn't in prison yet—her trial hadn't started. Unlike Brooke, she hadn't pled guilty, and given that her crimes involved her powers and that was a novel complication, she wasn't in prison yet, but it seemed an inevitability to me. She had, though, been forbidden from returning to Carterville. Last I heard she was in Tucson staying with an aunt.

At first when I heard that Brooke had pled guilty to her crimes, I was surprised, but then as I thought about it, it made sense. There were too many witnesses to what happened in the mine. She pled guilty because that was the way to get the shortest sentence.

But I wasn't thinking about that right then. My heart was pounding in my head and the room felt too damn small as I glared at Brooke. I wanted nothing more than to throw my coffee cup at her and storm out. Not true. I wanted to do a hell of a lot more to her than that.

Yes, my relationship with Annie had been difficult and tumultuous, and likely not that healthy. But there had been love, there had been sweet moments between us, and the breakup Brooke had engineered had been hell.

I didn't throw the mug, I gritted my teeth instead, put the mug down, and walked out of the room.

If the reason Brooke had visited that Navajo grandmother years ago was so that I would come here today and leave furious, so be it.

My idea of how to defeat Brooke seemed like a silly fantasy, given how I couldn't stay in a room with her for more than five minutes.

SEVEN

TUESDAY, JUNE 16. THE ARIZONA STATE PRISON, FLORENCE, AZ

THE REDHEADED GUARD HAD A LOOK OF SURPRISE ON HIS FACE as I stormed out of Brooke's room and slammed the door shut so hard that the metallic clang of it echoed down the hallway.

That look of surprise quickly melted into one of empathy. I suspected Brooke had done something similar to him, probably everyone here. I'm sure she had manipulated her way into her accommodations using her sharp cruelty.

The guard swallowed hard and said, "I... Ah... Ready to go?"

I was about to nod when the door cracked open. "I'm sorry, Chief," Brooke said. "Please come back in. I will answer your question."

Her voice sounded odd, like she was still that girl following her father around when I had met her eight years ago. She was a curious, somewhat precocious girl of twelve and wanted to be an archaeologist just like her father.

The guard's eyes widened, and he backed up a step, clearly

displaying his opinion of me going back in there. And a wise opinion it was.

I didn't turn around, I just stood there trying to think. If Brooke opposed my return to Carterville, and there was little reason to think she wouldn't, then the effort was doomed. But then why plant the seed so many years ago to bring me here?

"I have a lot of questions," I said, my voice seeming to steal out on its own. I hadn't meant to say it.

"I will do my best to answer them," she said, her voice now sounding contrite. The guard was blinking too much and slowly shaking his head like I was outside the lair of a predator being lured back in.

"You need something from me," I said, this time I was trying to speak. It was the only possible reason for all of this.

"Yes," she said.

"And you know what I need," I said.

"Yes," she said again.

"Is it possible?" I asked.

"Yes," she said for the third time, and despite the clear look of warning on the guard's face, I went back into Brooke Jennings's lair.

———

BROOKE WAS SITTING ACROSS FROM ME AT THE ROUND TABLE IN her room. I'm not quite sure what to call it. It wasn't her prison cell, there was no bed here, but the room clearly belonged to her, and it seemed like she spent a lot of her time here away from the rest of the prison population.

I had the coffee mug in my hand, and she had an iced tea sitting in front of her.

It was an odd scene. She was in her burgundy jumpsuit, and I had my cowboy hat back on—I felt no need to be courteous and take it off—both of us staring at our drinks.

The table was old with a scratched laminate top. I had to wonder why it was here. Given how small the space was, it took up quite a bit of room. Did Brooke regularly have the kind of meetings that required a table to sit across for someone?

How many small cruelties had she administered at this table, like what she had said about Annie and me? How many had it taken to make the guard outside so afraid of her, to get her the privilege of this private space?

Brooke and I were now playing another game. She had admitted to needing me and she might have admitted that there was a way for me to get back to Carterville, but her affect had changed once we returned to her domain. She was slouched back in her chair, her arms crossed in defiance. This was a different gear, but it was the same game, a game of wills.

She didn't want to speak first. She had already shown some vulnerability and wasn't about to show more.

Fine by me. The coffee was bitter and harsh, but I was okay sitting here sipping it, slowly doling it out from the carafe so it was still hot.

Brooke shifted in her seat, and I raised my eyes just enough to see her stance hadn't changed. This may have been childish, this may have been a game, but it was one that I knew how to play.

I sipped coffee until I had had my fill and then I stood up without a word and turned to walk to the door.

"Wait," Brooke said, her voice hushed like she was about to tell a secret.

I turned around and crossed my arms, echoing the pose she had been wearing. She sat up straight and relaxed her arms. I just kept standing there.

"You don't make this easy," she said.

I still didn't say anything. She knew what my question was, I had asked it multiple times, and I wasn't going to ask it again. I wanted to know why I was here.

She pursed her lips and narrowed her grey eyes as she stared at me. Was this to be a staring contest now? I could do that too.

"Look," she said, her eyes flicking away. "I need you to tell me what you want and where you are with it."

"Why?" I asked.

She shook her head and stared at her hands resting on the table. "This is delicate," she said. "I need you to talk first, so I know which future we're in."

A moment or two passed as my mind slipped out of gear, her words echoing. Believe me, I had had enough time to try to imagine what it was like to be Brooke, to spend so much time sorting through futures to find the one you want, like searching an impossibly messy house for the smallest of things, a challenge that would make "needle in the haystack" seem like child's play.

It must be hard and maddening. Maybe enough to drive you crazy. And maybe Brooke was already there.

Cowboy boots aren't meant for standing, even more so since the big five-oh, but I stood there trying to figure out if she was telling the truth. It was plausible, but was it just another one of her manipulations?

And did it matter? I was here. I had walked into the monster's lair. Might as well see it through.

"I want to return to Carterville," I said, my voice bland and boring. "I was just with Patty. She gave me some insights into Smitty and a general plan."

Brooke looked up and to the left, her eyes flicking like she was reading something in the air. This didn't last long, maybe the length of two breaths, and she looked at me. "Right. Good. Her information is sound, but not enough."

What the hell was going on? Was she seeing the future still, even away from Carterville? Had she memorized all these futures and was able to consult them at will?

"Look," she said, leaning forward. "Now that I know where we're at, I'll answer your questions." A smile played upon her lips, one that was half-predatorial and half-crazy. It sent a chill down my spine and made me want to run.

"Why am I here?" I asked.

She snorted. "In every damn future you are stubborn, Henry Carter. God, you are so stubborn."

"Why?" I asked.

She shook her head and sighed. "Because we both want the same thing. We both want to return to Carterville."

EIGHT

TUESDAY, JUNE 16. THE ARIZONA STATE PRISON, FLORENCE, AZ

Brooke Jennings wanted to return to Carterville. She wanted me to help her. This is what she needed me for. This was why I was there. This was why she visited the Navajo elder three years ago before she set my banishment from Carterville into motion.

My knees felt weak, and I wanted nothing more than to sit down and drink more coffee until excess caffeine drove this feeling away.

And what the hell was I feeling? Terrified, certainly. This woman and her ability to manipulate things made Smitty seem like a rank amateur. Awed that she had seen that far ahead in the future. And I even felt a bit hopeful. My flicker of an idea, the one I dare not say to anyone, the one I dare not even write down won't work unless we both return to Carterville.

I am sure my face registered surprise and a few other

emotions, but I quickly got it under control and asked, "Why?"

She shook her head. "Jesus H. Christ, Henry. You are like a toddler, a stubborn as hell toddler." She chuckled, got up from the round table, went back to the recliner and started knitting again, the clack-clack of the needles a thin bit of comfort in this madness.

She nodded at the table, and I walked over, moved the chair so I was facing her, and sat back down, my arms crossed. While it was clear she had some general knowledge of this future, her reactions made it seem like she didn't have much, or any, specific knowledge of this conversation. And that made it to my advantage for her to talk, not me.

She knit and I sat, the motion of the needles strangely meditative.

Without looking up, without stopping, she said, "I'm running out of runway here, Chief. You can't imagine how hard it's been to stay safe this long. I need some time in Carterville so I can see how to survive this."

"Survive?" I asked.

She stopped knitting and stared at me. "Yes. Survive. Think about it. I'm a freak here. I'm *the* freak. I'm the Fortune Teller. Everyone expects magic out of me, the reality of Carterville be damned. And it's magic they'll have or their pound of flesh. I saw how to create this space, how to get this far, but…"

Her hands dropped to her lap and she stared right at me with her grey eyes like she was trying to see inside my mind. She licked her lips and took a deep breath. "I don't need long. Just a few days in the zone of influence. You can keep me locked in a cell the whole time. I don't care. I just need some time there."

She looked young. She looked vulnerable. It was hard not to believe her, but I didn't.

"Who do you think I am?" I asked. "I'm an out-of-work cop. How am I supposed to make that happen?"

She rolled her eyes. "How hard was it for you to get in to see me?" she asked, but didn't wait for my answer. "It will take some convincing, but I know you can do it. You're the goddamn Promise Keeper. You are the most famous law enforcement officer in the country right now. You've been hiding in the forest typing away, but the world knows who you are."

I nodded. It had taken me one phone call to get in to see Brooke. What she was asking for was certainly possible.

"But I can't enter Carterville," I said, the words coming slowly. "I can probably enter the zone of influence, but even then, I don't think I'll be able to stay long. My exact promise was about Carterville, but I understood Smitty's intent so I don't think I can help you."

Brooke smiled and it was a terrifying thing. "That's where I come in," she said. "I don't know everything, but I can help you through a couple of the trickier bits and get you back."

My jaw hung open a moment before I got enough control over my face to shut it, but long enough for Brooke to laugh. It was a happy sound which was completely incongruous with where we were at.

"Patty already got you inside Smitty's head," she said. "Not that complicated, really. And I can get you past a few of the harder parts, and then we are back, baby. We are back!"

Her smile was no longer terrifying but genuine. It made

her look like a child that just saw a load of gifts under the Christmas tree. She wanted this. She wanted this so badly. And so did I. But her naked desire made me want to abandon going back myself. If making a deal with Brooke was what it took then I wasn't going to do it.

I stood up and stared at her for a moment and then said, "No. I can't trust you, Brooke. You don't just want a few days in Carterville and we both know it."

Brooke's smile dimmed but didn't disappear and I couldn't hold her eyes anymore, so I turned and walked to the door. I had my hand on the handle when she said, "But what about Annie?"

I stopped, a cold shiver running down my spine.

Brooke continued. "She's fighting the charges against her, but you know she's going to lose. You're going to testify against her, Chief, and make sure she does. And when she loses, she'll end up here, she'll be a freak like me, but she won't have anything to fall back on. What about Annie, Chief?"

The thing I've learned about Brooke Jennings is she never lays all her cards on the table, and this Annie thing was a hell of a card to play. It made me worried what other cards she had to play.

My shoulders stiffened and my stomach twisted, but I didn't take my hand off the door handle. "What do you want?" I asked, struggling not to spit the words out.

"I want seventy-two hours in the zone of influence," she said. "In your cell and under guard works fine for me. Actually preferable. Some decent food. A real pillow and some warm blankets. And to be left alone. That's all."

"And you'll come back to prison?" I asked, my back still to her. It had to be this way. I didn't want to see her face.

"Yes," she said.

"And you'll serve your term?" I asked.

"Yes," she said again.

"And you'll make sure Annie is okay?" I asked.

"I promise you, Chief," she said with a little too much emphasis on the word "promise." "I'll be good. I'll come back. I'll make sure no one messes with Annie. You have my word."

"I'll expect you to repeat those promises to me in the zone of influence," I said. "And a few more." Now I wasn't turning around because I didn't want her to see my face. I didn't want her to get an idea of what the card I hadn't played was.

"Of course," she said. "I will repeat these promises."

"And first you'll help me get Smitty to release me from my promise to him?" I asked.

"It kinda has to work that way, doesn't it?" she said.

I took a few deep breaths to steady myself, turned around, and looked at Brooke. She looked small in the old brown recliner, not like a monster that had lured me into her lair. She looked like a young woman in need of a second chance.

"I need you to explain one thing," I said.

She shrugged. "Sure. Anything."

"If you are willing to help me get back to Carterville," I said, trying to make my thoughts coherent. "And Smitty is sure to weasel his way back. That will leave your two 'Destroyers' back in Carterville. After all you went through, why in the world would you do that?"

She sighed and seemed suddenly very tired. She gestured with her knitting to the chair. "Please sit. You're making me nervous."

I nodded and sat down.

"I'm sorry if this doesn't make sense," she said, picking up her knitting, the rhythmic clacking sound starting back up. "English really isn't constructed for these kinds of things and what I will say to you will sound like it's in a foreign language."

I leaned forward and just stared at her. She wasn't exactly saying I was too stupid to understand but getting pretty damn close.

"When it was all over at the mine," she continued, "I told you that all outcomes led to my goal."

I nodded. I remembered. She was cuffed to a fence outside the east entrance to the Carter Mine when she told me that, when it looked like Smitty had died.

"That is still the case," she said. "That was what was so hard about what I did. That's why it appears as strange as it does. I maneuvered us through many thousands of possible futures to the set where Carterville survives, to where you and Smitty didn't end up destroying it."

"And I had to have my power used against me to remove me from Carterville?" I asked. I had meant to let her talk, but I couldn't help myself.

"And Smitty needed to screw up and get caught," she said with a nod. She stopped her knitting. "With where we ended up, it was the only way."

"And what did you 'save' Carterville from?" I asked.

She laughed and there was too much pressure behind that laughter and she sounded crazy. "Shit, Henry," she said. "We don't have long enough for me to list all the disasters. A central theme of them was that you and Smitty were almost always so preoccupied with your stupid pissing contest that you weren't able to save the town. Just like what happened to poor William."

I gritted my teeth together at the mention of William Reilly. Smitty and I were having a thing and if we hadn't been William would have lived. The teeth-grinding part of it was that Brooke maneuvered us into that situation.

"But if we both return, what will be different?" I asked.

She gave a half laugh and I decided I really never wanted to hear her laugh again. Each form her laughter took was terrifying. "You are different, Henry. You. That's what this was all about."

NINE

TUESDAY, JUNE 16. THE ARIZONA STATE PRISON, FLORENCE, AZ

I'm sure that Brooke Jennings sometimes tells the truth. I'm quite sure she does it with the same ease as she lies. I'm also quite sure that Brooke's power has messed with her in ways that could easily be classified as "crazy" but that would be much too simplistic.

I sat there in Brooke's deluxe prison day room and stared at her. For how long, I couldn't tell you.

She had just told me all the madness from Lila Chang's murder on had been about me. Changing me. So I was somehow capable of saving Carterville when the inevitable crisis or crises came, or at least not getting in the way.

I asked her more questions as she kept knitting. I won't attempt to reproduce them here. I'm having enough trouble getting her voice out of my head as it is.

She told me that the ideal result of all her manipulations would have been Smitty dying. Less ideal would have been both of us dying. Even less ideal, but still workable for

Carterville, would be the situation we were in. Smitty and I alive and Brooke heaping a truckload of guilt on me.

At one point she referred to me as "her expertly forged weapon." I almost left. I really should have. If not for Annie, I would have.

And those of you that read all that I wrote about Annie and me may be wondering why. To say our relationship was tumultuous is like saying the desert is dry—it doesn't begin to cover it. But that doesn't mean there wasn't love and real feelings along the way. Annie is… well, she's human, and she's complicated, and she's demanding, and she's fierce, and so loyal until she's not.

Annie was so mad at me, and much of it I do understand, but her betrayal still hurts. It hurts worse than Smitty's actions—we've hated each other for a long time. It stings more than the mayor Karen Winslow's implicit support of what happened even after all I did for that town.

I feel betrayed by Annie, on a level so fundamental I still don't know what to do with it. And don't get me wrong, Annie committed crimes, she was involved in the attempted murder of Patty and me, in Frank's stabbing, she lost her way and deserves to go to jail. I just can't bring myself to not help her when there is something I can do.

"She won't know it's me," Brooke said.

I shook my head. "What?" I asked, trying to get back in the game.

"Annie," Brooke said. "She won't know it's me, and by extension, she won't know what you did for her. I'll find a path for her, but I'll keep it all under wraps."

I nodded. "Thank you," I said absently. I hadn't realized I wanted it that way, but I did. I was dreading the trial and the media frenzy around it—I didn't want to see Annie again and I didn't want to testify against her, but it looked like it was going to come to that.

"So we have a deal?" Brooke asked.

Brooke had stopped knitting and I hadn't even realized it. She was leaning forward in her recliner, an eager look on her face like a gnawing hunger was about to be sated.

"Yes," I said. "We have a deal."

A shiver ran down my spine, but I was careful not to let it show. It felt like I had just made a deal with the devil, and maybe that's exactly what I had done.

"Catch," she said, tossing a small blue bundle to me.

I caught it and realized that it was what she had been knitting. It was a blue beanie, the kind you might wear in the winter. Inside of it was something hard about the size of a bar of soap.

"It's going to be a cold winter, Henry," she said with a chilling chuckle. "You might need it."

I peaked in the beanie. Inside was an old-fashioned flip cell phone, a burner phone to be specific.

"We'll talk soon," she said and unmuted the TV. I had been dismissed.

Out in the hallway, the redheaded guard gave me the kind of look you might give an old, sick person that was on their last leg.

"What happened in there?" he asked.

"I wish I knew," I said.

———

IT WAS HOT OUTSIDE THE ARIZONA STATE PRISON. THE JUNE heat in the desert can be deadly but I welcomed the blast of heat as I exited the prison and walked to my truck.

I started sweating, but it was clean sweat, real sweat, not the stinging, prickling sweat of fear that Brooke had engendered.

I tilted my head up to the sun and sighed. I've visited prisons before, this one before, and I have always felt this sense of relief on exiting, but this was on another level.

Brooke wanted something more than what she asked for, but I couldn't figure out what it was.

I didn't think it was to leave prison early. If that had been possible, she would have set it in motion already or avoided prison in the first place. I actually believed her that there was no way to create the future she wanted that didn't end up with her in prison.

I stopped on the hot asphalt when I realized something. I didn't ask her about the explosion in the mine, the one she was responsible for. There had to be something to that. It was part of her plan to save Carterville. It had to be. The size of the explosion was much more than she needed to set up her twisted "Who will Henry save?" game.

The burner phone that was still in the beanie buzzed and I almost jumped. I flipped it open and there was a text that said, *I'll answer that when we are both back.*

I just stared at the phone blinking. What the hell? How could she have this fine-grained a resolution of what was happening right now this many months away from Carterville?

Had she retained some semblance of her powers? And if so, how the hell was that possible? And this led to much bigger questions as to how her power worked. I was just standing there thinking these thoughts. Her power wasn't reading minds, it was seeing the future.

The phone buzzed again. *The answer to that one is easy. You'll figure it out here in a moment.*

I almost turned around, I almost marched back in there. These texts were a power play, pure and simple. Brooke was trying to make sure I knew exactly how powerful she was and exactly how useless it was to oppose her and the future she wanted.

I was in the middle of the parking lot and the heat had become oppressive, but still I stood there racking my brain. How did Brooke know what was going on in my mind?

"Shit!" I said as it hit me like a ton of bricks. Brooke was reading my memoirs. She had, somehow, seen them in the future. That's how she knew what I was thinking, that's how she knew what to text me. It wasn't mind reading at all, it was future reading.

But then that led to the question of how we caught her at all, how she hadn't seen Martin Lester coming. Couldn't she just have looked into the future and read that memoir and avoided it?

The phone buzzed again. *That would have created a paradox. Can't do that.*

A paradox? My brain hurt. If she read my memoir about how we caught her and then avoided being caught because of it, then that version of the memoir would have never been written, and that sure as hell does sound like a paradox.

I shook my head trying to clear it and resumed walking to my truck, an old Toyota 4x4, white and worn that stood out against a lot of newer vehicles.

"I guess it's a good thing I'm writing all of this down," I said aloud.

The phone buzzed once again. It was just a smiley face emoji, which was most certainly not the look on my face because I didn't know if I could trust Brooke. I didn't know if this paradox thing was real or just more manipulation, or both.

There was something about Brooke's power that was constantly surprising. I had experienced it before, and after she had been caught, I had done my best to forget about it. Back then, Brooke was headed to jail, and I needed to be able to live my life without wondering if every little thing I did had been seen by Brooke and was somehow what she wanted me to do.

I had shoved Brooke so far out of my mind that when Frank got stabbed and I made that deal with Smitty to leave Carterville if he saved his life, I hadn't even thought of her and her promise of what was to come.

But I didn't have that luxury anymore. I had to get back to Carterville and defeat Brooke, but it seemed I needed her help to do that, and I was quite sure there were a lot more surprises coming. More surprises than her using my memoirs to create the future she wanted.

The only hope I had was that this paradox thing was true. That if I was honest in what I wrote, wrote about what actually happened, then she couldn't use it to change things, only as a roadmap as to what she needed to do.

I guess I do have to keep writing all of this down.

I suggest you don't think about it too hard. It's the whole "which came first the chicken or the egg" thing. It's a hall of mirrors with infinite reflections. But it isn't, apparently, a paradox, just the out of order madness of Brooke Jennings's power.

I had been lost in thought and was standing in front of my truck staring at the burner phone in my hand. I was expecting another text, something pithy and sharp, something that made it clear that I couldn't beat Brooke.

But no more texts came. I unlocked the truck, got in, and tossed the beanie with the burner phone in it into the glove compartment.

I couldn't try to not think about Brooke, but I could think about something else. And the town that bore my name was always on my mind.

I put the key in and the truck roared to life, eager to get back on the road and get back to the mountain. I didn't know what was coming, but it felt like I was finally on the right path, the deal with the devil I had just made notwithstanding.

I rolled down the window a little, popped in an old Gretchen Peters tape, and headed back towards Carterville.

PART 2
FUTURE PLANNING

TEN

WEDNESDAY, JUNE 17. JUST OUTSIDE THE CARTERVILLE ZONE OF INFLUENCE

I couldn't see Carter Hill and the houses draped on its slopes looking to the north. I was on Carterville Road just outside of the zone of influence. Here it's all juniper and piñon trees, the road running through a dip and Carter Hill hidden behind a smaller hill.

My truck was parked on the narrow shoulder, and I was outside of it standing on the edge of the road staring in the direction of the town that bore my name. This is as close as I had come since I left.

The road was curving to the right, to go around the hill blocking my view of Carterville and just a few feet in front of me the zone of influence started. It was bizarre, really. Just a few steps and I would have my power back, but out here I was as normal as the next human.

No. Not *my* power. I think it was my time away but standing there I saw it differently. It wasn't *my* power, this Carterville phenomenon that made me the "Promise Keeper."

It was Carterville's power, I was just the one that got to wield it, but only in the zone of influence.

When any of us thought about our powers and how they worked, we couldn't help but think of the meteor that fell eight years ago and buried itself deep in the mine below Carter Hill. It appeared to be the source of our powers, although the evidence there is only circumstantial. Correlation does not mean causation, as the saying goes.

But that is not today's mystery. Today's mystery is simple enough, an exploration as to what the promise I made to Smitty will do if I enter the zone of influence.

There's no visible sign of the border, but I've felt it hundreds of times. When you leave the zone of influence, it's like this background hum suddenly goes away, like when your house loses power, and you feel a new degree of quiet now that electricity is not buzzing all around you.

I've never felt that much when entering the zone, more of a resumption of feeling normal, like when your power comes back on, but it had been nine months and I'm doing it this way because it seems somehow important. Since we got powers, I had never been away from Carterville for more than about a week.

I took a step forward, the cinders of the road's shoulder crunching under my cowboy boots. It was midmorning and the sun felt hot on my bare head. Somehow it hadn't felt right to wear my Stetson for this. I reached my hand out. I didn't think I was there yet, but I had never taken the time to do this and I wanted to feel as much as I could.

I felt nothing.

I took another slow step, my hand extended, hoping that no one would drive by and see this. I wasn't just some middle-aged white guy in jeans and cowboy boots. I was the exiled chief of police and the ancestor of the founder of Carterville. Word would spread fast.

But no one drove by, and I felt nothing.

One more step and I felt a faint tingle in the tips of my fingers. If I hadn't been going so slow, I probably wouldn't have noticed it. I pulled my hand back and the tingling stopped. I extended it and it started again.

This was it. The line was really that fine and I had to wonder if powers worked when we were only partially in the zone of influence. I would need someone with a more conventional power to find that out, like the Carterville PD's office manager Annabelle and her ability to levitate objects.

I took a half step forward so my body was just outside the line and felt with my hand. What was the shape of it? From personal experience, I knew powers worked at least a few hundred feet above Carterville, but there had to be an altitude boundary too, didn't there? It couldn't extend out into space, could it?

In my mind, I thought it might be a big sphere around that meteor below Carterville, but given how big a sphere that would have to be, my feeling around determined nothing. It would take GPS and walking through the forest to determine that was true. Some studies had been done early on, but I'm not sure I ever read them. Annabelle would know.

I extended my hand through, and the tingling left my fingers and settled around my wrist. I leaned forward and that slight tingling went up to my elbow.

Well, that was a new piece of information. I could only feel the tingling where my body crossed the border.

This was all interesting, but only in an academic way. I

was procrastinating. While I wanted to return to Carterville, was desperate even, parts of me were content with the simpler, slower life that I had been leading.

I had been writing a lot, hiking, sleeping under the stars and not dealing with emergencies all the time. It had been good for my health and still I longed to return.

Just a few days ago, when I had been in Pagosa Springs, Colorado, with Patty Walsh, helping her out with a mystery, she had given me the rough outline of a plan to return. She had also said, "I am hoping that now that you know you can go back, that you won't have to."

That was at play too. I had Patty's knowledge of Smitty and a rough plan. I had Brooke's future-seeing assistance, as distasteful as that was. I didn't expect it to be simple or easy and I expected there to be a substantial cost, but it seemed I could return, but did I really want to?

I don't know if this is a middle-age thing, but I seem to remember that knowing my mind was easier when I was younger. Sure, in part it was the hormones, but you know what I mean. With less experience, with fewer times getting knocked around by chance, it was easier to take a risk like the one I was facing.

Or maybe I had just had too much time on my hands and had been thinking about it all too much.

I shook my head and stepped forward into the Carterville zone of influence. I had been still enough, aware enough, that I felt that tingle pass through my body as I took that step, and as I stood on the other side, I could really feel it.

That's a poor description so let me try to do better.

It wasn't like I had just drunk a couple of cups of coffee or anything like that. It wasn't a buzzing feeling or even a feeling of power. It was more subtle than that and not really a physical sensation, at least not one I can describe. What I felt was the promise of power instead of power itself. It was kind of like the contentment that comes when you have enough savings in the bank so you know you can weather a storm. It was like my mind and my body were working just a tiny bit better, but what brought a smile to my face is that I knew there was another gear available to me if I needed it.

And I, somehow, felt less alone, like this power was glad to see me and I really was coming home.

I took a couple of deep breaths of the warm air. The power of my promise hadn't kicked in. I didn't feel even a little compelled to leave and that was a curious thing.

I thought I had understood my power and how it worked. But I had kept my power secret until it came out when Smitty and company arranged my exile. It's not like I could do experiments with it. My understanding was based on observation and I could be wrong.

A thought sparked in my brain, a hopeful, giddy thought. Smitty wasn't in Carterville and since he was the one I made the promise to, maybe I could return right now.

There was only one way to find out.

ELEVEN

WEDNESDAY, JUNE 17. JUST OUTSIDE CARTERVILLE

As a rule, I'm not much for hope. It's a tricky thing and it's a projection of what you want, not an acknowledgement of what is.

Look, I get it, hope is important, hope can get you out of bed in the morning and keep you in the struggle long enough to break through the toughest issue, but when hope is just wishful thinking, it can land you back in bed with the covers pulled over your head, your soul a dark void.

When hope goes up against reality, reality wins. Every single time. It doesn't care about our hope. But hope is human, so I felt it as I rushed back to my truck and felt the sensation of my newly restored powers leaving as I crossed out of the zone of influence. My heart was thumping happily along, and I was like a starving man who had just got his first scent of food. What I wanted, what I needed was right in front of me, I just had to go get it.

I fired up my truck, got back on the road, and shot back

into the zone of influence, happy to have the background hum of my powers snap back again.

Carterville is not a big town, maybe "village" is a better description, so it was a mile or so and minutes until I got to the city limits.

As I got closer, my hope started to sour and my mood started to darken. I had kept my power a secret, but promises had been made to me and I had never seen them falter while the promiser was in Carterville even if I was not.

Frank Paulson never started smoking again. Annabelle and Ortega never mentioned Brooke Jennings's name to me even after I left town. Bo Larson always called when he was coming to town.

Promises to me are like live explosives—powerful and dangerous—so I am very careful with them and use them sparingly, but enough promises had been made to me for me to observe the results.

At first, as I headed towards the city limits where I would be, literally, in Carterville, I didn't feel anything but excitement and hope. But as each curve brought me closer, as the road gained a little elevation and ponderosa pine trees started taking over from the juniper and piñon, I felt this growing anxiousness, the sense that something was wrong, that something about me was wrong.

My head started to hurt, and I couldn't roll the windows down far enough to get enough air to breathe. I felt like I was in a small space with the walls closing in.

Was this all in my head or was this my power coming to bear? Given that we didn't have one clue how our powers worked and given the nature of my power, it could be either.

We promise each other things to create and maintain

trust. We promise ourselves to try to do the things we know we should. But promises are normally insubstantial, like a wisp of a cloud in the wind. Circumstances change and that promise no longer makes sense and is suddenly gone like fog under the glare of the morning sunshine.

Except my power makes promises into steel, amplifying the power of will.

My sister and my friends gave me hell for not trying this the moment Smitty left town, like I was somehow abdicating my responsibility just because things had gotten difficult.

I can't say that they were completely wrong. I was wrung out, I had needed a break, but I was as sure as I could be that I couldn't return even with Smitty gone.

Right before the last curve where I would see the "Welcome to Carterville" sign, I pulled my truck over onto the shoulder. I was sweating and I was white knuckling the steering wheel, my heart clanging around in my chest like some toddler had gotten ahold of a bell and was ringing the hell out of it.

I was to the east of Carter Hill and could see the north-facing houses draped on its slope with the heights of the San Francisco Peaks framing it.

This was my home. This is where I had spent all but a few years of my life, but today it looked different. It seemed somehow out of place in the middle of the forest, houses instead of trees feeling wrong, and after my time at Four Corners, I could see why the Navajo and the Hopi didn't like it.

Mount Humphreys tops out at 12,637 feet and is the highest point in Arizona. It was easy to see how this mountain covered in a thick forest and capped with snow rising out of the surrounding desert was sacred to the Native Americans. The Navajo name for it, "Dook'o'oosłííd," means "the summit which never melts." The Hopi call it "Nuva'tukya'ovi" which means "the place of snow on the very top."

Easy to see why a mountain like that might be sacred in a desert like this—hell, it was sacred to me. We are not talking Colorado where there are so many peaks that they don't bother to name them all. This is Arizona and there are seven peaks that are part of this mountain, all of them named.

I felt this rage well up as I sat there staring and sweating. At Smitty for executing my banishment. At Brooke for engineering it. At my ancestor Samuel Carter for coming here in the first place and finding silver and giving the town his name. And mostly at myself for letting this happen.

Yes, these mountains felt sacred to me, and while the town looked a little out of place, all human towns do when they beat nature back. It wasn't just the Peaks that were sacred to me but Carterville itself. The land, the people, the history.

I got out of my truck, my boots crunched against gravel again as I walked forward. I wanted to do this on my feet. I didn't want to rush through in the truck fearing what that might do to me.

I died once, for just a couple of minutes. I had pitted my own power against another's power and my heart couldn't take it. I floated above my town and watched the scene, watched Isabella

Ortega enter Carterville even though she had promised me she would stay away that night.

Smitty healed me, with Ortega pointing a gun at him, and when I was alive again, the power of the promise Ortega made to me came to bear and she looked like she was suddenly barefoot and standing on hot coals.

So if I die, all the extra power leaves the promises made to me or by me. But if I leave Carterville, the power remains. My power is strange and I may not fully understand it, but some things are clear.

But it wasn't really my power, was it? It was the power of the meteor or whatever else created it. We were just conduits of that power. I fingered my bolo tie and gritted my teeth thinking that this sounded very much like Coyote at work.

And I realized that all the tourists coming to Carterville want to experience the power of it, hoping to taste it, actually could. Through me. If they promised me something they would experience the power of Carterville expanding their will so they could meet that promise.

So because of my power, my return, if it happened, would be complicated. I would spend a good amount of time with tourists promising me stupid things just to feel the power and me releasing them from their promises so they didn't hurt themselves.

That's what I was thinking as I marched forward, each step getting harder.

The words of my promise that exiled me weren't that specific. Smitty had said, "I want you to leave Carterville and never come back," and I had said "You save Frank, I'll be out of here in a week. I promise."

In retrospect, it's telling that Smitty didn't extract a more specific promise from me. But I had been a man of my word before the meteor and, like for many others, the power I was given amplified an aspect of me. At least for me, it wasn't the words that really counted, it was the intent of the promisor and the promise. I had been pushing it reentering the zone of influence, but crossing into the actual city limits was starting to feel impossible.

It was like I wasn't quite in control of my body anymore. I had to fight for each step, each breath had to be dragged into my lungs. I was sweating like I was at the end of a marathon—not that I would ever try to run a damn marathon—and my vision was beginning to tunnel in.

My power amplifies will, and I was trying to force myself to overcome that enhanced will.

I made it around the corner and saw the sign. "Welcome to Carterville. Established 1881." The sign itself was made of copper from the mine, the edges of it greening a bit as it hadn't been maintained in a while. The letters were silver-colored, made of stainless steel not actual silver or it would have been stolen long ago. The copper sheet hung on a frame made of large pine logs that sat in a base of dark volcanic rock.

I stopped when I saw it. It was just a fancy sign, one too fancy for our little town, but seeing it made me want to cry. I had opposed the expense, it seemed excessive, but Karen Winslow had convinced the town council to shell out for it a couple of years after the meteor hit when tourism was really picking up.

The sign was something of a promise. That the town past it was special, was different, was worth visiting.

And it was all those things, but it wasn't for me today.

I managed two more steps, with my teeth gritted, sweat dripping down my face, and my heart going faster than was healthy.

I think being middle-aged saved my life there. I am stubborn. I think a measure of it is required to get anywhere in this world, but I was too stubborn when I was young. If I had been twenty facing a challenge like this, I probably would have kept going until my heart gave out.

But I let the wisdom of age win and turned around, turned away from my town, and walked back towards my truck.

The change was immediate. I suddenly felt fifty pounds lighter, and something whispered in my mind that I had been silly to come, that I should go back to Patty in Colorado, that I should do anything else but come back to Carterville with all its troubles and tribulations.

But that was just my mind. My heart ached to be back and it was time to do what needed to be done.

TWELVE
A BIT OF HISTORY

Winston "Smitty" Smith was born in 1983 to Mary Elizabeth Evans and Wilson Smith in Cornville, Arizona. His mother Mary was a schoolteacher, his father Wil was a part-time grifter and a full-time criminal.

I could say something like "the apple doesn't fall far from the tree," but that would be too clichéd, so instead I'll just make a reference to it and let you all draw your own conclusions.

But I should pause and explain just in case anyone else does read this. When I was in Colorado, Patty Walsh told me some things about Smitty, helped me understand him better, helped me understand his fears.

Patty, when she was in Carterville, knew what you wanted before you even asked. That was her power and it made her one hell of a waitress, but, as I recently learned, there was a price to be paid. Her life in Carterville had been filled with everyone else's desires so much so that she had trouble knowing what she wanted.

But Patty knew what Smitty wanted and, by extension, knew what he feared.

So I'm taking a break from my narrative to take what she told me, what I know of Smitty's history, and form that into a short biography here.

During the "Destroyer" mess what had gotten Smitty to reach out to me were all the bizarre threat letters he was receiving. To return to Carterville, I need something different, something that would scare him even more, so that he will release me from my promise and let me return to my home.

Threat letters made up of letters cut out of magazines aren't going to do that. Repeating what had just been done would be amateur hour. So I am taking the time to try to understand Smitty. Not that I don't. I was a cop in the small town Smitty grew up in and learned to take after his father. I knew him as a cop knows a criminal, but this called for something else.

So, Smitty was born in 1983 in Cornville, Arizona. It's a small town in the high desert south of Sedona. Rolling desert hills with Oak Creek winding through it. These days they grow grapes on the hills above the creek, but back then there wasn't much going on. If you had money, you lived by the creek, if you didn't you lived in the open desert under the scalding sun.

Cornville along with Cottonwood and Camp Verde are part of a cluster of towns in the Verde Valley. On the Arizona heat index, it is about halfway between Flagstaff and Phoenix. Hot, but not "frying eggs on the sidewalk" hot.

His mother called him "Win." It wasn't until high school that he got the nickname Smitty. Win did what any smart, bored, curious kid did growing up in a small desert town. He poked around, got in trouble, made mischief.

I grew up in a much smaller mountain town and I did the same. But my father was a hard-working contractor that was very present in my life, probably too present, while Win's father was a hard-working grifter that abandoned him.

Win had hair so blond it looked almost white in the bright sunlight. He had freckles on his face brought out by that same hot sun. He has always been slim but he was positively gangly when he was just a kid. And he was a mama's boy, if ever there was one.

There are clichés here in Win's young life so let me just lay them out. His father was a drunk who, at first, paid attention to Mary Evans because her family had money. Just Cornville-level money, but that was enough to attract Wilson Smith's attention. Beyond the money, Mary had long honey-gold hair and a tall willowy frame that appealed to Wilson.

The courtship was intense and frowned upon by Mary's parents. She was cut off from the family money and Wil was gone by the time Win was two. Mary and Wil had never gotten married.

Even after Wilson left, Mary's family still wanted nothing to do with her, so Mary took a job in an old mining town north of Flagstaff. Carterville.

The job was as the town's only teacher. Carterville's lone community center was attached to the church at the top of Carter Hill, and at the time was something of an old-fash-ioned one-room school. Junior high and high school were in

Flagstaff, but the residents of Carterville liked keeping their young ones close.

That doesn't happen anymore, but there was a period of about ten years where Carterville had its own grade school.

So, Smitty moved from a small town in the desert to a much smaller town on a mountain and never saw his father again or his mother's side of the family. Cliché number one.

It was good for a while. Even though Carterville isn't all that far from Cornville, it was so different that it felt like a clean break to Mary. Her heart was broken by Wilson's departure, but she filled it up with a room full of kids to teach.

This really was a one-room schoolhouse with all grades in the same room, but Mary was that good of a teacher. She was well educated, had her master's in education, and could have gone just about anywhere, but the close-far nature of Carterville spoke to her.

The job was demanding enough, and Mary needed to be consumed by it, so she tutored after school and was pursuing her PhD on the side. Win was often on his own, something of a latchkey kid. Cliché number two.

This was a weird dichotomy for Win. He spent his days with a mother that had to treat him like every other student, his afternoons with her gone, and his nights with a mother that was there but wasn't really there.

Win didn't understand this, of course, but he looked a lot like his father, and that made it hard for Mary, leading to some of her less functional behavior.

This left Win to learn to fend for himself. Not such a bad thing, in and of itself, but the boy had literally been abandoned by his father, rejected by his mother's family, and now didn't get to see much of his mother, and when he did, he was mostly just another student.

All that loss changed him. He worried, as any kid would, that it was all about him. That he was the reason why his father left, that he was the reason why his mother worked so hard, even when she was at home.

Our childhood shapes us all and this is the childhood that shaped Smitty.

———

I KNEW WIN WHEN HE WAS A CHILD. HIS BLOND HAIR WAS usually too long and falling into his eyes and he would usually be running. Running away from the trouble he had caused or running towards the next mess he would be involved in. The kid was clearly smart, his sometimes green, sometimes hazel eyes reflecting intelligence along with defiance.

I was a police officer in my twenties, so I often got an earful of his exploits from angry residents. He wasn't that different from a handful of other kids, he was just a little more of it. Well… often a lot more of it.

Summers were the worst, of course, when he wasn't spending the day in the one-room school with his mother who was busy being something of a mother to an entire town of kids.

I remember one hot June day when I saw Win, then about eleven, dashing out between a couple of houses down on Aspen Street, shouts following him as he ran towards Main Street. He didn't seem to notice me, despite being dressed in police blues, and I grabbed him by his shirt, a ratty blue polo shirt. He had shorts and flip-flops on, his ability to run so fast in them rather impressive.

"Hey!" he shouted, batting back at me with his hand.

"Slow down, son," I said.

"I ain't your son," he barked. "Let me go."

The shouts were getting louder, a man's and a woman's and they were coming this way.

"So what did you do this time, Win?" I asked.

"Nothin'," he said.

I got a grip on his arm, the shirt was liable to rip, and chuckled. "We'll find out soon enough."

I walked more when I was younger, which seems like a silly statement, doesn't everyone walk more when they are younger? In any case, I walked the streets of Carterville more as part of my job. The town was quieter then, the chief of police, my predecessor, a man named Ren Thomas, was older, spent plenty of time at the station, and liked me being out and being seen.

Carterville was struggling economically then. The mine was open for tours and the town council was doing their best to keep Main Street nice and inviting, but we were just another old mining town off the beaten path, so it wasn't easy. We had a really good rock shop, a nice enough antique store to be on the circuit for those types, a decent restaurant, but not a lot else.

Most Carterville residents worked in Flagstaff, making this a distant bedroom community of that small city.

"Let me go," Win said, trying to wiggle out of my grip. "I didn't do nothin'. That old lady just has it out for me. I'm telling you, Officer, I didn't do nothin'."

We were on Aspen Street near Main. It was all residential at the time. The day was hot and I didn't have a cowboy hat on since Ren frowned upon it.

We were on the lower part of Carter Hill, with mostly juniper and piñon trees scattered amongst the houses with a couple of taller pines and some deciduous trees that had been planted with some of the houses.

It didn't take long until I saw who was yelling. It was Mary and William Reilly. Back then, Mary's hair was short and just going grey and she was already looking like your prototypical grandmother even though she was still in her fifties. William wasn't tall, but towered over Mary's four-foot-four, a friendly-looking man a couple of years older than Mary with dark hair.

They were both dressed in jeans and boots, with William in an old white T-shirt and Mary wearing a blue button-down shirt with yellow paint stains.

"Thanks for grabbing the little ruffian," William said.

I smiled and nodded, holding the squirming boy while they approached.

"Give it back," Mary said.

Win looked at me, his eyes wide and pleading.

"What did he take, Mrs. Reilly?" I asked.

"Henry Carter," she said with a shake of her head. "You are a grown man now, you can call me Mary."

"He took the keys to the new house," William said. "Took them right out of the door while we were inside."

The two of them had bought a couple of old run-down houses. Rumor was they were going to tear them down and create a small RV park.

I looked at the boy and he said, "They didn't see me do it."

He looked defiant, but his wide eyes showed his fear, and I could feel his heart thumping in his arm where I held him.

"We heard it," Mary said, staring at the boy, and even back then, before her powers, her bright hazel eyes were hard to hold when she was giving you the "look." "I opened the door and saw this one scampering away."

I knew those houses. They had been foreclosed on a few years ago and they had become an unofficial and unsanctioned hangout for some of the kids. I had cleared them out multiple times but they kept coming back. I didn't see anyone else, but I was pretty sure some of the rest of Win's little gang were watching us right now.

"Give the keys back, Win," I said.

"I ain't got no keys," he said.

"He doesn't have the keys," I said to William and Mary with a shrug.

William gave me a quizzical look and glanced at the kid's shorts. There was clearly something in his right pocket. The kid had the keys, but there were lines here that shouldn't be crossed.

"But you were trespassing, Win," I said. "I saw you on their property. If the Reillys want to press charges… well… I'd have to arrest you and take you into the station and…"

His eyes got wide. He was daring and bored enough to do what he did, but still young enough to be easily manipulated.

"I… Ah…" he stammered.

"But," I said. "If we were all to look the other way, and the Reillys' keys just happened to show up on that grass over there… well, then no real harm would have been done."

Mary caught my eye, her brow furrowing like she was

considering my unspoken offer and then she nodded. "We just want our keys back," she said.

I kept a hold of Win, and we all turned so we were facing away from the house we were in front of and its yard. There was a jangling sound and a small thump and Win said, "There they are. There are your stupid keys. Can I go?"

I let go of his arm and he was running down the sidewalk the moment I let him go.

———

THE BOY WIN COULD HAVE GONE EITHER WAY. LIKE I SAID, I wasn't that much different when I was a kid. I was a degree or two less mischievous, but not that much.

But I had two parents that were present, and Win didn't. I guess you would call this the main cliché of Win's upbringing, but a couple of years after the incident with the Reillys' keys, when Win was just hitting puberty, his mother Mary got hooked on painkillers after a horse-riding accident that left her with a serious back injury and an addiction.

His mother was no longer distant, she was needy, and this put the young Win in the position of caring for his mother.

The one-room schoolhouse experiment soon collapsed and Win and his mother had to move out of their nice house into a house not much better than the foreclosed one the Reillys had bought.

He went from being the neglected child to an unprepared caregiver in a few months' time.

Win loved his mother, fiercely. He became very protective of her, and at first it seemed like he took to the role he had been thrust into. He started working at the garage just north of the main part of town on Carterville Road. He started high school and then asked everyone to call him Smitty, the name change seeming to mark this transition in his life. It seemed like suddenly he was all over town doing odd jobs. But at the same time, there was a rash of petty thefts.

The thefts were cleverly done, and I couldn't pin any of them on him even though I knew he had done them, at least some of them. He got used to seeing me pretty often asking him a lot of questions about thefts in town, the ones he was part of and the ones he wasn't. I knew the kid didn't have a father, and I was aware that my interactions with him were paternal, like when I caught him with the Reillys' keys and just tried to scare him into not doing that kind of thing again. But I wasn't his father and it got twisted and that started to create the rift between us.

Don't get me wrong. I had empathy for the situation he and his mother were in. He was doing what he felt like he had to do to take care of his family, which was laudable—it's just that there are better ways to do it.

All of this backstory is so that I can understand Smitty better. It took me time to dredge through my memories, time to talk to others to put this together, but it confirmed what Patty had told me in Pagosa Springs, what the best lever was to use to get Smitty to need me again like with the "Destroyer" threat letters.

Smitty had daddy issues and that was my way in.

In retrospect, the tone of our conflict is totally informed by his daddy issues… and mine.

This is not my backstory, I suspect we'll get to some of that, at least, but suffice it to say that while I had a father, and while he tried, he wasn't actually around that much and when he was he tried too hard.

All of this is to say that to return to Carterville I would need to exploit Smitty's daddy issues and confront some of my own.

THIRTEEN
SUNDAY, AUGUST 9. FLAGSTAFF, ARIZONA

THE OTHER SIDE OF A MYSTERY IS, OFTEN, A CONSPIRACY. IT'S hard for a single person to create a compelling mystery.

Sure, Patty Walsh's neighbor pulled it off up in Pagosa Springs, Colorado, but he had time on his side and a limited scale to the "haunted house" mystery he was creating.

Instead of solving a mystery, this time I needed to create a mystery for Winston "Smitty" Smith, and I needed help to do that.

I was alone, pacing in a nondescript hotel room on the east side of Flagstaff, not far from the country club with a good pizza place right across the parking lot.

As I've rambled and camped, I have taken to staying in a hotel room every week or so. I'm getting used to my fancy camping pad, but I'm old enough that a real bed makes a big difference, and a long, hot shower feels like my best friend some days.

I've done this enough that every hotel room kind of seems

the same. A couple of queen beds, a TV, a table of some kind, short carpet in a variety of annoying patterns. You get it. It was just another hotel room. One I would soon forget.

Much of summer had slipped by as I researched and prepared. It was August, the sun was slipping to the south, and the days were getting shorter.

I paced and felt for the little cell phone in my jeans back pocket. I had developed a strange relationship with the burner phone Brooke had given me. It was like I was some kind of primitive version of a man and the flip phone was some kind of totem, a magical artifact the goddess used to communicate with me, to decide my fate.

Brooke giveth and Brooke taketh away.

This wasn't where my mind was with it. This wasn't a logical thing, but this was where it had gone emotionally. I hated it.

It felt like a chain around my foot, or, perhaps more apropos, a collar around my neck and a leash that Brooke held on to.

The phone buzzed, I pulled it out, and popped it open. "Relax," the text from Brooke said. "These are your people. They want to help. They want you back."

Except I had made a deal with the devil, and I was about to draw them into it. I wouldn't be a rational human if I didn't feel some doubts and some guilt.

When I had talked to Brooke in prison, she had indicated that much of her knowing what to do and what to say was from my memoirs. She didn't explain the mechanism, but she indicated that she could read the memoirs before I wrote them.

Which is fine. Seems like a bit of a cheat or a shortcut, but okay. Somehow her power lets her read books before they are written. Seems logical given what I know she can do. Seems smart, even.

The problem here is that while memoirs have dates in them, they lack precise times, yet her magical texts always seem to arrive at the right moment. I've learned this well over the last few months as her texts have nudged me onto the right path or kept me going when I would have quit.

So maybe she was future-reading my memoirs, this memoir to be precise, but that wasn't all she was doing. Her powers were greater and more complicated than that.

When there was a knock on the door, I jumped. I had been lost in Brooke-land.

"Is there some kinda password?" a muffled voice with a southern drawl asked. "'Cause I got hot pizza and that should be enough of a password to your little private club."

I couldn't help but smile and opened the door.

Annabelle Unger stood there holding a couple of boxes of pizza dressed in tight jeans, red heels, and a silky red blouse, a smile on her very red lips.

The smell of the pizza and her perfume was almost a blow, my stomach rumbling and my smile getting wider.

Annabelle was a few years older than me—I'm really not sure how much older, a gentleman doesn't ask these questions —but she was around sixty years old. It showed in the wrinkles on her face, those exacerbated by many years of smoking, but it did not show in her chemically assisted, purple streaked, bright red hair.

"You just gonna gawk, Chief, or are you gonna let me in?" she asked. "It's not like you ain't laid eyes on this since you left. We had lunch last month."

I felt my cheeks flush and stepped aside. "It's different this time," I said.

"You got your fancy plannin' done?" she asked as she strode by, her balancing in those heels seeming like something of a miracle. Annabelle is the dispatcher, office manager, CSI tech, and a bunch of other things for the Carterville Police Department. She's not an actual police officer but holds the station together. She started working for me a little bit before the meteor hit.

But, I guess, she didn't really work for me anymore, but hopefully that was going to change soon.

She put the pizzas on the small, round table and turned around and faced me, her arms crossed. "So, what the hell is this plan?"

I nodded toward the door that I was still holding open. "I think we should wait until the others come."

She shook her head. "I'm early and I need to know. Everything. Right now."

I opened my mouth to speak but didn't come up with any words. Clearly, she didn't work for me anymore and it felt strange. Not that Annabelle was ever shy about speaking her mind, but there was something different here.

She walked over, pushed on the door, and I let it go and she shut it and then stood with her back to the door. "You need me to run this show from Carterville, right?" she said. It wasn't really a question.

"Right," I said.

"Then I need you to tell me everything. Now," she said. "Start with the part you don't want to tell everyone else."

I blinked and swallowed. This wasn't a power or anything like that, Annabelle just knew me, but I started to feel that pressure on my chest, like the elephant was just starting to transfer its weight on to me. She took my arm and guided me over to one of the beds and I sat down. She sat on the other bed across from me.

"You been locked in your head, on your own, for just about a year, Henry," she said, her use of my name not my former title getting my attention. Her brown eyes through the forest of her fake eyelashes were a mix of compassion and concern. "You need to get it out. You know you do now. Spill the tea."

I nodded. She was right. I had been thinking and writing, but I hadn't been speaking it. And there were certainly parts that I didn't want to speak.

I cleared my throat and nodded, sweat beading on the back of my neck. "I… I made a deal with Brooke."

———

THEY SAY CONFESSION IS GOOD FOR THE SOUL, AND I CAN SEE that, but I'm not sure they were thinking of someone like Anabelle Unger when they made that saying up.

Annabelle is as good at cursing as a songbird is at singing and she let loose a string of curses as she surged up and started pacing the bland hotel room, the same path I had been pacing before she came.

I won't bother to try to record Annabelle's expletives. I don't think I could do them justice and I'm not trying to write a book filled with f-bombs and much more creative cursing than that.

"Are you crazy?" she asked me when the barrage was slowing down.

I shrugged. "Maybe. But you haven't heard it all. She planted something for me at the Four Corners Monument. She did it three years ago before all of this started." I fingered the turquoise bolo at my throat. I was keeping the trickster, Coyote, close.

She kept up her restless pacing as I filled her in on what happened at Four Corners, on what I had learned about Smitty, about trying to return to Carterville, about my deal with Brooke, about the preparations I had made in the last few months.

In the state she was in, Annabelle was more likely to say "shit" or something worse than the usual "mmmhhmm" or "okay" that someone would do when you told them a long story.

When it was over, she slumped down on the bed opposite me. "She 'future-read' your memoir?" she asked. "Is that what you are callin' it?"

I nodded.

"So, she knows about this here conversation," she said.

I nodded. "As long as I write about it."

Her brow furrowed, the fine lines from her years of smoking putting on a display. "Then why the hell don't you sit down, right here, right now, for as long as it takes, and write the memoir with the ending you want?"

The idea slammed into my brain. I had thought a lot about Brooke and her power and what I was writing—all of it making me dreadfully self-conscious—but I hadn't thought about that.

"Ahh... I...," I began, my brain trying to process the novel thought. "I don't think her power works that way."

Annabelle cocked her head to the right. "Explain."

"She sees the future," I said. "She doesn't create it. If I record what I want the future to be, if she reads it and assumes it's correct, then she won't take the actions needed to create the future she wants."

She snorted. "Well, that don't sound like such a bad thing."

"But what we want aligns," I said. "At least until we both get back to Carterville."

Annabelle bit her red lip, her eyes wandering around. "So she'll take you to that place, to where you are both back, and then what? Won't she have prepared something else that… that… Oh, hell, this shit just makes my brain hurt, but you know what I mean."

"I have a plan," I said.

"Then what the hell is it?"

I shook my head. "I can't say. I won't say."

Her brow furrowed again and she nodded to my laptop which was sitting on the low dresser. "Just tell me and don't write about it."

I shook my head. "I can't. She's doing more than future-reading my memoir. She has to be. If I tell you then she'll know."

Annabelle sat there blinking, her eyes unfocused for a few breaths, and then she shook her head like she was trying to clear a disturbing thought. "I ain't got one little clue how you are managing this, Chief, not one. But I am here to help."

She leaned over and hugged me and I felt a wave of relief. I wasn't alone in this anymore.

FOURTEEN
SUNDAY, AUGUST 9. FLAGSTAFF, ARIZONA

THE NONDESCRIPT FLAGSTAFF HOTEL ROOM WAS CROWDED. People were eating pizza, drinking sodas, and chatting, but these weren't just any people, these were *my* people.

Bo Larson, he's a sculptor of reclaimed metal and looks it with a big barrel chest, rough, scarred hands, and kind eyes under his mop of curly, overlong blonde hair.

He's in his early twenties and ran into a lot of trouble with his powers, so he doesn't live in Carterville anymore but outside of it in a nearby off-the-grid area called the 40s.

Frank Paulson, my best friend, was sitting next to him, his shaved head bent low as he talked to Bo. He was taller and bigger than Bo with kind blue eyes. He's the cook and owner of the Carterville Dinner.

My older sister Wendy was sitting in a chair at the round table and her brown eyes caught mine. She gave me a small smile that raised her cheeks and highlighted the splash of freckles there. She had shoulder-length brown hair, that's still fully brown, unlike mine, since she had the help of Lady Clairol.

Wendy was sitting next to and talking to Martin Lester, who I often call "the quiet man." Because he's quiet, and because of his power where if he doesn't want to be noticed, he's not. Martin was in his early sixties, tall and slim with dull blue eyes and a prodigious steel grey mustache.

"It's kinda nice, ain't it?" Annabelle asked me. She's standing next to me near the door.

I nodded. The murmur of voices, such familiar voices, was a wonderful comfort. But we were not here just to eat pizza and catch up.

"You didn't eat much," she said. "You lost your appetite for pizza, Chief?"

I shook my head. "Just worried about what I have to say."

"And you have to tell them everything," she said. "You don't, I will."

I looked at Annabelle, her brown eyes were serious. She was always the mother of the department and so now it appeared she had appointed herself the mother of this conspiracy.

And it was not lost on me as I stood there that I was going to write about this. I really hate to. But if this memoir sees the light of day, I'll be surprised. I have to write this for Brooke. It needs to exist for her. But I don't know if I want anyone else reading it.

This is all personal. I don't know if I want anyone else reading any of my memoirs beyond the one that the publisher already has.

"I'll tell them," I said with a sigh. "They have a right to know."

"You got this," she said, her tone low, and then she cleared her voice loudly and the chatting stopped, and all eyes were on me.

Annabelle gave me a smile and went and sat on the bed with Bo and Frank, giving me an encouraging nod.

"Thank you all for coming," I said. That many eyes on me after so much time alone felt strange and I started to sweat. My job has always been in the public, but I have always recharged when I was alone, usually on my deck watching the light play across the desert as the sun goes down. I guess that makes me something of an introvert who has always had an extroverted kind of job.

"I know I've been rather mysterious and rather absent for the last couple of months," I said. "Something happened at the Four Corners Monument after I was in Colorado visiting Patty. Something that sent me to Florence to visit Brooke Jennings."

Everyone started talking at once, expressions of surprise, outrage, and worry. Everyone but Annabelle, who sat there with a little grin on her face because she knew what was coming.

———

IT TOOK A LOT LONGER TO GET THROUGH IT ALL WITH FIVE people instead of one. Even Annabelle had more questions, but I recounted what happened at Four Corners and since. I explained Brooke's offer and gave them an outline of what getting Smitty to release me from my promise would entail.

My sister, Wendy, asked the fewest questions. She sat there with her arms crossed most of the time staring at me.

She was mad. She was my big sister and expected me to come to her first with this kind of thing. And maybe I should have, but it was just a tenuous idea for a while, and then I wasn't sure, and then… Well, it was time to start it up.

She has the same brown eyes as I do and there are some similarities in our faces. If I squinted, it almost looked like it was me there giving me the stink eye. And I guess there was something to that. There was a lot about this plan that didn't sit well with me.

"Wait," Bo Larson said, rubbing at his curly blond hair. "Let me see if I got this right. So Smitty, he's got daddy issues. Least surprising thing in the world." There were a few chuckles at that, and Bo grinned and sat up a little straighter. "So, we're gonna pretend his old man is roaming around Carterville waiting for him to come back."

I nodded.

"What's his father's motive?" Frank Paulson asked. He was fond of murder mysteries, had read everything Agatha Christie had ever written, so this wasn't a surprising question. "Why would Smitty's father be wandering around Carterville texting him?"

I shrugged. "Doesn't really matter. Maybe he's got cancer and wants Smitty to heal him. Maybe he's broke and needs money. Maybe he's old and lonely and wants Smitty to take care of him."

"Or all three," Martin Lester said with a grin and a rub of his mustache.

"Right," I said. "Hints and innuendo are all we need. Just enough to drive Smitty a little bonkers."

"More bonkers, you mean," Annabelle said and there were more chuckles.

Bo nodded and said, "And so Smitty, still in prison, will have some people investigate. Try to find the old man."

I nod. "Right. It may take a few months, but it will happen. And when the texts keep coming and the investigators can't find anything, he'll really be upset."

Bo's brow furrowed and he crossed his arms. "Upset enough to call you?" he asked. "Upset enough to release you from your promise and send you to Carterville to investigate?" He shook his head. "I don't know. He really hates you."

Wendy caught my eye and the look on her pursed-lipped face seemed to say that maybe Smitty had good reason to hate me or that the feeling was obviously mutual. I looked away and scratched my face, making sure she could see that I was wearing the fitness tracker she bought me after my heart scare a couple of years ago. I meant it as a placating gesture, to show her that I did listen to her, but then I realized I was scratching at the scars Patty gave me that terrible night and she might take the wrong message there so I quickly dropped my hand.

"Umm… He'll need someone who knows Carterville," I said. "Someone who can get to the bottom of it. There's just not that many of us."

"Will he call me?" Lester asked. "I hope he does so I can tell him to go to hell, you know."

There were no chuckles at that one because the first part of his question brought the specter of Brooke Jennings back into the room because we all figured that Brooke knew the answer to that and pretty much any other question we might have about this.

"I don't know," I said, and everyone knew that meant that Brooke knew but she hadn't told me.

There was a moment of silence as everyone dealt with what we were up against in their own way. Maybe a few flirting with the existential crisis that such ponderings can bring. The blank look on Frank's round face made me think he had gone there, or maybe he was back living the trauma of his stabbing.

Wendy leaned forward and licked her lips. "What about Isabella?" she asked me, her voice quiet but tight.

"Smitty knows better than to ask her," I said.

"No," she said. "Why isn't she here? We've got your Carter's Six, or whatever you want to call this thing, but no Isabella Ortega. She doesn't want the job you left her. She wants you back as much as any one of us. Why isn't she here?"

I won't pretend to understand my sister's motivations here. She was irritated with me, to some degree, and that may have been a factor, but as uncomfortable as it was, this was a question that needed to be asked.

I nodded, took a step forward, and came and sat on the dresser in front of the flatscreen TV, a sigh escaping me. "It's better for her if she doesn't know what we are doing."

"Better?" Bo asked, looking around. "Are we doing something illegal?"

"Maybe," I said. Bo opened his mouth to speak and I held up my hand. "Look, if we were doing all of this to extort money or directly harm Smitty, then yes, we would be committing a crime. Fraud, to be specific. But all we are doing is trying to get him to release me from my promise. We are going to intentionally manipulate him for that purpose, but… it's hard to see that as a crime."

"That's criminal," Wendy said. "What about civil? Could Smitty sue us?"

Maybe this was "tough love" from Wendy. These were my people and they needed to know what they were getting into, but I would have preferred to do it in my own time.

"Smitty don't need any kind of excuse to sue us," Annabelle said with a chuckle that didn't spread.

"Yes," I said. "Smitty could sue us for pain and suffering. We are going to put him through something. He might even have a case against us." Mouths opened and about three people were going to speak, but I kept going. "But we have a case against him for what he did. Frank," I said nodding to the big man. "He was responsible for your stabbing." I pointed at my face. "And my scars and Patty's trauma. He intentionally addicted people to his power and extorted them. None of these are crimes he was convicted for."

I stood up and squared my shoulders. "Honestly, if what we do causes him to sue us, we'll just sue him right back. We've got a much better case. Much better."

There were nods and murmurs of agreement.

"Here's what I don't get," Frank said when things had quieted down. "Say this works. Say Smitty releases you from your promise and you go 'investigate.' What then? There's nothing to find except our own little…" The right word was conspiracy but that's not what he said, he said, "…whatever you call this. What will you tell him?"

"Honestly," I said. "I'm not sure yet. We'll cross that bridge when we get there."

FIFTEEN
SUNDAY, AUGUST 9. FLAGSTAFF, ARIZONA

I solve mysteries, I don't create them. But all my time thinking about and investigating the strange had led me to have some insights on what makes a good mystery. My previous memoirs have all revolved around untangling a mystery, not creating the tangle.

In that hotel room, my non-answer on what to tell Smitty if he released me from my promise went over just fine with almost everyone. Maybe it would make sense just to tell him outright, let him really feel what it was like to be taken advantage of. Maybe we would come up with a plausible scapegoat and redirect his ire. Whatever it was, we would deal with Smitty when I was back in Carterville since that was, in many ways, one of the main things I was going back to deal with.

But Wendy wasn't having it. At all.

"And when we are back in Carterville?" Wendy asked. "After you've given Brooke her few days and returned her to prison? How long until Smitty finds out? How long until renewed hate for you, his hate for us, drives him to try something again?"

I opened my mouth to speak, but she was shaking her head. She stood up, and the look on her face stopped me. "Are you and Smitty going to draw guns on Main Street, the town not being big enough for the two of you? Make no mistake. He wanted you gone, and when that failed, he tried to kill you. He won't stop, and neither will you.

"How does this all end, Henry? How does it end?"

She sniffed and walked past me and out of the room. I looked back at all the faces staring at me and suddenly Wendy's actions all made sense. She wanted me to be able to come home to Carterville, but she wanted me alive and well even more. She was my big sister. She had been trying to look out for me ever since I was a kid.

Annabelle's eyes widened and she gave me a small nod. I took the hint and followed Wendy.

Out in the hallway, I found her a few doors down crying. "I won't go through this again," she said. "I won't."

I wasn't sure which "this" she was referring to. Falling from the sky while chasing a murderer—Carterville powers can lead to some crazy situations. Having a burning building fall down around me. Barely escaping an explosion that collapsed much of the old Carterville mine. There were plenty to choose from.

"What am I supposed to do?" I asked her. "Let this be? Never return to my home?"

She looked up at me, her tear-streaked face hardening. "Yes," she said. "Isn't being alive outside of Carterville better than being dead there?"

"This isn't just about Smitty," I said. I know, obvious, but in the moment it felt like a revelation.

"Oh no, it's about him," she said. "You two hate each other so much, this will go on until one of you is dead."

My face flushed hot, and I wanted to yell at her. Of course I hated Smitty. Look at what he had done. Look at what he did with his real live superpower. He could do so much more, be so much more. He had squandered it all on his ego, tried to recreate Carterville in his image, but he had gotten himself exiled when he exiled me.

Before I could find any rational words, Wendy stood up straight, pulled her shoulders back, and said, "I must not hate. Hate is the mind-killer. Hate is the little-death that brings total obliteration. I will face my hate. I will permit it to pass over me and through me. And when it has gone past I will turn the inner eye to see its path. Where the hate has gone there will be nothing. Only I will remain."

It was a recitation, a familiar one. As my mind struggled to grasp what it was, Wendy closed the few steps between us, kissed me on the cheek, and said, "I can't be a part of this." With that she turned and walked away, her words about hate hanging in the air like heavy overly strong perfume. The kind that lodges in your nose and you can't get rid of.

———

It was quiet when I walked back into the hotel room. Too quiet. These were people who had all known each other for many years. This wasn't a quiet group.

Annabelle got up, led me over to the bed, and I sat down opposite Bo and Frank, and Annabelle sat next to me. Martin scooted his chair closer and it felt a lot more intimate.

"I hate Smitty," I said. I kind of expected there to be chuckles or snorts of agreement but there wasn't. "I really, really hate him."

Annabelle took my hand and squeezed it but stayed silent. This feeling of hate wasn't some big revelation. Brooke's whole "Destroyer of Carterville" madness was about getting Smitty and me out of town so our hate for each other wouldn't destroy it. Well… it's not that simple. She indicated that our hate would distract us when a crisis came and that crisis would destroy Carterville.

Wendy's words rang in my head, "Hate is the little-death that brings total obliteration."

I knew it wasn't right, that quote, but it rang true. Hate destroys. It can do nothing else.

"I can help you," Bo said gently. I was staring at my hands slumped over. I looked up and his brown eyes were just peeking past his overlong bangs. "You helped me," he said. "When I was angry all the time. When I got my power. When it was causing others to get violent with each other… I can help you."

Bo's power was an odd one. When he was angry, and he was an angry teenager when the meteor hit, that rage would spread to others. We had random outbreaks of violence that we couldn't explain until we realized Bo was always in the area. I had helped him get a place near Carterville out in the 40s. I had gotten him counseling and help.

I nodded.

"I hate him, too," Martin Lester said. His chair was near enough so he was leaning into the tight circle. "I hate Brooke more, but I hate that smug, condescending bastard too, you know. But I don't give it no air. I just stay away and do my best not to think about either of them."

I had promised that I would never ask Lester to return to Carterville after the last time. And I hadn't. I had actually seen a lot of him lately as he had been helping me investigate Smitty and his father these last few months.

"Everyone hates Smitty," Frank said, his blue eyes intense. "How do you do this, Henry, how do you come back and not let the hate destroy you?"

I shrugged and then everyone was looking at Annabelle.

"What?" she asked. "Of course I hate him and I ain't ever goin' to feel bad about it and I ain't never going to stop. Henry, you're a kind soul, and I can see how hate might mess with ya. But me? It just fuels me."

I nodded and took a deep breath. It's one thing to be fueled by hate and it's quite another to realize that is what has been keeping you going. Rather it was what was keeping me going. I hated Smitty. I couldn't bear to let him win. He couldn't have Carterville, not while I was around.

My main criticism of Smitty is that he makes it all about him, and if I do this because of hate, I'm really no better than him.

"Wendy is out," I said. It needed to be said and I needed to change the subject.

"We got enough folks in Carterville," Annabelle said.

"Lisa will help," Frank said. "You know she will."

Lisa Paulson was Frank's wife and I had known her as long as I had known Frank.

I nodded. "Thanks. There's more to talk about, more to plan, but…" I didn't finish. I didn't need to.

"Come back home with me," Bo said. "Stay as long as you like."

"Thanks," I said. I had been camping around Flagstaff when I could have been staying with friends or family. I knew this, but I hadn't understood why, I had just needed to be alone. Now that the ugly truth was out, I didn't want to be alone. "I have to do something first, but I'll come out."

The conversation turned into Smitty stories, ones that painted him in a particularly bad light. I got what they were doing, they were trying to make me feel less alone, but it didn't feel right. Smitty was the wrong focus. I needed to get back to Carterville to serve the town, to protect the town, to protect the people.

Things were changing. We had gotten so much exposure in the media, it was turning into something of a circus. Or, at least, that is what I had heard. It's not like I had been there to witness it.

I quickly said my goodbyes and left. I really did have something I had to do.

SIXTEEN

SUNDAY, AUGUST 9. FLAGSTAFF, ARIZONA

FORTY POUNDS OF GRANDNEPHEW PLOWING INTO YOU WILL change your state, that's for sure.

Ian was four years old with a round, cherubic face and dark rumpled hair. "Grand!" he screamed when he saw it was me and made like a mini-linebacker and charged.

My knees didn't protest too much and I was squatting down when he slammed into me, both of us laughing.

"He misses you," my niece Lilly said. "You should come around more."

Still holding the boy who was bracing his heels against the threshold of the door and grunting, I glanced up and nodded. Lilly had long dark hair, pale green eyes, and a sharp Carter chin. She was dressed in scrubs having followed her mother into the medical field. She was a nurse now but studying to be a nurse practitioner.

"Mom came home upset," Lilly said. "Really upset. What happened?"

I looked down and grunted myself as I resisted the boy's assault. He was sure to be a real linebacker someday, or maybe a wrestler. I grabbed him and surged up, my knees popping as I did and I had a wriggling grandnephew in my arms, as hard to hold as some huge slippery fish.

"Smitty," I said to Lilly.

She nodded and her face soured. "She didn't like your big plan?"

I shook my head. "She doesn't like the thought of us both being back in Carterville."

Lilly raised one eyebrow and gave me a small nod.

I wrestled the boy inside, walked into their small living room, threw him down on the couch, and started tickling him.

"No, Grand," he said as he laughed. "No, no, please no."

When the boy was younger he had called me "Grandpa" and that, obviously, didn't sit well with any of us. With Wendy's husband deceased, I was the older man on this side of the family. Granduncle doesn't come slipping off the tongue but "Grand" was something Ian could manage and we could live with.

"Grand" didn't really sit well with me either. It hinted at Carterville and the powers there. The boy was always pestering me to tell him stories of people with powers.

"Stop, Grand. Stop! Stop!" the boy yelled while he was giggling.

When his tone changed from playful to distressed, I stepped back and he lay there panting.

"Come on, Ian," Lilly said, walking over and sitting next to the boy and tousling his hair. "Let Grand be. He needs to talk to Grandma. Let's find out what Bluey is up to."

———

As I left Ian and Lilly watching some animated show about a blue dog, I lingered in the hallway and looked back. I should come around more often. Ian's father was never in the picture, Lilly didn't have a partner, and that really put me in the position of the older male in the boy's life.

Ian giggled at something that was going on on the screen and I felt this longing for family, for something other than Carterville. My son, Tom, was still in college in Phoenix. I suspected it would be a while before he started thinking about a family.

The truth was, I hadn't visited enough, not nearly enough. Before Smitty extracted that promise from me, it was the job that kept me so busy, and after I had been obsessed with returning to that job. I had been spending time writing these stories when I could have been spending time with my family.

But what if I did return? Could I find a way to be more balanced? To take time off? To not feel like every single bad thing that happened in Carterville was on me?

Yes, I am something of a workaholic and the job pretty much demands it, but the truth is, work is easier a lot of the time. All that external pressure, those external constraints make it pretty clear what you need to do and how you need to fill your day.

My months without all that pressure have been challenging. Not only was my job taken away from me, but my home, and both of those took plenty of attention. That left me in a void that I could have filled a lot more with rambunctious grandnephews, my sister, my niece, my son, my family.

I have written how a job can make you more than you

thought you could be, and that is true, but it can also make you less than you should be in other areas of your life if you let it.

———

Wendy had her own room in the house. Both Wendy and Lilly owned it, and Wendy was there a lot because of her long shifts at the hospital and helping out with Ian. Moreso since I left Carterville.

I would say her room looked rumpled but not messy, with the bed only sort of made, papers and books stacked on the small desk, books arranged a little haphazardly in the bookshelves that lined all available space. There was no TV in here and her laptop sat closed on her desk.

Wendy loved books and it showed. She was sitting on the bed crossed-legged, a well-worn paperback in her lap, when I entered. I didn't recognize the book, but I did remember where her quote came from.

She was obsessed with the novel *Dune* when we were kids. I wasn't much into books when we were young, but she insisted that I read it. And I liked it. Kind of. It was something of a fictional history of a conflict between two families, with knife fights and sand worms and lots of other strange things.

When it comes to fiction, I am more partial to Westerns, although change the trappings a bit and *Dune* could be almost viewed that way. But more than fiction, I like to read histories. I like to learn about the real world, not made-up worlds.

Wendy was staring at me, her face neutral. She had told me to come in on the first knock and she was waiting for me to start the conversation.

"It's fear," I said. "Fear is the mind-killer. That's the quote from *Dune*. It's not hate."

A smile briefly turned up her lips until she suppressed it and returned to her neutral mask. She had a fuzzy blue robe on and the freckles on her cheeks looked darker in the dim light.

"But I get your point," I said. "Hate is a mind-killer too. I must not hate."

She nodded, but still didn't speak.

"But Smitty is so damn hateable," I said, and she finally cracked a real smile.

"That he is," she said, patting the bed.

I sat down on the edge of it. I was in better shape than I had been, but sitting cross-legged in cowboy boots wasn't pretty. This left me twisting around to look at her.

She sighed, put the book down, and scooted so she was sitting on the edge of the bed too and I felt this wave of déjà vu. How many times had we sat like this as kids and talked. How many times had my big sister tried to help me out as I dealt with bullies or girls or having the name Carter?

"I want to do better," I said.

She arched one eyebrow and said, "What do you mean?"

I shrugged. "I want to spend more time here, with you and Lilly and Ian. I want to see Tom more. I want to go back to Carterville, I really do, but I want to find a way so that it is not all that I am anymore."

"Good," she said, but I could hear the doubt in her voice.

"But the thing you don't understand is that Carterville, the town, the people, they are my family too."

"I do understand that," she said. "I feel it too, the pull of that strange little town and its people. I would hate to be in your situation."

I nodded. "It's Smitty then?" I asked.

She shrugged. "Oh, there's the normal cop stuff multiplied by ten because of the powers, but, yeah, it's Smitty. That town really isn't big enough for the two of you."

I sighed and nodded again.

"If you are both back there, you will try to destroy each other," she said. "I think Brooke is crazy, but her essential point about you two was correct. She might have made it worse, but it would have gotten to where it did on its own. It would have just taken longer."

She was right. I was the town's cop and Smitty was the town's petty criminal. At least that's what it was before the meteor and our powers. Now he was a superpowered healer dedicated to reshaping the town into something that served him.

"Do you really think the governor will commute his sentence?" Wendy asked.

I gave her a look. While she had her head in books, I was always wading into the real world. Of course the governor will commute his sentence. Smitty only needed to find someone the governor loves that needs to be healed and one was readily available. And it didn't really have to be the governor. It could be someone that had leverage on the governor. This is why Smitty pleaded guilty. He didn't want the trial, which would have been garish and painted him in a very poor light.

"Yeah," she said with a nod. "He's coming back."

"And what happens to Carterville if I'm not there to resist him?" I asked.

"Others will take up the fight," Wendy said. "It doesn't always have to be you, Henry." I opened my mouth to speak but she forged on. "And don't give me your 'I'm a Carter' speech. It's just a name. You still have a choice."

"What I was going to say," I began, "is that I know others will take up the fight. Ortega. Anabelle. The Marins. Frank and Lisa." I sighed. "I know it's silly, maybe even horribly old fashioned, but I'd rather be there standing between the people I care about and Smitty."

She pursed her lips and nodded, and I could see something in her eyes. Sadness. Resignation. Fear.

"But I want to be here more too," I said. "I want to be around until little Ian is big enough to truly tackle me. I want to be there for Lilly when she graduates and becomes a nurse practitioner. I want to be around for everything Tom has coming.

"But I'm not whole right now. Can you see that? I'm not myself without Carterville. I need to return."

She smiled—it was a shy, brief smile. "But hate is the mind-killer," she said. "How do you do all this and not do it out of hate?"

I was still for a moment trying to remember the words. "I... I will let it pass through me and when it's gone, there will be nothing. Only I will remain."

Wendy laughed. It wasn't pure laughter, it was fueled by stress and a little too loud, but it filled my heart to hear it. She grabbed my arm and leaned her head against my shoulder. "Not quite there, little brother, but close. Please keep talking to me about this. Please."

SEVENTEEN

SATURDAY, AUGUST 22. THE 40S

I HATE TO MEDITATE.

Bo tells me that makes me human and that tells me that I am on the right path.

I still hate to meditate.

And hate is the mind-killer and I am trying out this meditation crap so that I can deal with this Smitty situation out of love for Carterville and its people, not hate for Winston "Smitty" Smith.

So, this new thing I hate is designed to help me not hate my enemy. Is this stupid or what?

"Just breathe," Bo said, his voice all Zen-calm and I hated that too. Bo was a teenager with anger control issues when the meteor hit, now he was acting like some Sedona guru teaching me to meditate.

"Just focus on your breath," he said. "Let the thoughts come up, but don't pay attention to them. There is no stopping your thoughts, but you can disconnect from them. You can know that they are not who you are."

And who the hell was I? A Carter that had been exiled from Carterville. A cop without a beat. A middle-aged man without a partner.

We were sitting on yoga mats—seriously!—on the concrete pad that was originally built as an RV shelter on Bo's acreage out in the 40s. The wind had kicked up and all his whirligigs and other moving metal contraptions were squeaking as they turned, the sharp scent of juniper trees making me think of gin way more than I had in a while.

Actually, meditation made me think of drinking more than I had since I left Carterville and the job. And it made me think of Lila Chang and the look of need on her face the night she died, the night I was too preoccupied with my own troubles to see that she needed help.

And that made me think of Annie Smith who the media dubbed "Blackout." Her trial was starting in a few months, and I would be testifying. And that brought images of her from high school all the way up to her betrayal.

And that made me think of—

"Breathe, Chief," Bo said. "You aren't breathing."

I cursed, trying to imitate Annabelle's fluency and falling short, but it was enough to elicit a chuckle from Bo.

Not only was I sitting crossed-legged on a yoga mat, my boots were off as was my cowboy hat and I wasn't even wearing jeans but sweatpants.

"I'm too damn old for this," I growled.

"Tell your monkey mind, 'Thank you for sharing,' and just breathe," he said. "Listen to the wind, feel the cool air on your face. Smell the desert."

It was early, stupidly early. It was late August and we had beat the sun up. I cracked an eye open, and Bo was sitting there peaceful as can be, a relaxed expression on his face making him look a lot like the teenager he once was, his rumpled blond hair contributing to that impression. He was good at the lotus position, his legs relaxed and flat on his mat while my knees were up in the air because I wasn't very flexible.

Bo had offered to teach me some simple yoga stretches to help with that, but I had told him to go to hell.

I had been doing this every day with Bo for almost two weeks. This was what he had done years ago when he needed to get his anger under control. He claims that I had been the one that suggested he try meditation, but I don't remember that. I absolutely do not.

Some days it seemed I got somewhere with it, but not today, although Bo assures me that there is no place to go and it's "the practice of the practice that counts."

I think it's Annie. I'm going to have to face her when I testify. I'm going to have to see the pain in her piercing blue eyes. She betrayed me, but that look will tell me that I'm the one betraying her.

We have history, God do we have history. First, she was my high school girlfriend, my first love, and then my on-again, off-again girlfriend after my divorce. We had betrayed each other at one level or another for years, as lovers often do, but her being involved in a conspiracy that escalated into attempted murder trumps everything that came before. But knowing Annie as I do, she will somehow make me feel like I'm the one betraying her when I testify.

"Just let go, Chief," Bo said.

"I can't," I growled.

The idea of "letting go" had never worked for me. Bad things always seemed to happen when I "let go." Maybe it was my profession, having to always confront the bad things people were doing. Maybe I was a control freak. Maybe I was defective. Maybe—

"Just let go of thinking about letting go," Bo said, and I just wanted to hit him.

"You're just messing with me now," I said.

He chuckled. "I am. But tell the truth, that's exactly where your mind went."

"Don't know why I ever decided to help you out, all those years ago," I said. "I used to think you had potential."

"I'll take that as a 'yes,'" he said. "Now come back to your breath. Feel the air filling your lungs, feel it as it flows over the back of your nose."

He droned on and, without thinking about letting go, I was able to let go. It took a long time, but I eventually hit what I call the "jump."

This isn't some guru term, just my experience. When it's right, when I'm actually meditating, there's a jump. Often a physical one, like a mild startle reaction, but really, it's a jump in time. Like I wasn't aware of the passage of time for a moment, like I couldn't remember what I had just been thinking about, like I could sense how things were slightly different than I remembered.

It's not like falling asleep, although that can produce a jump. It's different, it's more nourishing somehow.

The jump is the result of truly letting go and I'm left feeling relaxed, but a little vulnerable. Both of which, I think, are good for me.

"Ready for today?" Bo asked when I opened my eyes after the "jump." He was sitting there watching me.

"No," I said.

He smiled. "Everyone just wants to help."

I nodded. Today we were redoing what we started in that hotel room before Wendy stormed off. She wasn't coming, but I had been over to their Flagstaff house a couple of times for barbeques and Ian's fifth birthday party.

"Everyone's been talking about me," I said. And they had been. I know they had been. Wendy was the one that had said something, but everyone had been worried about me, apparently. I'm the worrier, not the one people worry about.

But that was a stupid old thought. Of course people worried about me. It wasn't my job to take care of everyone and not be cared for by anyone.

Bo nodded and smiled. "Just let it go, Chief."

He wasn't quite close enough for me to reach, but I leaned forward and swatted at him. He gracefully rolled back and got up. Bo was a stocky, barrel-chested guy that wrestled with metal for a living, but all this yoga and meditation had left him quite limber.

"Need more today?" he asked.

I nodded. I wanted another "jump." Honestly, I wanted to jump past all of this until I was back home, but wishing the world worked the way you wanted doesn't do anyone any good.

"Good," he said. "I'll be back in twenty with coffee."

I closed my eyes and let the squeaking of his metal contraptions take me away.

———

THE ENVIRONMENT WAS AS DIFFERENT AS IT COULD BE FROM that bland hotel room in Flagstaff. We were under the former RV shelter in the middle of Bo's chunk of land surrounded by twisting junipers and piñon trees. His metal sculptures were mostly still—the breeze had died down as the day wore on into the afternoon.

There was a six-foot folding table set up with chairs around it. I had a box of gear in the middle and there were laptops and notepads on the table. Around the table were some of the most important people in the world to me.

Bo Larson dressed in jeans and an old Def Leppard concert T-shirt, his considerable musculature on display.

Annabelle Unger with her purple-streaked red hair with a silky blouse that matched.

Frank Paulson, his bald head gleaming in the light, his bulk contrasting with his wife Lisa's willowy build and grey-shot dishwater blond hair.

Martin Lester, leaning back in one of the metal folding chairs far enough that it looked like he might topple over backwards, rubbing at his epic steel-grey mustache and staring at me.

And around us, looking like strange alien guardians, were Bo's sculptures. Some of them simple whirligigs and weather-vanes, some of them symmetrical twirling wonders, others of them multi-armed contraptions designed to turn in ways you didn't expect. He used reclaimed metal, but you would never know it. These were high-end pieces, plenty of which he hauled down to Scottsdale to decorate the very expensive yards there.

It was a strange image, the six of us, Bo's contraptions, the green forest around us, and the San Francisco Peaks hunched down on the horizon as if watching us.

I was on my feet pacing while the others were sitting. We had gathered and eaten, the empty pizza boxes and bottles scattered on the table attested to that, but we hadn't talked about the plan, about the conspiracy.

"So what's changed from a couple of weeks ago?" Lester asked.

I smiled and nodded and noticed his dull blue eyes tracing my steps. Lester was quiet but he was observant and a good judge of people.

"Me, hopefully," I said.

Annabelle tucked some of her red hair behind her ear and said, "Don't you dare tell me you're ready to give Smitty a big hug and sing kumbaya with him?"

That made me smile. "No. I'm a terrible singer. There's been no magical transformation. I still hate Smitty but now I'm more aware of it. I am considering my choices in that light. I'm…" I looked at Bo and he gave me an encouraging nod. "God help me, I'm learning to meditate, and that is helping. I think."

Lester's eyes aren't intense eyes. He's the quiet man. He's an observer. But rocking back on his chair, his eyes were very intense. It seemed like he had taken the role Wendy had taken on before she left our little "conspiracy."

"Don't seem like that changes much, you know," he said.

I looked around and all the eyes on me were intense. I felt the flush of shame light up my face. They really had been talking about me. They had planned for this planning session.

I stopped my pacing and stood facing the table. "I take it Martin is speaking for all of you," I said.

Frank and Lisa looked away, but Annabelle sat up straight and said, "He does."

"And you all think Brooke Jennings had a point in her characterization of Smitty and me?" I asked.

"We do," Annabelle said.

I nodded and said, "And I agree with you."

They all looked at each other, unspoken words of relief passing between them. My knees felt a little weak when I realized that this had been a test. Something they had planned. A conspiracy within the conspiracy.

I felt my face flush again, first in anger and then in another dose of shame, but I took a deep breath, closed my eyes, and gave it a moment to pass. I wasn't trying to meditate, I was just remembering what it had just felt like to meditate, hoping that would bring me calm.

But I couldn't blame them. I would have done exactly what they did in the same circumstance. So I decided to lean into it but I needed to move so I started pacing again, glad to have my cowboy boots back on.

"I don't understand Brooke," I said, "but I know she believes in what she did. It landed her in jail and, from what I can tell, it's going to keep her there for a while longer. Smitty without powers was a problem and a challenge, but Smitty with powers is a poison for Carterville. But Smitty and I fighting each other? Well, that's some toxic stuff."

"Then what happens when you're both back?" Frank asked, his voice low and deep. "How do you stop it from becoming 'toxic'?"

"Politics," I said.

There were a few murmurs and they looked at each other. "That ain't clear," Lester said. "You mind bein' clear?"

"Smitty's hold on the town is via Karen Winslow and the town council," I said. "He's got something on all of them. We either find a way to get Karen out of office and get Carterville a new mayor, or we get something on them that we can use to counteract Smitty's leverage."

"That sure as hell sounds toxic," Annabelle said.

I nodded. "Agreed. Politics is not pretty, but it's not Smitty and I going at each other. The only other choice is to allow Smitty to return and allow his rot to slowly destroy the town we love."

"And what if Smitty gets out of line?" Lester asked. "'Cause he'll get out of line, you know." He wasn't rocking in the chair anymore but leaning forward, staring at me.

I stopped pacing and held his gaze. "We let the law take care of him," I said.

"But you will be the law again," Lester said.

I nodded and started pacing again. "The actual law. He breaks a law, he gets arrested. I've had a few conversations with some people I know close to the governor. While he is sure to be getting out of jail soon, it won't be without strings. The amount of evidence we had against him was huge, not just for what he did to Patty and me, but many other things. There are other laws he broke, other ways to keep him in line."

"But only if you are there?" Lisa asked. Her voice was quieter than Frank's, but with her that gave it more power.

I stopped my pacing, faced them, and shook my head. "If this doesn't work and Smitty returns and I don't, I'm still here to help. I'll still be here for Carterville whether I'm physically there or not."

All eyes were on me. It wasn't comfortable, but I took it in.

This had never been just about me but the time slowing down and reflecting had made that clear. I hate Smitty, God knows I do, but I love Carterville a hell of a lot more. Carterville is not "my" town, it's just my home and I'll do all I can for it.

But there was something we hadn't talked about but needed to. Instead of waiting for them to ask, I took a deep breath and said, "Mary Reilly is dead because of Smitty. He corrupted her with intent. I realize that Brooke intensified the situation, but that was Smitty doing his Smitty thing. And if Brooke hadn't stirred the pot, it would have been someone else besides me feeling Mary's power.

"I still feel the gun in my hand, I still dream about shooting Mary. And does that make me hate Smitty? Hell yes. He was willing to use other people's lives in his narcissistic game. He deserves to stay in jail for the rest of his life. He should never feel his power again. But he will. And I want to be there to resist him, to see when he will next step over the line, because you know he will."

"Seems there's a hell of a lot of hate there still," Lester said.

I nodded. "But I will keep working on it." I glanced at Bo and he gave me a small nod. "I will weigh my actions, I will talk to and listen to others, I will obey the law and do things by the book."

"After this here little bit of madness," Annabelle said, gesturing at what was arrayed on the table.

I nodded. "Yes. After this bit of madness." I sighed and my shoulders fell. "I don't have this all figured out. I'm still very human. But that thing I wasn't looking at, the way my hate was driving me, I'm looking at it every day now. I'm being as honest as I can be with myself and you. This may all turn to shit, and I don't blame any of you if you don't want to be a part of it, but I have to try. For Carterville, I have to try."

There was silence and I met each one of their gazes. It wasn't comfortable, it made my stomach twist, but I loved these people, and if they felt the need to test me, then so be it.

When it went on too long, I asked, "So, did I pass your test?"

EIGHTEEN

SATURDAY, AUGUST 22. THE 40S

WE SPENT THREE MORE HOURS UNDER THAT RV SHELTER ON Bo's land. It was hot, but since it was late August the promise of cooler temperatures was there, and the sun had moved noticeably to the south.

Seasons change. When Brooke had tossed me that blue beanie, the one that was still stuffed in the glovebox of my truck, she had said, "It's going to be cold winter, Henry. You might need it." At the time, I didn't think this would take so long, and now I was starting to believe her.

We went over the plans, the timing, what everyone's part was. It was a relatively simple plan, this con we were going to attempt.

"So," Lester began, stroking at his mustache when we had been over it all twice. "We use your burner phone there." He nodded at an old-fashioned flip phone in the middle of the table. "We show up at the right place at the right time and

Annabelle uses the remote-control app thingy that sends a text while we look as innocent as can be."

"Are you sure you want to go back?" I asked Lester. As I promised, I hadn't asked him to go back to Carterville, but he had volunteered. It had been close to three years since Lila Chang's murder and maybe enough time had passed.

He nodded, a quick bob of his head signaling that there was nothing else to talk about on that topic. "Timed texts at set locations to Smitty," he continued. "No one ever looking like they are texting."

I nodded.

Annabelle said, "And these texts appearin' to come from his father, because the poor boy has daddy issues like nearly every other man I know."

"Yes," I said, ignoring what might or might not have been a jab at me. "The locations are important. Smitty has the means to acquire the phone records with the cell tower location data."

Lester leaned forward. "Texts first. Calls later. We drive him crazy pretending dear old dad is in Carterville. So crazy that he hires investigators at some point. The texts and calls continue, but his people can't find the old man."

I nodded, stood, and fished the drone out of the box. "And we'll use this so Smitty thinks his father is in his house."

"And that'll do it," Annabelle said. "The boy loves that gaudy monstrosity. With his investigators comin' up empty, he'll be forced to turn to you, the one person that knows Carterville inside and out, the one person who solved his last mystery."

While I was searching for words, Bo said, "But *will* that do it? I know Brooke told you it would. But will it? Could this be leading to something completely different?"

"She's not exactly trustworthy," Frank said.

"Agreed," I said. "But she wants something from me. If this doesn't work, she doesn't get what she wants."

"Her three days back in Carterville," Annabelle said, a sour look on her red lips. "Where she can use her power and plot her future."

I nodded.

"Is it worth it, Henry?" she asked. "How much damage could that baby-girl do with what she learns?"

I met Annabelle's brown eyes. This was *the* question. Was me returning to Carterville worth the risk of what Brooke will do with her powers? She said she's done with Carterville, that she "saved" it. But can we trust that?

I shrugged. "I can't see the future, but I hope so. I want to believe it."

"And that's the danger, ain't it?" Lester asked.

It wasn't a comfortable moment, but I was actually heartened to see they had been thinking about this madness too. Since so much of it was focused on me, it's easy for me to get lost in that, to not realize how much Brooke's manipulation shook the whole town.

"It is," I said. "And I'm too close to this to see clearly. We have a plan and there is definitely risk, but you decide if it goes forward. I'm too close."

Frank nodded at me and said, "But you want to go forward."

"Yes," I said.

"And what if Brooke wreaks havoc with her time in

Carterville?" Frank asked. "What if things end up worse? Can you live with that?"

I took a deep breath and let out a long sigh. "God, you all really did talk about this, didn't you?"

"We did," Annabelle said. "This here all comes from love."

I smiled, or tried to. "Tough love," I said.

"Can you live with that?" Frank asked again.

I stared into his blue eyes. He's a big guy, 250 pounds, with a shaved head. Behind the grill of the Carterville Diner, he looks like he belongs, but if you met him in an alley on a dark night you would want to avoid him, except for his eyes. They are kind in a way that you just can't hide.

He was my best friend, had been since high school, and he was asking the toughest question. Could I live with what Brooke does with what she gets being back in Carterville?

I swallowed and said, "I don't know, Frank. How can I? Brooke swears this is about getting her through her time in jail, giving her a soft landing on the other side. But she isn't trustworthy. But I…"

I looked around the table. I still didn't feel comfortable thinking much about the one card I had to play, much less speaking about it.

There was silence around the table, all eyes on me. The wind kicked up a little and Bo's metal contraptions sounded loud.

"We have to assume Brooke is here with us right now," I said. "That her power is that strong. So all I will say is that I have reason to believe what she can do in those days is limited."

"There will be unintended consequences," Bo said. "You know that."

I nodded and felt something shift in my gut. I did believe in this. I knew there would be fallout but there was a chance that this would make things better, and not just for me. "I know," I said.

"Why don't you take a walk, Chief," Annabelle said. "Let us talk it through."

I nodded and got up and walked away, letting those I love decide my fate.

NINETEEN
SATURDAY, AUGUST 22. THE 40S

I can't see the future and I am glad. I truly believe that Brooke's power is a curse. She sees the many futures and tries to find the actions she can take that will lead to the future she wants.

As humans, I think we often have trouble making choices because we can't see the future, we can't know the outcome or the wisdom of our choices until they are far in the rearview. There is always risk. There are always unintended consequences, no matter how thoroughly we plan.

But I'll take that over seeing the future any day. Well… most any day. That day, walking down the winding dirt road to Bo's land past the twisty juniper and occasional piñon trees, I wanted to see the future. I wanted to know what my friends would decide and, if they agreed to go ahead with this, how it would all turn out.

I also thought through what I would do if they said no. I hadn't set them up, I hadn't given them a choice that really wasn't a choice, but I am human. Walking down the dusty, sandy road, I considered going this alone. Well… I couldn't do that. I needed people in Carterville acting on my behalf, but it didn't have to be these people. It would get more complicated—who else could I trust?—but it was still doable.

I felt bad about it, but that's just where my mind went. Smitty needed to be checked. And that needed to be by me. No one else knows him and his tricks as well as I do. No one else knows Karen Winslow and her plans for the town like I do.

"No," I said to the trees and the sky and the mountain. "It doesn't have to be me."

I thought about Patty Walsh up in Colorado and how she had implied when I left—that if I wasn't going to return to Carterville—maybe there was a chance for us.

That was a fine thought. Patty was kinda the one that got away, but Patty shouldn't be anyone's second choice. She deserved better than that. She didn't deserve a cop without a job pining to return to his hometown. Because that's what I would be if this plan didn't move forward, if I didn't return to Carterville.

Since I had had time on my hands, I had started working on getting a private investigator license. I loved it because it was a backup plan, I hated it because it was admitting defeat was possible here.

It would take a hell of a lot of meditation to make this okay and I wasn't built to be some monk meditating all the time. Hell, I couldn't even sit in a proper lotus position, not that that counted one bit towards meditation. Let's just say that when you think meditation you don't think of someone in cowboy boots and a cowboy hat that is used to having a gun at his side most of the time.

As I wandered, I really wanted Brooke's power, a limited version of it, for just this one thing. Would they say yes? Would it work? Could I live with the consequences?

I pulled the flip phone out of my back pocket, the phone Brooke gave me. She knew. I could ask her, and she just might answer and she just might tell the truth.

"No," I said again out loud, stopping in the middle of the road and staring at the phone. "No."

Brooke knew the future and that was a hell of a temptation. Is this what she felt? Did she use her power casually like when she saw someone in a bar that caught her attention, did she close her eyes and see what would happen, not just that one night but for the next thousand nights, or the next ten thousand nights? Or the many possible futures that could occur based on what she did.

How could she not, and what the hell kind of life was that?

Her life must feel a little like a TV show and she's just an actor in it reading a script. Except, of course, she helped write the script, but still, it must be stifling.

But if Brooke was here right now asking me if I wanted to know what my friends were saying, what they would decide, could I say no? Could I turn away from it?

And then I knew what was coming if this all worked out and I brought Brooke back to Carterville for her three nights. She would tempt me. She would make me an offer I couldn't refuse, tell me how to create the future I wanted if she only got more time with her power.

"Shit," I said, kicking the dirt, shoving the phone back in my pocket, and walking down the road again.

My friends were going to say yes, this was going to work, and then she was going to tempt me. I was sure of it. It was like, for a moment, I could see a tiny bit of the future.

Except, I couldn't really see the future, it just felt like I could.

———

THEY WERE SILENT WHEN I RETURNED TO THE RV SHELTER, ALL of them staring at me.

I was hot from the walk, sweat trickling down my back, and my own thoughts had been tumultuous enough that I wasn't very patient.

"Well?" I asked.

"We need your word before we continue," Frank said. "We need you to promise us that you will abide by our decision. That during this, if we decide to pull the plug, that it will end."

"Do we need to go into the zone of influence for this?" I asked. My tone was a little strident and I regretted it immediately.

Frank blinked and then shook his head. "No, Henry. You are a man of your word, but we must have it."

"As long as this continues to be a discussion," I said. "As long as I can try to convince you otherwise if I believe your decision is wrong."

Frank looked at Lisa and Annabelle and then Lester and I was afraid I had gone too far. I had been wrestling with the specter of Brooke's power and I wasn't at my best. But let me be honest here, I was used to being the boss, being the one that makes the decisions for others, not the one accepting the decision of others.

Frank turned back to me. "That is reasonable."

I nodded and kicked at the cement with my boot, took a deep breath, and looked back up at them. I felt a little like I was cheating. I was left with the feeling that I knew what their decision was, because it was inevitable just like every situation Brooke turned her power and her will to.

I took a deep breath and said, "I promise to abide by this group's decisions regarding this plan to get Smitty to release me from my promise to never return to Carterville."

Frank held my gaze for a couple of breaths and then nodded and said, "Good. Thank you." He looked around at the others and I was mildly amused that my former colleague Martin Lester had been chosen to give me the bad news and Frank Paulson, my best friend, the good. "Let's do this," he said. "Let's get you back to Carterville."

I had felt it coming, so it was somehow anticlimactic. Was this another moment of empathy for Brooke and her power? Were the highs not very high and the lows not very low because she could see them coming?

"Thank you," I said, and I meant it, but I felt strangely hollow.

"We want to go over everythin' again," Annabelle said.

I nodded, pulled up a chair, and sat down.

"And there's one thing you haven't told us," Lisa said.

"What?" I asked.

"Well… someone has to call Smitty and play the part of his father," she said. "We are faking some photos of this person in Carterville. That can't be any of us. Who is it? Who is playing the part of Smitty's father?"

I nodded and bit my lip. "That's… well, it's a bit complicated, but I have someone that is the right age and has the right look."

"Who the hell is it?" Lester asked.

I swallowed and said, "My uncle. Elias Carter."

Annabelle's eyes got wide and she swore, Frank's brow furrowed, and Lester shook his head.

"Wait," Lisa said. "You haven't talked to him in years, right? Decades?"

I opened my mouth to answer but Annabelle said, "You just don't make things easy on yourself, do ya?"

I looked at Lisa. "It has been decades, but Brooke told me I would know who it was and to trust my gut." I turned to Annabelle. "No, I do not, but he's still family and I got to think he might want to help."

Annabelle gave me a pursed-lip look as she shook her head. She had never met Elias Carter, but she had heard the history.

Annabelle was right, I certainly didn't make things easy on myself.

PART 3
PAST REVISITING

TWENTY
FRIDAY, AUGUST 28. GLOBE, ARIZONA

Arizona is full of small towns. Most of them full of cactus, unlike Carterville. People think of Arizona, they think of vast and sprawling desert, which it certainly has plenty of, with houses huddled here and there.

During my exile, I had spent a lot more time in the desert, and had gotten more used to it, but not today. As I drove into Globe, Arizona, in my old pickup, my stomach was tight, and I couldn't play the music loud enough to drive out my restless thoughts.

Family, at its best, can be your greatest strength. At its worst, it can be your greatest weakness. But there's a spectrum here with most people having different parts of their family on different parts of that spectrum.

My sister was on the strength end of the spectrum. My parents were both gone, but when they had been alive, they had been, for the most part, on the strength side of things.

While I have a policy of telling only the things that I need to in these stories—I'm telling enough secrets as it is—it's other people's secrets I have trouble with. Driving into Globe, I know I'm heading deep into the wrong end of family and secrets that aren't mine to tell.

Globe is about ninety minutes east of Phoenix and about a thousand feet higher in elevation. It's sprawled amongst cactus-covered hills in sight of the Pinal Mountains. Globe is the county seat of Gila County, and although there is no copper there, there is in its sister city of Miami where it's all about copper.

The Globe area went through a lot of boom-and-bust years because of the price of copper. There's a lot there, most of it dug out of pit mines near Miami and farther to the west in Superior. These days it's become something of a retirement community. It's close enough to Phoenix, but is a small town and not quite as hot.

The Pinals top out at about 7,800 feet in elevation, not much higher than Flagstaff, but you can get up into the forest if you want to. Lake Roosevelt is nearby giving you the option of water if that's what you want.

But I wasn't here to sightsee. I was here to see one of those that had retired here. Someone on the weak side of the family spectrum. My uncle, Elias Carter. I hadn't seen him in a couple of decades, not since he had left Carterville.

I don't know the whole story. I do know that Elias is the twin brother of my father, and he was born a couple of minutes earlier, making him the elder Carter male after my grandfather died.

Carters like their tradition and it should have been my uncle's lot to own the house on Carter Hill that my sister and

I now own. He was the one that should have stayed in town to represent our family.

Well, it's not like there's a rulebook or anything, but I know my uncle felt the pressure from his father just like I felt the pressure from my father. This was something I didn't put on my own son, Tom. If he wants to come back to Carterville, I will welcome him. If he wants to do something else, then fine.

Having expectations for your children before they are even born is a surefire way to end up on the bad side of the family spectrum and a good way to get your kids to do the opposite of what you want for them.

This is all natural. Parents want the best for their children and have opinions as to what "best" is for them. Children need to become independent and distance themselves from their parents, after all they won't always be there, and they have to learn to function on their own.

Elias Carter came under the expectations of his father and what it meant to be a Carter and that didn't go so well. My father took his place, but he always felt a little like an imposter even though he was only a couple of minutes younger than Elias.

Which makes the patriarchy seem just a little insane. Two boys from the same womb born minutes apart and one is the heir apparent and one isn't. I mean, you've got to pick, but it seems more than a little silly.

Uncle Elias's house sat on a hill not far from the high school. It had a view, mostly of Globe with a few hills on the horizon, but at least it was a view. I couldn't imagine living in a house that didn't have one.

I pulled my truck up and stared at the house. It was old,

probably a hundred years old, white, two stories high, simple with a small, covered porch out front.

I saw the drapes move and my stomach clenched even tighter.

I needed something from my uncle, and this was the wrong way to do this kind of thing. You don't just show up after decades asking huge favors that are sure to open back up deep wounds.

But I couldn't trust a stranger with this, and he could just say no… or just not open the door.

I left my cowboy hat in the truck and got out, rubbing my sweating palms on my jeans. It was hot and dry, the sky a dusty desert blue.

There were a few steps from the sidewalk up into the small grass yard. The cement was worn and well past the need to be repaired or replaced. The grass in the yard was too long and half weeds. As I approached the house, I could see the white paint wasn't so white anymore and was peeling here and there.

When I got to the door, I didn't have to knock.

"You're the goddamn spitting image of him, you know," Elias Carter said.

He looked different than I remembered. Which I expected, but the reality of it was still a punch to the gut.

He was tall, taller than me, but stooped, his hair thinning and grey, his face sagging with deep wrinkles and about a week's worth of grey beard, his brown eyes dim. He was still fairly slim, the ratty brown bathrobe he wore hung loosely on him, but there was a noticeable bulge around his middle.

"Who?" I asked. I should have said hello, even after his lack of greeting, but I was too busy evaluating his looks and seeing if it could work for our conspiracy.

"Don't play stupid, boy," he said, turning and shuffling into his living room, like he was afraid to lift his feet lest he fall out of those cheap black slippers.

"I'll get coffee," he called as he shuffled through the small living room into the kitchen. "I know you like coffee." He ended in a little chuckle that just put my nerves on edge.

He had, clearly, been reading about me. My first memoir was done, soon to be published, but the first few chapters had been released here and there. The first thing I talk about in that book is coffee.

Uncle Elias's living room was crowded but neat. It's small with bookshelves along two walls where there aren't windows, old hardwood floors covered by oval braided area rugs in shades of brown. There was a couch, covered in a brown blanket, a recliner with a crowded side table, a TV, and one of those towering, carpeted monstrosities that cats love.

The overall effect was a little claustrophobic for me. There was just too much stuff in too little space. If it had been messy, though, it would have been much worse.

I wandered by the bookshelf. The books were old, mostly hardbacks, mostly history, American history, particularly the southwest. A couple of books on mining in the Old West, one specific to Carterville. There were a couple of books on Tombstone and half a shelf on Custer's last stand at Little Bighorn.

The books were, somehow, comforting. Elias Carter had been a high school history teacher, just down the hill at the Globe high school for twenty years before he retired. Noticeably lacking, though, was the history of Carterville that he had written when he was younger and still in Carterville.

"It's important to understand the past," he said as he returned with two mugs of coffee. "You don't know the past and it's going to be your future, like it or not."

I nodded and took the mug. It was thick and white, stained on the inside from long use, and only half full. He had read that first chapter.

He shuffled over to his recliner, sat down, and nodded at the couch. "Sit, boy," he said. "Ask for this mysterious favor. I'm not going to bite. I won't hold you to account for the sins of your father even though you look just like him."

I sat down holding the warm mug like I needed the comfort of some heat even when it was plenty warm outside. It was in the seventies in here so he must have had some kind of air conditioner.

The couch was lumpy and it must have been old, which is why it was covered with a blanket.

"How are you?" I asked.

He held my eye for a second and looked away. "I'm old and alone. How do you think?"

"I was sorry to hear about Aunt Claire," I said.

He snorted, but it was half-hearted. "Not that I saw any of you then."

I nodded and looked down. The "sins of my father" may be the reason Elias Carter left Carterville, but it was my sin to be so distant with this part of my family.

"I wish I had done something," I said. "I wish I had come."

"Wish'n don't do any of us any good, so just stop that shit, Henry," he said. "I wish I had done a lot of things differently. I wasn't there when your mother died, and…"

He looked away and I had to guess he was blinking back tears. My mother was the "sin" of my father's he was referring to. She was the wedge that drove them apart.

He took a deep breath and continued. "And I wasn't there when your father died. So we have established that we are both imperfect humans. We don't need to catch up. We don't need to reminisce. What do you want?"

I needed a moment to think, so I took a sip of the coffee. It was good, smooth and with a bite. This wasn't the cheap stuff or instant. This was real coffee, which somehow made me feel more at home, more at ease.

"I want to return to Carterville," I said.

He nodded in encouragement, which surprised me. I knew it was something he could relate to but didn't know if he'd be interested in helping.

"To do so," I began, licking my lips and leaning forward, "I have to convince my enemy that his father is alive, that his father wants something from him, needs something from him. Something he won't be willing to give. Something his father will do anything for."

Uncle Elias took a noisy sip of his coffee and leaned back. He was slim and the chair was big, so it kind of seemed to swallow him. He may have been my father's twin, but he wasn't his identical twin, which I was glad for on many levels.

Today I was glad that he was tall and thin and long ago had dishwater blond hair. The planes of his face weren't as sharp as Smitty's but the wrinkles were enough to cover that up.

In truth, he looked more like Smitty's father than mine.

"You done looking me over like a cut of meat?" he asked.

I nodded and looked away, embarrassed.

"Aren't I a little old to be your enemy's father?" he asked.

I caught his eye and there was a grin on his face. He pulled a manuscript off the side table that had a few remotes, a small stack of books, a couple of half-filled water glasses, and a bottle of Tums. He slammed the manuscript on the arm of the couch. The title was "The Blood of Carterville."

He had a wicked grin on his face while my jaw hung open.

"Your publisher hired me to fact check this," he said. "So you want me to play the part of Smitty's father. Aren't I a little old for that role?"

I nodded, still stunned. I shouldn't have been. Brooke Jennings was involved, and while she hadn't said anything about using my uncle, she hadn't done anything to change my path either.

I've written a lot more about Carterville, but hadn't turned in any other manuscripts yet. I wasn't sure about letting all of this out into the world, but I was also living off the advance from that first book.

"Yes," I finally said. "Smitty's father was ten years older than his mother, so that works. But… there's more. Smitty just might be the easy part."

"The Fortune Teller," he said. While my book about that wasn't out, Brooke had been headline news back when it happened and she is mentioned tangentially in *The Blood of Carterville*.

It was disconcerting. Uncle Elias didn't have a power, not a Carterville power, but he had a sharp mind and, apparently, publishing connections.

I nodded and pulled the piece of paper out of my back pocket and handed it to him. Explanations were no longer necessary.

The sheet of paper had a couple of dates on it and sketches of conversation.

His brow furrowed as his eyes quickly scanned the paper. "There's no dialog here," he said.

"No," I replied. "It needs to feel real, feel spontaneous. Those are the prompts that will lead you to say exactly what you need to say."

His sharp brown eyes met with mine for a moment and I saw… Well, it's hard to explain. For a moment, those looked like the eyes of my father and that brought a flood of complicated emotions. But I also saw the intelligence there and compassion.

"Oh," he said, his mind trying to grasp how Brooke works. "This is from *her*."

"Yes," I said.

"And you trust her?" he asked.

"Hell no," I said.

"But you have a plan?"

I nodded. "Not one I can talk about."

His eyes wandered back to the paper. "Because she'll know," he said.

I felt another wave of emotions flood over me. My father and I used to be like this, when I was a kid before the hormones kicked in. He just seemed to get me without a lot of conversation or explanation.

I took another sip of coffee and when I looked back up, he was staring at me.

"You keep in touch with Abby, I hear," he said.

I nodded. Abby was my cousin, his daughter. Uncle Elias and his wife hadn't been married very long and it had been an ugly divorce. His wife kind of got Abby in the divorce.

Claire was his second wife and they didn't have any children.

I nodded. "Yeah. Her kids are just a little younger than Tom. We visited a lot when they were all growing up."

"Well at least your generation is doing better than mine," he said.

I shrugged. "Don't know about that. My ex-girlfriend was involved in a plot to murder me."

He chuckled and shook his head and then his face got serious. "I'll do it, but I have a couple of conditions."

I just sat there blinking. I hadn't even had to ask. Brooke hadn't given me anything for this encounter besides the notes for the Smitty calls.

"Why?" I asked.

He shrugged. "You're a Carter. You should be in Carterville if you want to be."

I felt another wave of emotion that is, again, hard for me to describe. Gratitude. Connection. Fear. Guilt. Uncle Elias had exiled himself from Carterville and I hadn't expected such understanding.

But family trauma almost always leads to regret. Clearly, he had plenty.

"What are your conditions?" I asked, worrying it would be more than I could give.

He picked up the manuscript. "You're writing histories," he said. "I would like the opportunity to review the manuscripts before you turn them in. Give some suggestions that you are welcome to ignore."

Yet another wave of emotion hit me. I'm a cop and I felt way out on a limb writing these memoirs. His condition was something I didn't know I needed.

"I would love that," I said.

He nodded. "Good. And I want to meet your son."

I blinked, taking a moment to absorb it. He had met Tom, but the boy had been a baby and that's not what he was talking about. He wanted to know who his grandnephew was.

"Sure," I said. "I mean… that's up to him, but I'll do everything I can."

He smiled and it was like he looked twenty years younger and I felt another wave of guilt. This one deep and stabbing. He was a Carter who craved connections with other Carters. He was in his last act and wanted the comfort of family. This was an obvious need and one I hadn't even considered.

All my fears driving out here had been unfounded. I could see there was some bitterness there, maybe a lot, but it wasn't directed at me, despite the fact that he had started this conversation telling me I looked like my father and that couldn't be easy.

And he hadn't even tried to extract a promise from me. He knew my power and even though it doesn't work unless I'm in Carterville, I expect a lot of people to try to get me to promise things.

There was awkward silence as we drank coffee together. We were family, we shared a name and DNA, but we hadn't shared much of our lives.

I thought of talking to him about Frank Paulson, my best friend, because he was a Civil War nut and I had to wonder if that was an early influence of Uncle Elias's. But then I remembered he had read the manuscript and he already knew that.

This is one of the problems with pouring yourself into a memoir. Suddenly other people know all about you. And the book wasn't out yet and this was just the beginning. I could tell I wasn't going to like how this felt.

"I don't know if I should keep publishing these," I said, nodding at the manuscript. "Airing our dirty laundry for all to see."

His eyes narrowed and he stared at me for a moment before looking away. "Cat's out of the bag, boy," he said. "With your power, people are going to talk about you. At least this way you can do what you can to control it."

His manner had changed. He was guarded for some reason. My eyes wandered to the bookshelf, to the place where his volume on the founding of Carterville should be. It covers the first tumultuous twenty-five years until 1905, but I had a vague memory that there was supposed to be several more volumes.

"Are you still writing?" I asked.

He swung back around and looked at me, his eyes a little too wide. "Did she tell you that?"

There was no need for him to elaborate on "she."

"No," I said. "She didn't tell me anything about this conversation. She just gave me the notes."

He sighed and sank back down into his recliner. "Don't know how you function with her…" he ended in a shrug.

"I don't know either," I said.

His eyes narrowed and he got a look on his face. He wanted to know about my plan. He wanted to know I could do something about Brooke, but he didn't say anything.

"Yeah," he said. "I have more Carterville histories. I just can't seem to finish them."

"Maybe I could read your manuscripts," I said, my voice

low like I was a kid again asking for what felt like a huge favor.

He smiled and said, "That might help."

"And you will probably need to ignore my suggestions," I added.

We both laughed and that seemed to break the ice and we drank coffee and talked for about an hour. Mostly of the old days when he was still in Carterville and I was a kid.

It felt good and strange at the same time.

I left feeling like this had been much too easy.

TWENTY-ONE
FRIDAY, AUGUST 28. OUTSIDE GLOBE, ARIZONA

Life isn't easy.

This seems like the most essential fact, one that many seem to have trouble accepting. Don't get me wrong, I think life should have moments of ease, we all need to relax and unwind, and there are moments where things are much easier than you expect, but life is not easy.

I don't think it's supposed to be. Survival isn't the struggle it used to be—we're not out there with crude spears chasing large mammals just so we can eat—but there is still always struggle.

Humans see the world differently and are constantly trying to make the world more like they think it should be. This leads to inevitable and endless conflicts. Families can be your deepest connection, but they are often the hardest one.

My encounter with Uncle Elias was easy. Not emotionally, it was damn hard going there with my fears of what it might be bouncing around my head, but the encounter was decidedly easy. He agreed to play the role I needed him to play. He didn't want to rehash the past. He didn't ask much from me, the two things he did ask are things I want too.

So let's put that another way. My uncle, who had a huge beef with my deceased father and who had self-exiled himself from the town that bore his name, was nothing more than a little grumpy as he agreed to do something that could potentially be illegal so that I could return to the town he exiled himself from.

"Too easy," I said as I rolled down a two-lane road outside of Globe heading towards Lake Roosevelt. I wasn't in a big hurry and wanted to avoid the Phoenix metro area, so I was taking the scenic route.

"Brooke," I said, slapping the steering wheel. Brooke had to be involved. Brooke had to have contacted him, maybe promised him something.

I wanted to turn around, but the shoulders were narrow with guardrails on both sides of the road, craggy desert hills rising to my left and falling away to my right. It was dry and desolate with the occasional saguaro cactus standing like a sentinel.

I turned the music down, an old Eagles album had been playing on the cassette player, and let the hot air blowing through the window wake me up a little bit.

I think we all want life to be easy. We want our difficult encounters to go smoothly. Part of us think they should. I certainly wanted my encounter with Uncle Elias to go smoothly, but something had bothered me about it and it took me this long to realize it.

I wanted to turn around, right there, but I kept going. I needed to think about it. I needed to let the whipping wind and the buzzing tires help me think. I needed to relax around this realization and not fight it.

Brooke could not be fought straight on. There was no beating her that way. That was more than obvious.

There were many odd things that stood out about that encounter now that I wasn't just basking in the relative ease of it. The first one was that he had my manuscript. He had said, "Your publisher hired me to fact check this."

His last name is Carter, he is a notable historian of Carterville, so it was plausible, but was it probable?

It didn't feel like it was. The kind of crap that was published about Carterville and those with powers had no fact checking. This stuff was being released as quickly as possible to capitalize on the world's fascination with Carterville. The world has a short attention span and would undoubtedly become fascinated with something else soon.

Even this morning, there was an email from the publisher begging for the next manuscript, the one about Lila Chang's murder. They were desperate to get it into production.

So, while it was plausible that he would be used as a fact checker, it was not probable. And if it wasn't probable, Brooke was probably involved.

"Shit," I said as the realization hit me. There was no one there to hear me, which was something I had become entirely too used to. I was much more inclined to talk aloud to myself since my exile from Carterville.

There seemed to be two things I could do. Turn around and confront Uncle Elias and find out how involved Brooke was, or keep going and accept that Brooke had broken the trail for me, that I was still her puppet.

Well, that last part, the puppet part, was hard to deny no matter what.

A few miles later there was a rare turnoff to my right, I slowed down and pulled off the road. I didn't want to drive back. I had other things to do, but I couldn't let this stand.

And then I realized, I wasn't in the middle of a movie or some TV show and I didn't need to be in Elias's presence to get the information I needed.

I pulled out my cell phone, the burner phone Brooke had given me, and called him. He picked up on the third ring.

"You forget something, boy?" he asked. "Or are you worried I'll lose my nerve? I won't. I can play your part."

"Were you working off a script today?" I asked, ignoring his questions. "Like the one I brought."

There was a quick intake of breath and then silence. This was, somehow, reassuring. It let me imagine that he was off script. But if that was true, it didn't really matter. Brooke didn't have him working from a script because the encounter didn't need her manipulation.

"I'd also like to know what's in this for you," I said. "What she offered when she contacted you."

More silence.

"I have to know where I am at with this thing," I said.

He cleared his throat and said, "Will you do what you said you would? I do want to read your manuscripts and I really want to meet your son."

I felt a flash of anger. At Brooke and at him. He should have told me. She should have told me. How could this little revelation possibly be needed?

"You can read the manuscripts," I said. "And as for Tom,

that's up to him. I will encourage it, but I will also tell him the whole story."

There was another moment of silence and then he said, "I told her you would figure it out, but the kid said this was the only way."

"When?" I asked, as my heart pounded harder in my chest

"Four years ago," he said.

This was before the Lila Chang murder, before she had bought the bolo tie for me that I was currently wearing, before Brooke had set things in motion in Carterville, when she was still a teenager.

"What's in it for you?" I asked.

"Claire had just died," he said. "The medical bills were about to kill me. I was going to lose the house. She gave me the script and a stock tip. Told me exactly when to buy and sell."

Now it was my time for silence. My uncle, my blood, had known there was a person that could see the future, a person that was manipulating me, and he hadn't said a word. He had bought his stock, gotten out of trouble, and had not said one goddamn word.

What if he had warned me, would Lila Chang still be alive? William Reilly? The feud between Smitty and me would still be there, but probably not nearly as bad. I would most certainly not have been exiled from Carterville.

"And what else did she offer you?" I asked, my teeth clenched. I knew there was more. The stock tip was her calling card, proving she could do what she said she could do. There had to be something else holding him to this path.

There was silence as my heart clanged and my face felt hot. I took some slow, deep breaths through my nose. Since the exile and the trauma of those few years leading up to it, I have found myself having panic attacks now and then. The world closes in, it feels like I can't escape, my heart sprints along in my chest. But this wasn't quite that. It had the physical components but it was fueled by rage instead of fear.

It was infuriating, but it wasn't particularly surprising. Of course Brooke had known about the bad blood between Uncle Elias and the rest of the family. Of course she had known he would take his money and keep her secret. But did that matter? Shouldn't I expect more from my family, even if those bonds had been shredded years ago?

Now I was truly dedicated to sending him the other memoirs I had written. I wanted him to see the destruction and death he had been complicit in by staying silent.

"What else?" I asked, my teeth still clenched.

"She… she told me that," he began, his voice carrying every single year of his age. "She told me that if I did this, I… that I would spend my last days in the Carter house on Carter Hill."

My rage flashed even brighter and I wasn't even very aware of my surroundings. The implications of that were clear. If Elias Carter was living in the family house that would mean that my sister and I were…

I couldn't even finish the thought right then. It was too unthinkable, and the craven nature of my uncle in this was unacceptable. It was clear when I called him that this was a betrayal, a huge betrayal, but I could never have imagined the full magnitude of it.

"Just do your part," I said and snapped the phone shut.

TWENTY-TWO
FRIDAY, AUGUST 28. ROOSEVELT LAKE, ARIZONA

My sister Wendy and I would need to be dead for Uncle Elias to be living in the old Carter home on Carter Hill.

That was the thought I couldn't finish when I was on the call with Uncle Elias, but it didn't take long for it to fully form.

I had planned to drive back up north and camp near Flagstaff—I wanted a night alone before returning to Bo's place—but I couldn't. I drove to Roosevelt Lake, grabbed a camping spot, and set out on foot, walking the shoreline of the greenish water and trying to cool off.

Well, cool off emotionally. It was hot, about 98, and it wouldn't be cool enough tonight to sleep well, but I was in no state to be on the road.

I have written before about this feeling of fate bearing down on me when I know I'm in Brooke's machinations. It's this oppressive feeling, this weight, this claustrophobic drowning sensation. And it's no surprise that I have panic attacks because of her manipulations.

I felt it then as I kicked at the sand with my cowboy boots and shuffled along, hardly seeing the miracle of water in the middle of the desert, the tough cactus and grass clinging to the dry land, the thirsty bushes growing near the water, the rolling craggy hills all around.

Brooke had seen this coming, seen all of this coming. She must know my hand, know the card I think I can play against her, but how can that matter? How can anything I do or say matter? Whatever it is, it's what Brooke wants.

My life has prepared me to be her pawn, and if she was telling Uncle Elias the truth, I won't be that pawn for much longer.

But what of Wendy? She only lives in Carterville part-time, but I don't see her giving up the house, especially not to Uncle Elias, unless she's dead too.

A plot to remove me from Carterville, one that turned into an attempted murder when I started to figure out what was going on was one thing. But to threaten the life of my sister? That was another thing entirely. It made me want to go back to Florence and burn down the prison with Brooke trapped in it. It made me want to do the kinds of things that I have put people in jail for. It made me want to wring my uncle's neck with my bare hands.

I would get angry as a kid. I have a thing about injustice. It drives me crazy. This life is hard enough without all those that take advantage of the system and of everyone around them.

The anger I felt would quickly turn to shame once I

calmed down. My mother used to tell me, "You are not your thoughts, Henry. You are not your thoughts until and unless you act on them."

And that's a good thing. Because if I was my thoughts as I strolled along the lake, kicking at the sand, throwing rocks into the water, I would be a very, very bad person.

———

I'VE WRITTEN ABOUT REALITY BEFORE. HOW IT DOESN'T CARE one little bit about what we think and what we believe. Our beliefs most certainly affect what we see, our perception of the world. Our beliefs can help us change the world, if they let us see that as a possibility. But our beliefs, our biases, often prevent us from really seeing the world as it is. And that is dangerous.

Uncle Elias's betrayal isn't new even though it feels new to me. My assumption that Wendy and I would have to be dead for him to be in the old Carter home is just that, an assumption. It rests on the shaky foundation of Brooke Jennings actually telling him the truth and not just telling him what he wants to hear.

Brooke is an "ends justify the means" type of person. She doesn't care who gets hurt or killed if it leads to the future she wants.

All of this is to say that all I really know is I don't have a good view on what was real.

Brooke will do that to you. Hell, life will do that to you.

All of this came to me when it was dark and the stars were shining above and I had a fire going in my campsite on Roosevelt Lake.

The flames and the sparks were mesmerizing. The smokey smell was comforting. It wasn't cool yet, but it wasn't hot anymore, either.

The reality was that I had a team and a plan. Elias Carter was part of that plan, in it for his own reasons just like anyone else. I believed my plan could work. It had a good chance of getting me back to Carterville. The rest of it, the card I was holding close, I pushed it away. The thoughts of where Brooke was taking this, I had to push that away too.

Brooke and her power are an existential crisis making machine. I had to push everything else back to not feel that crushing weight on my chest, to not feel my heart clanging around like it was trying to escape. I had to push it all away to keep going.

But how can I help but feel that my life doesn't have meaning when Brooke has seen the future we are rushing towards and is doing everything in her power to make it happen?

How can what I do matter when it has been predetermined?

I'm not going to have some long debate on these pages about fate versus free will. In some ways, with Brooke, it's moot. I have free will, but she already knows what I'm going to do and my fate has been seen.

I poked the fire with a stick, sparks rising into the air in a crackling burst. I heard the sounds of a distant radio and the chatter of children from other campsites, but I felt pretty much alone here.

I felt that way in this whole thing. Sure, I had Carter's Six or whatever you want to call them, but they weren't dealing with Brooke. They weren't getting her expertly timed texts with the perfect information. They weren't dealing with family betrayal at a fundamental level.

"Isabella," I whispered to the sparks, talking to myself again. She was noticeably absent from the team. She felt like the daughter I never had. In many ways, she was my reason for all of this.

When Brooke had the people I loved the most tied up in the Carter mine with a ticking bomb, it had been Isabella Ortega that I had untied first. Not my crush, Patty Walsh, or one of my oldest friends, Lisa Paulson. It had been Ortega.

I had told Smitty it was because she was young and had the most life to live. True enough, but not the whole story. It was these paternal feelings that drove my actions.

I still felt them despite my time at the Four Corners Monument when it became clear she had her own reasons for being in Carterville. Reasons I didn't understand and she had never shared. Reasons that, with the influence of Brooke, couldn't help but make me suspicious.

But the suspicion was swamped by the paternal feelings. I knew her. I knew her character. She was a good person. And while it was clear that she hadn't told me everything, didn't that just make this even more of a parent/child relationship? Kids are always holding back from their parents.

And while maybe my fate was sealed, I was hoping that hers wasn't. That I would have enough wiggle room in the straitjacket of Brooke's machinations to save her. And to save my sister.

Maybe Elias Carter would spend his last few years in the old Carter house, but if I had any say about it, Wendy would be alive and well and so would Ortega.

I poked the fire again and watched the sparks shoot up into the night trying to shake off the existential dread so that I could do something here. So that I could fight. So that I could, just maybe, surprise the Fortune Teller.

TWENTY-THREE
FRIDAY, AUGUST 28. ROOSEVELT LAKE, ARIZONA

Promises can be tricky things, as slippery as the fish being pulled out of Roosevelt Lake if you let them. I had promised to let Frank, Lisa, Annabelle, Bo, and Lester have veto rights on this conspiracy, but I hadn't promised to tell them every little thing.

Not that that was even possible, right? I couldn't communicate every detail, every nuance, every word said, could I?

The answer to that is a simple and easy "no." But, what I could do is tell them the essential facts. I said at the beginning that I was writing these entries every day as part of my processing this process. So, I could do one better, I could send them what I had written, full of typos as it was, and let them decide.

Transparency is a great principle but a damn hard one in practice. It takes guts to let others really see us, especially those we love, those whose respect we want.

So, I meditated on it. Which is a silly thing to say now that

I have my tiny little bit of experience. Meditation, at least the way Bo taught me, was not about staying with a topic or a thought, but letting go of all the crap running through your brain.

When I am camping, if the weather is nice, I just sleep in the back of my truck. A tent is good to keep the water and bugs off you, but it also keeps the stars away and I like the stars.

It was a clear night and nothing was biting me, so after I wandered the lake and poked at my fire contemplating the madness of all this, I lay awake in the back of my truck watching the stars for the longest time. And then in the morning, after taking care of a few essential biological needs, I sat there with my legs crossed as well as they will cross and focused on my breath.

There was the smell of smoke from the previous night's campfire and the chatter of families waking up and getting breakfast, but that was pleasant accompaniment.

My thoughts were actively pinging around from Isabella Ortega's mysterious reason for wanting to be in Carterville, to the Navajo grandmother I had met up in Four Corners, to my visit with Brooke, to all the planning, and finally to my visit with my uncle and his desire to return to Carterville too.

It took time, plenty of time, but when the "jump" came and I opened my eyes, I didn't think about it. I grabbed my laptop and emailed what I had written about my visit with Elias Carter to my co-conspirators. With it I added a note:

Things just got more complicated, one of those "unintended consequences" you mentioned, Bo. But I believe that this is still the path forward. Elias wants his place back in Carterville too. Maybe he deserves to be back. Maybe he's pushing the boundaries to get back just like I am. Maybe he will end up back in the Carter home.

I am giving you these rough chapters in the interest of transparency.

I don't know what's coming and I'm glad.

I stared at what I had written for a long time before sending it. It wasn't right. It wasn't enough or maybe it was too much. Whatever it was, I didn't once think about that burner phone and Brooke on the other end who could tell me if it was the right thing to say.

It was a small victory, but I'll take it.

TWENTY-FOUR
SATURDAY, AUGUST 29. THE 40S

Bo greeted me with a beer, and Yaki, his dog, greeted me with a happy bark, a sloppy lick, and a wagging tail. I took it as a good sign that I had been here long enough so that the big Lab didn't consider me a threat.

"You read it," I said, seeing the pinched look on Bo's face.

He nodded as we sat down on a couple of folding chairs that faced the San Francisco Peaks. "We're divided on moving forward," he said.

My stomach tightened up but then I took a deep breath and tried to remember what it felt like to meditate. Bo didn't ever mention doing something like this, and I don't imagine this is new or anything, but it kind of helped. Like going to your "happy place" in your mind, except this wasn't a place, just a state.

And if you think about it, happy most certainly isn't a place at all. Sure, maybe a mountain with fresh powder or a tropical paradise with an umbrella drink is the place you were the happiest, but it's not the place you need to summon but the state.

"Not too surprising," I said.

"That was a lot," Bo said.

"Yup," I said with a grin, clinked my bottle against his, and took a sip. It was ice-cold. Bo prioritized his limited solar power wisely. The beer was always cold.

"Frank and Lisa are against," Bo said after he took a swig. "Martin and Annabelle are for."

"And that makes you the deciding vote," I said. I thought I should be stressed out, like my heart should be racing or something, but I wasn't. I was calm. Maybe it was summoning the meditative state. Maybe it was the Brooke effect and knowing she had already seen this and knew that it would turn out her way.

"Her way" is the important part of that last sentence. All of this manipulation was about her, the Fortune Teller. It was not about me, and I was just her pawn, which means I was an easy sacrifice in her larger game.

"I am," Bo said. "Frank and Lisa know your uncle, I take it."

I nodded. "Martin does too."

"The whole thing was about your mother," Bo said.

I nodded and took another sip, staring at the Peaks.

"Which is interesting, considering what you and Frank went through with Annie," he said. "You and Frank being like brothers and all."

That caused my stomach to clench and my heart to speed up. Frank, Annie, and I had been something of a love triangle when we were in high school. Well, not "something of." Annie was with Frank and then Annie was with me. She's the only thing that ever came between Frank and me. He broke my nose over it.

"Just ask what you need to ask, Bo," I said. I didn't mean to be impatient, but with Annie's trial looming this was a tender spot he had just poked.

He shrugged his strong shoulders. "You kinda freaked out at first, thinking for your uncle to be back, both you and your sister would have to be dead."

"True enough," I said.

"So…?" Bo asked. "How much of a possibility do you think that is?"

I looked at him, his head tilted down a bit and his brown eyes hiding behind his blonde bangs a little more than normal. He was being honest. This was what his vote hinged on.

I slid the beer bottle in the holder on the chair, pulled the flip phone from my back pocket, and Bo's eyes widened. I got it. Brooke was the Fortune Teller, some kind of oracle. She could answer questions none of us could.

I had been very resistant to using her, but here it felt right. I freaked out on hearing about the deal my uncle made. While those thoughts were real, they were just thoughts. I can't objectively come up with odds.

I flipped it open and said, "Wait for it."

Bo blinked and looked at me. "What…?" he said

"Just wait for it," I said. "Earlier when we were all gathered, when I said we have to act like Brooke is here, I wasn't kidding. I meant that literally."

My phone chimed and a text appeared, *Hello Bo Larson.*

His jaw practically unhinged when he read the text. I had

told them about this but now he was experiencing it, which is something entirely different.

It chimed again. *Elias Carter will end his days in the Carter home with Wendy Carter caring for him.*

I didn't need to remind Bo that my sister was a nurse. Hospice wasn't her specialty or anything, but she was well versed in palliative care and is exactly the person you would want around when you were dying.

"Shit," Bo said.

"Welcome to my world," I said with a grin that was half grimace. I snapped the phone shut and shoved it back in my pocket.

I hadn't thought of my uncle coming home to Carterville to die, but it made sense. Elias Carter, despite the history—or maybe because of the history—was family. In the end, we would take him in if that is what he asked for.

And I guess I didn't pull the phone out just for Bo but for me. My initial reaction had been so strong, it spooked me too.

"So this is happening, then," Bo said. "You are going to get to go home."

I took another swig of the beer. "Yeah. I guess it is."

Bo took a long pull on his beer and finished it. I couldn't tell you exactly what was going on, but his demeanor changed. He was leaning away, he wasn't looking at me in the eye.

"What is it?" I asked.

He took a deep breath and sighed. "There's something else the five of us talked about. And agreed on."

I felt my face flush and looked around like I was being watched. Of course, I was, but not here. The five of them were talking about me. I had agreed to it, and I had invited it, but it sure as hell didn't feel good.

"And you all chose not to let me have a say," I said. I hadn't thought it through, but it had to be true.

Bo nodded, still not looking at me.

I looked around again and noticed some dust in the air down the road and heard the distant rumble of a muscle car. I swore under my breath and said, "You told her."

Bo met my eyes, but only for a moment, and nodded his head. "She needs to know. You need to talk to her."

With that Bo got up, called Yaki, and went into his single-wide.

There was no mystery here. I hadn't wanted to involve acting Chief of Police of Carterville Isabella Ortega, but clearly they had.

I would love it if this thing just didn't keep getting more complicated.

TWENTY-FIVE
SATURDAY, AUGUST 29. THE 40S

Isabella Ortega slowly drove her 1988 Ford Mustang down the dirt road to Bo Larson's place. She loved that car, and the washed and waxed red exterior attested to that, but just don't look at the inside of the car. It's full of food wrappers, unopened mail, and other kinds of junk.

Ortega is not the neatest person in the world, by which I mean that she is a slob.

As she drove closer, I stood and walked towards her, reflecting on the very human dichotomy of taking such good care of the outside of your vehicle but not the inside.

And she wasn't just Officer Isabella Ortega anymore, she was acting Carterville Chief of Police Isabella Ortega. The mantle had fallen to her when I left Carterville and there hadn't been another election yet.

She was young, 26 now, and a by-the-book cop. I had, of course, seen her since I left. Talked to her and texted with her pretty often as she wrestled with the weirdness of Carterville and everyone's powers, but things had changed since Four Corners. Since I started this plan to return, since I realized she had kept something from me about why she wanted to be in Carterville.

I hated the distance. I loved the girl, thought of her as the daughter I never had, but she had hidden something from me and I had hidden something from her.

And I guess that made us normal, but it wasn't comfortable and it showed in the growing distance between us. Me being exiled hadn't done it, the secrets had.

I was fairly calm, though, I wasn't even trying to remember the feeling of a meditation "jump." I think this was Brooke. I wasn't worried about the outcome as long as I was going with the flow of Brooke's will. I wasn't even really that mad at Bo and the rest of them. Why would I be? It was like I had the perspective of hindsight brought on by my confidence in the outcome.

But as the car drew close, as I caught sight of Ortega, my guts started to clench up. There was nothing about Brooke's machinations that said anything about this relationship that was so important to me. There was no reason for it to be preserved, Brooke's ends could be met with this relationship, and all the other ones that really counted, lying in tatters.

That brought me back to being human and my heart started doing a quick two-step in my chest.

Isabella Ortega is short and strong, she's a powerlifter and it shows. She's a third-generation Mexican immigrant with a Navajo grandmother, she—

Wait. Was that Navajo grandmother I talked to up at Four Corners her grandmother? Normally I'd discard such suspected synchronicity, but Brooke Jennings was involved so such things were much more likely. Why? Because it would delight Brooke, there need be no other reason.

When Ortega got out of the car, her warm brown eyes were hidden behind a pair of aviator sunglasses. I think she picked that up from me, but hers were the expensive variety, not from a dollar store like mine.

Her long black hair wasn't in its usual ponytail, but cascading down her back, making her look younger. The hair down and the jeans and a loose black T-shirt made it clear that she was off duty, as well as the lack of the department SUV and the low-clearance Mustang being out here. She was by-the-book and wouldn't take the SUV for something personal even when her car wasn't made for these roads.

"Good to see you, Isabella," I said with a tip of my cowboy hat.

"You look well, Chief," she said. "Did you lose more weight?"

I looked down and my belly was a much smaller protrusion than when I was really chief, but it didn't seem significant. "Maybe," I said. "Listen, I had good reason to keep you out of this."

She nodded. The sunglasses were still on and I hated it. I wanted to see those eyes, but this was a trick I had taught her. When you are the one that needs the questions answered it's sometimes easier when you know they can't see your eyes.

"Yeah?" she asked.

I nodded and pointed to the chairs Bo and I had just been occupying. There was now a small cooler sitting between them. Bo must have snuck it out while I was waiting for Ortega.

She walked over, looking strange to me in jeans. I was

used to her in uniform with the bulk of the utility belt on her waist. She looked so much younger, more like a teenager.

She sat, pulled a bottle from the cooler, and popped the top, taking a long drink.

I sat next to her, but I left my beer where it was in the arm holder. I wanted to be sharp.

"To be clear," she said. "I know there's a plan to get you back, but I don't know what it is. Explains a lot, though."

That was a relief in some ways—my friends hadn't totally betrayed my trust—and not a relief, this was all on me now.

I sighed and stared up at the mountain. "It would be better if you didn't know anything."

"Better for who?" she asked.

"Better for you," I answered.

She nodded. "Don't care about that. So how many laws are you breaking? And are you breaking any of them in my jurisdiction?"

I had to smile. In some ways it seemed like she was born to be a cop. This seemed natural to her. I picked my chair up, moved it in front of hers and sat back down.

"I'll answer your questions honestly," I said. "If you answer my questions honestly."

She looked around like she might be afraid we were being watched or something and then she looked back at me. "Your questions?"

I took a deep breath and let out a long sigh. "I need to know why you wanted to come to Carterville. I need to know the real reason."

The sunglasses were a good shield, but I could see the motion of her blinking behind them. There was something there. I hadn't been making things up at Four Corners.

She took another long swig, probably to give her time to think, and looked at me. "Does it matter why I came to Carterville?" she asked. "I've done my job. I've been a good cop."

I leaned back and nodded. I found I had crossed my arms, so I uncrossed them and took a deep breath. "It matters to me. Since Brooke started pulling the strings—and she started in earnest right before you came into the picture—it feels like there's a double meaning, like there's two things going on, and I can never keep up. So it matters to me, a lot."

She took a deep breath and hid behind the beer bottle again. There was something there, and while this wasn't a huge reaction for a normal person, it was for her, and I wasn't sure I wanted to know anymore.

She sighed, nodded, and said, "I guess I owe you that, but… Not now. Not today. Not here." She looked up at the Peaks, the place that was sacred to the Navajo side of her family.

I thumbed the bolo tie I was wearing. I had kept Coyote close all these months like the Navajo grandmother had told me. I really can't tell you why. I'm not the superstitious type. But if there was magic beyond the kind granted to us in Carterville, maybe the Native Americans had some of it.

"When?" I asked.

"After," she said.

"After what?" I asked.

"After all of this," she said. "After you are back or after your plan fails and you won't be coming back."

I felt a flash of impatience, a restless wave of energy that made me want to get up and walk away. I needed people to be honest with me and I really needed my protege to be honest with me.

"Why?" I asked.

"Because it will be better this way," she said, a grin prying its way past her pursed lips.

"Better for who?" I asked, echoing her question.

"Better for you," she said.

I smiled, I couldn't help myself. She wasn't treating me like her boss or her teacher. In fact, she hadn't called me "Boss" which she always used to do. I couldn't say that I loved that I was on the receiving end of the more mature Isabella Ortega, but I loved that she had gotten there.

"So how many laws will you be breaking?" she asked again, but with a smile on her face this time. "Are you going to break any of them in my jurisdiction?"

"One or two," I said, smiling back. "Yes."

"Do you think it will work?" she asked.

"I do," I said. "I have it on good authority that it will work."

She opened her mouth to speak and then coughed like what I had told her caused her to suck some spit down the wrong tube.

"Really?" she asked when she could talk again. "Her?"

I nodded. "She left something for me at the Four Corners Monument that got my attention. She left it for me over three years ago."

She didn't cough again but covered her mouth like she was afraid of what she might say. She lowered her hand and bit her lip for a moment and looked around. Smart girl. She was realizing that if Brooke was involved you had to assume she was listening, that she knew.

"I see..." she said. "Yeah. I see." She took her sunglasses off and I finally got to see her eyes and realized there was another reason that she had been wearing them. She looked tired, real tired. I had seen that look in the mirror plenty of times when I was a cop in Carterville.

She stood up, so I did too.

"Be careful, okay?" she said, and she was suddenly the shy girl I had met three years ago. "She is so dangerous, so…" she looked around again. "I really hope this works, Boss."

And then she was hugging me, and I bit back the wave of emotion that I was feeling. I had really missed her. I hated the distance between us. But it seemed like it was better this way.

She didn't hug me for long and then the glasses were on, and she was walking away.

When she was about ten feet away, she turned around and said, "Just don't get caught. I will arrest you and anyone involved if you break the law in my jurisdiction."

I tipped my hat to her and held my smile until her back was turned and she was walking away.

PART 4
PRESENT CONCERNS

TWENTY-SIX

TUESDAY, OCTOBER 6. OUTSIDE CARTERVILLE, ARIZONA

It's been a while since I've written very much. Well, I have been writing every day, but it's been more in the vein of journaling, not that kind of thing anyone else would read or would go into a book. Boring stuff like what happened today in our slow-burn plan to get Smitty to release me from my promise.

And I'm finding that being on the inside of a mystery is, at times, nail biting, but it's not that interesting. In fact, it's rather slow going and boring. At least this one is.

Carter's Six have been about their job. The texts started in late August, just a couple, and then got more frequent in September.

Annabelle has been coordinating the passing of the burner phone with the remote-control app. Frank, Lisa, and even Lester a time or two, have carried it to the proper location.

I have remote access to it all and have been sending the texts and seeing Smitty's replies. Or lack of replies, at first.

In mid-September he finally got curious.

I don't know who this is, he texted. *But you will pay.*

You know who I am, we texted back.

You can't be him, Smitty texted.

Try me, we texted.

For this exchange, Lisa had the phone in her purse and was at the Carterville Brewery having lunch with some friends.

Where did you meet my mother? he asked.

Courthouse, we texted. *Waiting to be arraigned.*

It was this kind of detail that Lester and I had spent months researching and Brooke had filled in the occasional gap.

What's my favorite ice cream as a kid? he texted.

This was a trick question, one of the ones Brooke had to help with. *You wouldn't eat ice cream*, we texted. *Weird kid.*

There was a pause then and I thought for a moment that we had lost him, that Brooke had been wrong. I mean, what kind of kid doesn't like ice cream? What kind of adult, for that matter? But then the phone bleeped again.

Why did you leave? Smitty texted.

Bad people were after me, we texted.

This wasn't true, at least not as far as we could tell, but it was what Smitty needed to hear. We think his father left because that's who his father was. He didn't stay put for too long.

Bullshit, he texted.

Bad people were always after me, we texted.

The conversation went on from there. Sometimes they were tedious, just following Brooke's script. Sometimes it was nerve-racking when we didn't have a script. Sometimes it was boring with days between texting.

I split my time between Flagstaff, staying with Wendy, Lilly, and Ian or out at Bo's place. When it was time to text, I wasn't at either. I'd drive to some place with a good view and good cell reception so that I could focus.

In October, Smitty sent two different private investigators. Martin Lester used his power and shadowed them from a good distance. They didn't find Smitty's father because his father wasn't there. But the texts continued.

In late October, on Smitty's birthday, Elias Carter made the first call. We were sitting in my truck just inside the zone of influence with Carter Hill in view. I had gone to Globe and gotten him. The remote-control application that I had acquired—and it wasn't cheap—allowed voice calls. We didn't need to be here, but it was Elias's condition.

I didn't trust him, not as far as I could throw him, but he was the one to play this part. The betrayal still felt fresh although it was now months old. He had a ratty down coat on, despite the fall day only being cool, and he hadn't shaved in about a week.

Even though he wasn't my father's identical twin, he looked enough like him, like that older version of my father that wasn't meant to be, and that wasn't easy.

"Happy birthday, boy," he said, his voice gruff but he sounded believable. He had the phone on speaker and held the script on his lap.

"Who are you?" Smitty asked. It had been a long time since I had heard his nasally voice, and right then I knew it hadn't been nearly long enough.

"Who the hell do you think I am?" Elias said.

"You can't be him," Smitty said. "He's dead."

Lester and I had investigated this and we came to the same conclusion. There was a fire, in a single-wide trailer, a meth lab, down near the border of Mexico. The bodies had been burned beyond recognition but it was believed that Wilson Smith had been one of them.

"It's me, Win," Elias said with a sniff. I stared at the older man. That sounded like real emotion. "It's me. I'm sorry it had to be like this. I just want to—"

"Go to hell," Smitty said, cutting him off. His voice was thick and even more nasally. "Whatever you want from me… just… just go to hell." He hung up.

Elias looked at me, a grin on his face and said, "Even the worst man wants his daddy back. The fish is hooked."

TWENTY-SEVEN

WEDNESDAY, NOVEMBER 18. PHOENIX, ARIZONA

It really does look like it's going to be a cold winter, a big storm blanketing the north country in early November, but I haven't worn the blue beanie Brooke Jennings knitted for me. I don't really know why. It just seems wrong. In all the ways that Brooke is manipulating me, if I can resist this one way, then maybe there is hope for all of this.

Silly, I know. But sometimes silly is important. Sometimes silly is all that keeps us going.

I'm not going to write about Annie Smith's trial—no relation to Winston "Smitty" Smith, by the way. I can't. I won't. There was plenty of media coverage of it, so have at it if you are curious.

Because of the complex nature of the case, the trial wasn't held in Coconino County, in Flagstaff, but in Phoenix in the United States District Court for the District of Arizona.

The trial occurred in early November in the midst of this

slow-burn plan with Smitty. The texts and the occasional calls had continued, the plot thickening, as it were.

It turns out that in our storyline, Wilson Smith is dying and needed his super-powered son to heal him. That's what this is all about.

I know. Not a big plot twist or anything. Rather obvious, really. Smitty was used to people from his past coming out of the woodwork when they needed to be healed, but he had spent his adult life believing his father was dead and we had conjured the illusion of his father being alive in danger of dying if his long-estranged son doesn't help him.

I know, I know. If not for the powers and the conspiracy, it sounds like some sappy movie on a second-rate cable channel where everyone reconciles at the end and sheds a well-earned tear or two before riding off into the sunset.

Annabelle had taken over managing communications while I was in Phoenix for the trial. I was there for the whole thing. I only had to be there for a day, for my testimony, but I had to see it all. I couldn't help myself.

I sat there in the uncomfortable wooden benches, which seemed way too much like church pews to me, and watched Annie sit there stiff-backed the whole damn time. She didn't look around, almost as still as a stone.

Unlike Brooke and Smitty, she was fighting for her life, fighting for fewer years in jail. Because it was clear she was going to jail.

It was hard for me to sit there for those two weeks, nearly impossible, so it must have been that much worse for her. She had to sell the Carterville Inn—to the mayor, Karen Winslow, no less—to fund her defense and still in the end she was found guilty.

The sentencing hearing hasn't happened yet. I'm not coming back for that. I can't watch it. I can't see the gavel fall and hear how many years she will be locked up with Brooke. I think my doubts about this "deal" with Brooke would get the best of me.

But as I said, I'm not going to write about the trial, but there are a few encounters that need to be recorded.

"Any more ghosts?" I asked Patty Walsh with a grin. We were meeting for dinner at a little Italian place in Phoenix the evening before her testimony. About five months ago, I had been in Pagosa Springs, Colorado, helping her deal with an apparent haunting.

"Not a one," she said, her smile dazzling, her green eyes bright. "Just some noisy geese."

I had been staring at Annie Smith's back for over a week at this point. Annie was short, slim, and dark, while Patty was taller, curvy, and a redhead. Patty had let the grey invade her long curly red hair while Annie chased the grey away vigorously, leaving her hair raven's wing black.

Patty was dressed simply in jeans and a green blouse that accented her eyes and her God given curves, but she had put a little makeup on and pulled her hair back, her freckles on fine display. Patty had this real-world beauty that had caught my eye from the moment I met her.

Annie was my past and I had once hoped that Patty was my future, but the trauma of Smitty, Annie, and Mary Reilly using their powers to try to stage our deaths was too much. For the longest time, I thought it was too much for us. Mary had used her powers on me and tried to force me to strangle Patty to death, after all, but in Colorado Patty had indicated otherwise. But only if I could leave Carterville behind and go be in Pagosa Springs with her.

"Glad to hear it," I said, sitting down across the small table from her. "I take it your neighbor hasn't returned."

She shook her head. "No. He hasn't been caught yet either. But it's back to being peaceful on the lake. I'm painting a lot."

"More faces?" I asked. When I had gotten there, her living room had been a gallery of Carterville faces, all of them stylized to bring out the qualities of the subject. It was part of her working through her Carterville trauma and had been a lot for me to deal with. She had painted me as transparent with the San Francisco Peaks showing through me.

"No," she said. "Landscapes. Tourist fare."

We continued on with the small talk for a while and after the wine came and some had been drunk, she asked, "How are you holding up?"

I cocked my head and stared at her. I wasn't sure if this was about Annie or Carterville or the underway plan she was the genesis of but didn't want to be a part of.

"All of the above," she said. We weren't in Carterville, Patty didn't have her power, but she had always been a very empathetic person and she knew me.

I sighed and nodded. "It's been hard being here every day. Hearing the testimony. Annie hasn't turned around once and…"

"What was it like to testify?" she asked.

"She stared at me the whole time," I said. "Those blue eyes of hers like lasers. Way worse than anything the defense's cross put me through."

"How bad was that?" she asked, her eyes flitting away, which was understandable. She was going to meet Annie's defense attorney face-to-face tomorrow.

"Bad," I said. "He made me feel like I was on trial. Like Carterville was on trial."

She pursed her lips and nodded. "So that's their defense?" she asked. "The powers made me do it?"

I shrugged. "It's a little more subtle than that, but yes."

"And it won't work?" she asked.

"No," I said. "Smitty isn't testifying, but he has a sworn deposition that has been read to the jury, part of his own plea deal. It lays out the whole conspiracy."

At the word "conspiracy" her right eyebrow arched in question. She was wondering about the conspiracy I was running.

"That's going to work out fine," I said in answer. "I don't like it, but as my uncle said, 'the fish is hooked.'"

She bit her top lip and looked away.

"This isn't on you," I said. "You got the ball rolling but…"

"Brooke," she said, a frown darkening her face.

I nodded. I hadn't told her yet, hadn't told her anything, which seemed like the deal in Pagosa when she told me about Smitty from the perspective of her power.

"Plot twist," I said, with what I hoped was a silly grin.

"Hardly," she said. "Brooke's still using all of us."

We were silent for longer than was comfortable. I suddenly wasn't hungry anymore and I wanted something a lot stronger than wine to drink.

The truth will do that. It was an obvious truth, one I had been living with every day, but to hear it declared so openly just made it way too real.

"I'm happy for you," Patty finally said. "I'm glad you are going to get to go back home."

Patty had a smile on her face but what she wasn't saying was there too, and it was dimming that smile. She wasn't saying that this truly meant that there was no future for us. I was married to the town, to the job, and since I couldn't leave it, that was going to be my life.

At least that's what I think that she wasn't saying. I'm not Patty, I could be wrong.

"How hard will this be?" Patty asked. She must have seen the look on my face and was changing the subject to her upcoming testimony and cross-examination.

"Annie is fighting for her life," I said. "They are going to pull everything they have."

She took a deep breath and let out a long sigh. "But she's going to jail?" she asked.

"Yes," I said. "For a while. Her powers were used in Frank's stabbing, in our..." I trailed off. I didn't have words to describe it. "Yes. She's going to jail."

What I didn't tell Patty, what I couldn't tell her, is that I made a deal with Brooke so that Annie would be okay in prison, that she would get through it, somehow.

I hadn't told anyone that. I couldn't. I didn't feel like it painted me in a very flattering light, but I was there that night. Annie hadn't wanted to be a part of what was happening, but things had gone too far, there was too much momentum.

Frank's stabbing, she went into with eyes open, but not Patty's and my attempted murder.

I knew Annie. She was a hard, demanding woman, often

unreasonably so. I had hurt her, deeply, multiple times in our on-again, off-again relationship. And, no, I am not excusing her actions, I'm just trying to explain my own. I had to do something to help Annie if it was within my power.

When the food came, we veered off into more pleasant topics. She told me about her life in Colorado and her painting, invited me to come up and stay anytime I liked. I told her how I had just gotten my private investigator's license, partially out of boredom, partial as a just-in-case. I had even put some feelers out amongst the people I knew in law enforcement.

"But you are going back?" she asked. "The… the Fortune Teller is on your side. It's going to happen."

I nodded. "It looks that way, but…"

"But what?" Patty asked. I couldn't tell if she just didn't know or if she wanted to hear me say it.

"But I need something to fall back on," I said. "You know. Just in case."

I felt my cheeks flush, and Patty smiled widely so her freckled cheeks pushed up and narrowed her green eyes. "Just in case, what, Henry?" she asked and now I knew she just wanted to hear me say it.

"Just in case Carterville doesn't feel like home anymore," I said. "After all of this time away and all of this…"

She looked shyly away and nodded. I didn't want to give her false hope. I was fighting like hell to return. But I had been away over a year and survived. There was clearly life for me outside of Carterville. Or maybe I could reclaim my home, but not the job, and not be so tied down.

These things had been fairly abstract thoughts, but with

Patty sitting across from me they seemed like possibilities, not just idle fantasies.

Brooke was helping to get me back to Carterville, but after that, wasn't it up to me?

I smiled, really smiled, because just thinking I had a say in my own future was the happiest kind of thought.

TWENTY-EIGHT
THURSDAY, NOVEMBER 19. PHOENIX, ARIZONA

"Got to hell, Henry Carter," Annie Smith said.

She was seated alone in a small room in the courthouse dressed in a black skirt and blue blouse that echoed the color of her eyes. Her arms were folded and her mouth was such a thin, tight line it almost disappeared.

There was a small round table in the middle of the room with some nondescript Arizona landscapes photos hanging on the bland white walls. This was a room where attorneys and clients met.

"Don't worry, Annie," I said with a grin. "There's a good chance of that."

We were alone, something that had been surprisingly easy to arrange. All the whispers about Carterville had given me more clout than I expected.

"You were never funny, Henry," she said. "Especially not under pressure, so don't even try."

I nodded and leaned against the wall. Since I was in the

courthouse I had on dark slacks, a white button-down shirt, and a black suit jacket, which made me feel entirely uncomfortable. I rubbed at the bolo tie, it and the cowboy boots the only thing that seemed like me.

"How are you?" I asked.

"Jesus Christ," she said. "What are you doing? Why are we talking?"

There was never any warm-up with Annie. It was all or nothing, and I have to admit that could be rather exciting under the right circumstances. But now? This was all her disdain, all her hate, all her anger that she was throwing at me.

But I knew Annie, really knew her. Not many people did, and I knew under that bluster she was terrified.

"I wanted to see you," I said.

She shook her head, the look she gave me withering. "Why? The last time we saw each other…" she began, her lips pursing and then her blue eyes losing their intensity.

"You were trying to kill Patty and me," I said, finishing the thought for her and now it was my time to be angry. I had arranged this hoping for… God, I don't know what. Annie wasn't the kind of woman that was ever going to be easy, the kind of woman you didn't want to be easy. We had had our problems, many of them, but what happened was still hard for me to reconcile.

I think maybe I thought that if I saw her, if I spoke to her, it would somehow all make sense.

Well, that was silly.

"What do you want, Henry?" she asked between clenched teeth.

I almost left. I almost let it be, but I couldn't. Too much

had passed between us, much of it good. "I just want to understand how we got here," I said, my voice quiet but sounding loud in the small room.

Her brow furrowed and she looked at me like I was a child asking the stupidest question in the world. "Really?" she asked.

I nodded. "Really."

She sighed and I swear to God she rolled her eyes like some bored teenage girl. "We got here one stupid choice at a time, one small step at time, until we went over the goddamn brink, Brooke Jennings manipulating me into this disaster."

"The cowboy hat," I said.

She pursed her lips and nodded. It was a Christmas gift Annie had given me right before our final breakup. Brooke Jennings, still a teenager then, had made an idle comment, just the right comment, and that had prompted Annie to make a big gesture of it on Christmas Eve a few years ago and that had revealed the fractures in our relationship.

That very night, Lila Chang was murdered, and Annie was a suspect because of my friendship with Lila and Annie's very obvious jealousy.

"So this is all Brooke's fault?" I asked, trying to keep my tone even.

"I'm not fourteen," Annie said. "Of course it's my fault. I made the choices, but that little witch set the groundwork to make my choices inevitable. The whole rotten series of them that brought me here."

I just stared at her, processing her words.

"You know I'm right," she said with a sharp smile. "That girl maneuvered us both out of Carterville."

I imagined Annie's reaction if I told her I was working

with Brooke, that I had made a deal with Brooke to make her prison time livable. The word "apocalyptic" came to mind.

My phone rang, not the burner phone but my phone, and I jumped. I needed a moment, so I pulled it out and it said, "Unknown Caller." Since I had feelers out for work as a private investigator, I had been answering my phone pretty religiously, with mostly scammers and salespeople on the other end.

"Hello," I said as I felt Annie's glare. And I got it. I had arranged this so we could talk, and here I was answering the phone.

"Hi, Henry," a nasally voice said on the other side. "Bet you never thought you'd hear from me again."

I blinked and it suddenly felt like this room was too hot, too small, and getting hotter and smaller.

Brooke had not prepared me for a call with Smitty. She had left much of the details of this conspiracy unilluminated, and my brain froze for a moment.

"Henry?" Smitty asked. "You there?" He chuckled and the sound made my skin crawl. "If I just gave you a heart attack, I guess that wouldn't be the worst thing."

I found my voice and said, "Go to hell, Smitty." I hung up the phone, muted it, and found Annie staring at me, her eyes wide.

A question formed on her lips, but no sound came out. I looked down at my phone.

I had come in here looking for some kind of closure, some kind of way to help me deal with her betrayal, but I just felt more betrayed. Brooke had known this was when the call would happen. She knew what kind of state I would be in and how I would react to Smitty's call. I wasn't acting. I had zero desire to talk to him under the watchful eyes of Annie Smith. And Brooke knew all that and let it happen without any warning.

When I looked back up at Annie, her eyes were narrowed and she was leaning forward. "Why in the world would Smitty be calling you?" she asked.

I held her gaze. Annie would know if I lied to her and for some reason that still mattered. Maybe for good reason, Annie wasn't powerless, she could still cause me trouble if she figured out what I was up to.

"How could you agree to Frank's stabbing?" I asked, going back to why I had come in here, going back a number of steps in the conspiracy she was part of with Smitty.

She pursed her lips and just stared at me for a few breaths, her arms crossed, but then she sighed. "Fine. Have your little Smitty secret. Trust me, don't trust that bastard."

"How?" I asked.

She sighed and said, "You've been here for the whole damn trial. You know the answer."

I was wondering if she had known I was here, so one small mystery solved. And I guess I did know the answer, but I wanted to hear it from her. "It was going to be Patty," I said, only partially succeeding in keeping my voice calm. "You and Mary were going to have a tourist stab Patty not Frank."

I remembered the painting Patty did of Annie. In it her face was elongated, a bit misshapen, her eyes tinged red making her seem like jealousy personified.

She looked away and said, "Yes. Smitty thought it would produce the most leverage."

"And how did he get that idea?" I asked.

She met my eyes this time and they were so fierce that I

almost looked away. "That boy is not half as clever as he thinks he is. I told him. Mary backed me up. The whole town knew about your big, huge crush."

I was sweating, my heart beating hard, but I kept going. I was getting at what I needed to know. "And how did that change to Frank?"

Annie sighed, seeming like a teenager again despite being over fifty. "Mary lost her nerve. Everyone loved Patty. She knew what you wanted without you even asking, so how could they not love her."

It was plain what Annie left out, that she didn't love Patty.

"When did the plan change?" I asked. These details had all come out in the trial, but I needed to hear it from her. I needed to see her face. I needed to know I had done the right thing in making that deal with Brooke.

"That morning," she said. "We had a fight, the three of us. When the target changed to Frank, I wanted out, but Mary… she…" Annie's eyes darkened and she looked up at me. "Mary really hated you because of William's death. She blamed you, not Smitty the man that was keeping her Alzheimer's at bay. She wouldn't turn back and I refused, so she made me punch myself in the stomach. Hard. I had no choice, Henry."

I bit back a torrent of words. Of course she had a choice. She could have come to me. She could have gotten the hell out of the zone of influence where Mary's powers wouldn't work. But I had been at the trial. I had seen the timeline. Annie didn't really have a chance to get away from Mary before the stabbing, but couldn't she have used her powers to put Mary to sleep and changed everything?

I let that question go, there was nothing to be gained. It

wasn't the choice she made and I am quite sure our tumultuous history was a big part of the reason why.

"And after?" I asked, keeping my voice as gentle as I could. "Why didn't you come to me?"

She sighed again. "Because, Henry, I thought we were done. I thought we had succeeded and finally rid the town of you."

I smiled but I'm sure it was a scary sight. Part of me got it, when small town romances go bad, you can't get away from your ex. And perhaps I gave Annie good reason to hate me, but there was no excuse for this.

"You're not going to stop with these questions?" she asked. Her shoulders slumped and she looked tired, looked her age, which was a rarity for Annie.

I shook my head. "I need to understand."

"Why?" she asked.

I nodded and walked over to the small table and sat down across from her. "I loved you, Annie," I said quietly. "And you were involved in…" I couldn't say the words. What the three of them had done, Smitty, Mary, and Annie, was beyond the pale. I can see there was a bit of a slippery slope for Annie, but she jumped on it with glee… well, rage, really.

"I'm sorry, Henry," she said. "I truly am. I…" Her eyes clouded and tears formed.

Annie wasn't a crier and my knee-jerk reaction was to comfort her, but I swallowed that and just stared at her.

"Fine," she said with a sniff. "I'll tell you everything. We were done, the three of us, you had promised to leave town if Smitty healed Frank. You were leaving town. But you couldn't let it be. You couldn't let the tourist take the fall for what happened to Frank and you were getting close." She shrugged.

The tears were gone and there was a fierceness to her that made me want to back away. What was even more chilling was how blithe she was about their conspiracy putting an innocent person in jail.

Back when things with Annie and I started going to hell, right after Lila Chang was murdered, Annie became a suspect. And with good reason. I had known Annie all my life, but there was darkness there that was still surprising.

"Your little doting protégé, Isabella," Annie said, "called Mary. Told her what was happening. How stupid was that?"

I didn't take the bait and come to Ortega's defense.

Annie held my eyes for a moment and continued. "Mary called Smitty and told him. It was his plan. And then Mary came to get me. I had no choice."

I leaned back in the chair. Maybe this was understandable, but it sure as hell wasn't closure.

"So you are the victim here?" I asked.

Her lips pursed and she crossed her arms again. I was baiting her this time. She hated the thought of being a victim. "Yes," she said. "I had no choice."

I nodded. "I get that is your defense, Annie, but do you believe it?"

Those blue eyes of hers drilled into me, but there was enough water under the bridge that they weren't quite as effective on me as they used to be.

"Yes," she said, her voice tight. "I believe it."

I nodded again. "I can kind of see that," I said. "Mary was powerful. I died when I put my power up directly against hers. I get how you couldn't quite bring yourself to defy her. But there is one thing you left out."

Her brow furrowed and she said, "What?"

"This may have been Smitty's plan," I said, speaking slowly and choosing my words carefully. "But you were the genesis of it. The starting point. You volunteered all the key information. None of this would have happened without you."

She blinked, furrowed her brow again, and said, "What the hell are you talking about?"

"I'm sure Smitty came to you one day," I said. "Probably at the Inn when it was slow. Complaining about me and how the town would have been better off without me."

She nodded tentatively but still looked confused. "Something like that," she said.

"Smitty is smart enough, sometimes even clever, but he didn't know my power," I said, and Annie's mouth formed an "O" and I nodded at her. "No one knew my power, at least I didn't tell them, not even the woman I loved. But you have always been observant, and we spent so much time together. You saw how careful I was about making promises, you figured it out, Annie. You told Smitty what it was and how it could be used against me. Maybe you were Mary's victim, but you started all of this."

Her mouth moved, she didn't speak, but I could see it in her eyes. I was right. She had told Smitty what my power was. She had helped him figure out how to use it against me. None of this would have happened without her.

I slowly got up and said, "You didn't wield the knife that was plunged into Frank's back and you didn't use your power to try to make me choke Patty to death, but you might as well have."

As I turned and walked to the door, I was surprised that Annie wasn't yelling at me, telling me how wrong I was. I took that as a sign of how right I was.

"Why?" she finally asked as I reached for the doorknob.

"What do you mean?" I asked, not looking back. I didn't want to see her.

"Is this spite?" she asked. "My life is, essentially, over. Why come here and do this? You never used to be cruel, Henry."

I took a deep breath, but didn't turn around. "It's not spite," I said. "And it's not cruelty. I need to be sure of what happened. I'm doing this for you. I hope you understand one day."

TWENTY-NINE
THURSDAY, NOVEMBER 19. PHOENIX, ARIZONA

I didn't tell Annie what I was doing because it wouldn't have done any good. She would have rejected the thought without even considering it. I knew her well enough to know that.

I had wanted to understand what happened from her point of view, but the whole victim thing needed to be confronted. Annie Smith is not a victim, at least not the Annie Smith I grew up with and loved. Until she embraces her part in all of this, she won't be able to heal.

As I sat in the courtroom that afternoon, uncomfortable on the hard wooden bench, I thought about this and wondered if I had cast myself as a victim in Brooke Jennings's machinations.

I was too tired to contemplate fate versus free will in the context of Brooke again, but I wasn't too tired to vow to learn from where Annie went wrong. I wasn't the victim of Brooke

Jennings. I made my own choices. Even if those choices happened to have been seen by her before I made them.

I'm not about to say that we are not victims of fate. We all are. The world does what it does without our permission or consent, and we are changed by it. And biology is, in the end, unkind, each of us having our brief moment on this planet. But that's not what I'm talking about. I think it's more about agency, the ability to make a difference, to do things that matter.

Brooke's power does not take away my agency.

I think I proved it that night on my deck with Mary using her power to try to make me choke Patty. I fought her. It almost cost me my life, but I fought her, I did something, and even if it hadn't worked it would have mattered.

I kept my phone muted for the rest of the day, and after I was out of court and back in my hotel room sitting on the bed, I looked at it. Smitty had called eight more times.

I had been so involved in that conversation with Annie and then the ruminations, and then watching her trial, that I had forgotten. The conspiracy to get Smitty to release me from his power fading away for an afternoon.

We had gotten to our last stage, where the drone with the phone was flown from my deck onto the roof of Smitty's gaudy house and Elias Carter had called him through it.

This had happened a week ago. Annabelle had let me know that they had spotted more private investigators in town.

I stared at my phone. I didn't know what to do. I pulled out the flip phone from Brooke and almost opened it, but said, "No."

I was sitting on the bed looking at both phones. I didn't want to lean on Brooke for every decision. That was a choice, to be sure, but it wasn't me exercising my agency. Consulting Brooke on every little thing would ruin me. Consulting the Fortune Teller with every decision I made would be crippling.

So, I put the burner phone away and thought about what I would do if I wasn't the reason why Smitty was calling. What would a Henry Carter not involved in all of this do if Smitty couldn't take a hint and kept calling?

I chuckled and blocked the number. That seemed counter-intuitive, like it wasn't leading towards my goal, but it's what I would have done. I really have no desire to ever see or talk to Smitty again.

And that gave me the path through with Smitty, one that didn't require consulting Brooke. Just go with my gut. Let the hate and resentment show.

I didn't sleep much. All of it swirling around in my head. Brooke and her chess-playing machinations. Smitty and his cruder but effective attempts to shape the world in his image. Annie on her way to jail and playing the victim. Patty and what could still be if I could turn away from Carterville. My admitted hate for Smitty but somehow not letting this drive my actions and take me over. My uncle and the deal he made with Brooke. Fate. Free will. Agency.

I tried to do what Bo had taught me and meditate, but it was useless. My thoughts were too strong and I was still pretty new to meditation.

I'm tempted to say something like, "I'm just a simple Arizona boy and this was all a lot," but let's face it, after that meteor hit and everyone in Carterville that night gained powers, I stopped being just a simple Arizona boy and a small-town cop.

I'm not exactly sure how to characterize myself now, but "simple" and "small town" no longer capture it.

THIRTY

FRIDAY, NOVEMBER 20. PHOENIX, ARIZONA

Having only gotten a couple hours of sleep, I was groggy and jittery sitting for Annie's last day of trial. Groggy from the lack of sleep. Jittery from the coffee to try to compensate, but those two things didn't really seem to account for what I was feeling.

Any thoughts of premonition that I might have looking back are just misplaced hindsight, but I really felt like something was wrong. I missed my utility belt that I wore for so long. I missed the weight of it and the holstered gun and taser. I kept looking around, the courtroom mostly filled with media, their eyes hungry from the drama that feeds them and their insatiable news cycle.

Patty was back in Colorado and no one else from Carterville was here. Annie was her usual stiff-backed self and didn't turn around. The lawyers gave the closing statements, not nearly as dramatic as on TV, and nothing untoward happened, but I couldn't shake the sense that something was wrong.

And my thoughts never went to our little conspiracy and returning to Carterville. Everything felt, somehow, much bigger than that.

I eventually tossed it up to a bad night and too much caffeine and paid attention to the trial. After it was over, out in the cavernous hallway of the courthouse, the murmur of too many people talking, I checked my phone.

There was a text from my niece Lilly, *Have you heard from Mom? Probably nothing but she wasn't here this morning.*

My jaw worked like I needed to say something, needed to express myself, but I couldn't. Lilly was a mom herself now, so she was something of a worrier, but she knew her mother. Wendy wouldn't make a dramatic change in plans without telling her daughter.

The crowd had spilled out into the courthouse's huge open area, it was six stories tall fronted with all glass. This wasn't an old-fashioned columns and granite courthouse but was built in 2000 and more modern.

It was a huge echo chamber and some reporters were eying me, so I hustled outside, and started the walk towards the parking lot and my truck.

Most of the reporters had figured out that I wasn't going to talk to any of them and had satisfied themselves with pictures and the fact that they could report on my presence and speculate on my reasons.

Despite it being fall, the air was pretty warm and I was sweating, my heart sounding too loud in my head. I am several decades beyond where lack of sleep is something you can just shrug off. I wasn't right. I needed sleep. But I needed to know my sister was okay much more than that.

I glanced back and saw that I was being followed by two people. The woman had a microphone in her hand and the man was lugging a camera.

I sped up. She had heels on, and I knew I could outpace them.

I unlocked my phone, found Lilly in my contacts and called her.

"Uncle Henry," she said when she picked up.

"Did Wendy show up?" I asked, my heart getting louder in my head. I really had drunk too much coffee.

"No," she said. "But… I'm sure it's nothing." The kid wasn't a good liar, something I liked about her.

"You called? You texted?" I asked.

I glanced back and the reporters were still following but farther behind.

"Yes," she said. "Nothing. Maybe… I don't know. Maybe something finally happened between her and Abel."

Abel was a nurse she worked with. Wendy lit up when she talked about him. I slowed down just a little bit. Maybe I was being paranoid. Maybe this wasn't about me. Maybe Wendy was finally allowing herself to be human and care for someone since her husband died.

Yeah, right.

"No," I said. "She would have at least texted. You know she would have."

"I guess…" Lilly said, doubt in her voice.

Something wasn't right. I thought back through our conversation, what Lilly said, what she sounded like, and I realized that I was on a speakerphone. That, in and of itself, wasn't unusual. A lot of people use speakerphone. But would Lilly put me on speakerphone when she was talking about her missing mother and her son could overhear?

I ran back through it again. I hadn't heard Ian at all and that was more than unusual.

I sighed, doing my best to make a show of it. "You are probably right. I'm just… this trial… you know."

"That has to be so hard," she said.

"Just let me know when you hear from her," I said.

"Of course," she said.

We hung up and I would have smashed the phone, but I needed it. Something wasn't right. Lilly was not being herself. Wendy had disappeared.

I looked back and the reporters had fallen farther behind. This was downtown Phoenix, the buildings all at least a few stories tall, the sidewalks wide, the craggy humps of distant hills visible here and there.

My heart was still beating too fast, so I slowed down. What I needed to do was call Brooke, but I hadn't brought the burner phone with me. I didn't want it to be a temptation and I didn't want to be seen using it in a room full of reporters.

Brooke would know what was going on. But why the hell wouldn't she have told me? And why would she have let something happen to my family like this?

Something really wasn't right. I sped my pace up again.

THIRTY-ONE
FRIDAY, NOVEMBER 20. PHOENIX, ARIZONA

By the time I got to my truck deep in a parking garage in downtown Phoenix, I was a sweaty mess, but the exercise seemed to have done me some good. I wasn't quite so jittery, and my mind was focused.

I was pretty sure I had lost the reporters, so I pulled the flip phone out of the glovebox and dialed the one number in it. In my contacts it was labeled "Fortune Teller." I didn't do that, the phone came that way.

I started the truck while the phone rang so I could get some air-conditioning. Brooke usually texted, we had only talked twice in the last couple of months and both times she had called me. This wasn't protocol, but a text wouldn't do.

After six rings, I hung up and texted, *Call me now. Urgent. 911.*

I sat there for a few minutes staring at the silent phone.

"Shit," I said. I was doing it. Doing what I promised I

wouldn't do. Leaning on Brooke and her knowledge of the future. But this wasn't about me.

I thought I heard something and spotted the reporters now in the garage and heading towards me. My truck kind of stands out. It's a white 1992 Toyota King Cab pickup. Kind of easy to spot in a sea of newer vehicles.

I fitted my phone onto the holder on the dash and pulled out. I couldn't wait for Brooke. I had to get to Flagstaff, see what was going on with Lilly and Ian, find my sister.

————

HEADING OUT OF PHOENIX AS THE SUN WENT DOWN, THE sprawl of it creeping farther and farther north like some kind of relentlessly spreading rash, I could only think of my family. Gone were thoughts of returning to Carterville and this whole Smitty conspiracy. It didn't matter. All that mattered was Wendy and Lilly and Ian.

Once the outlet mall was past and the desert hills had become ghosts in the darkening light, I started talking on my phone and calling people.

"Hey, Chief," Annabelle said, her southern accent and the energy in her voice making her sound cheerful. "Did the verdict come in yet?" There hadn't been any love lost between Annie and Annabelle, not for years. Annabelle was working for me during many of the "off again" phases of my relationship with Annie and got to see that side of it.

"Don't know," I said, my voice clipped. "Don't care. Wendy is missing and something isn't right with Lilly."

Annabelle cursed briefly and said, "Wadda ya need?"

I gave her instructions, and in a strange way it felt good.

Not that my family was in trouble but because it felt more like old times, like I was really "Chief" and Annabelle was working for me.

Maybe "good" is the wrong word. It felt more right, like it was the way things should be.

Which again sounds strange. Annabelle is smart and capable. She could find many other jobs if she wanted, but we had always had a good working relationship and that was something that I valued.

I called Lilly again and started talking as soon as she picked up. "Listen," I said. "I know I was planning to spend the night up there with you guys, but I'm beat."

That was a lie. My plan had been to head to Globe, since I wasn't far away, and camp somewhere out in the desert. I was supposed to check in on my uncle tomorrow.

"Oh, that's okay," she said, her voice sounding a little distant and I knew I was on speakerphone again. "Ian will be disappointed but I'm sure we'll see you soon."

That did it. Lilly had a good memory. She knew I wasn't planning to be there. I slept on the pull-out couch in the living room and some prep was required so I never surprised her with it.

"No doubt about that," I said, trying to sound cheerful. "And I've been thinking about Wendy. Do you have Abel's number? It's probably that, but… you know. My life is strange enough that I really need to check on her."

I couldn't blow off my missing sister. Whoever was on the other end of the line listening, if they knew me at all, wouldn't buy it. Wendy and I were close. She wasn't answering her phone.

"I… I don't," Lilly said. "Sorry."

"No worries," I said. "I'm sure I can come up with it. I'll keep you posted on my plans."

But there were many worries when I hung up. I hadn't heard Ian. I was a cop, so my gut on this was to call another cop. I knew the Flagstaff chief of police. I could get them there in minutes with sirens blazing, but that didn't sound smart. Wendy and Ian were in danger. There were other people there. There could be no doubt.

But who would be doing something to them and why?

I was going to make another call when my phone blipped. It was a text from Wendy. *I'm fine. Just need a break.*

Whoever was behind this conspiracy, the one involving my family, wasn't very smart. They hadn't covered for Wendy's absence. They relied on me not knowing my niece was not herself. Sure, I was distracted with the trial, but not that distracted.

I used the voice command on my phone and texted her back, *No doubt. Give me your code word and I'll leave you alone.*

Wendy and I didn't have a code word, she would have given me hell if I had suggested it, but it was plausible. A banished cop coming from a town as complicated as Carterville setting up a code word with his sister sounded quite reasonable and I was annoyed that I hadn't thought of it before this.

The traffic was thinning out and I was able to speed up. I kept my eye on the road. I focused on my driving. And my mind churned through what little I knew.

Wendy was kidnapped. There was little doubt now.

Lilly was in trouble. Whether she was in her home or not was anyone's guess. I couldn't tell.

Ian was a complete unknown, but I was beginning to think

he wasn't with Lilly because she put me on speakerphone and I hadn't heard him. It was too early for him to be asleep and that boy was a noisy one.

It took a little while for the text to come back, which told me something too. Whoever had Wendy's phone was probably not with her and that complicated things. The text was a single word. *Portabella.*

Wendy hated mushrooms so that gave me some hope that she was okay. But why would she use that as her fake code word? It was her one opportunity to communicate something to me and it had to count, but what could portabella mean?

I let the hum of the tires and my focus on driving lull my brain so it could put things together. This wasn't meditation but it was kind of like meditation, if you know what I mean.

I was a cop for decades. I had arrested a lot of people, both before and after the meteor hit and we got our powers, which meant I had plenty of enemies.

But the ones that needed leverage on me right now were Brooke and Smitty.

Brooke because maybe she had figured out what I was thinking of doing, because she wanted more than just a couple of days back in Carterville so she could see her way through her time in jail.

Smitty because his dead father was haunting him, and I had blocked his calls, but that was only a few hours ago and that would be an awfully big swing for him to take so quickly. From jail, no less. That could explain the general sloppiness of what was going on.

My phone rang and it took me a moment to figure out it was the burner phone, not my smartphone mounted on the dash. It was still in my back pocket. I slowed down, carefully pulled it out, flipped it open, and put it on speaker.

"What did you do with her?" I said by way of greeting. Not my best moment, I will admit.

There was silence for a couple of breaths, and I was about to say something when Brooke said, "Hello to you too. And who the hell are we talking about?"

"Wendy," I said. "She's missing. And something is wrong with Lilly."

"Wait… what?" Brooke asked. I really wished we were in the same room so I could see her face, because she sounded genuinely confused.

"My sister Wendy didn't go home to my niece's house this morning after her shift," I said. "Lilly, my niece, is acting strange. Something isn't right. You must know this."

There was silence on the line.

"And why the hell didn't you warn me that Smitty was going to call while I was talking to Annie?" I asked. "How could that have mattered one bit to the future?"

"What?" Brooke asked, sounding not just confused but lost.

"Did I not speak clearly?" I asked, my hands gripping the steering wheel hard as the road started winding up a steep hill.

"Tell it to me again," she said. "Slowly."

What I wanted to do was throw the stupid phone out the window, but I did as she asked and slowly told her what I had already told her. I left out certain details, like the code word trick, but I summarized my calls with Lilly.

"And Smitty called you today?" she asked.

"Yes," I said. "Today. In the middle of my conversation with Annie."

"Wait," she said. "You talked to Annie?"

"What the hell is going on, Brooke?" I asked. "I know you are not stupid, but you sure as hell are acting like you are."

"I'm… I'm sorry," she said. "We are… Oh, God. We are not in the future I thought we were."

The hum of the tires and the whine of the engine got loud, too loud, and it felt like the cab was closing in on me. I had spent a lot of time contemplating Brooke's power so what she said registered.

She had seen multiple futures, many of them taking one small change to create. She had chosen the one she wanted and done her part to make sure it came to pass. But she had been away from her powers for over a year and was working from her memory of those futures.

If you think of the many futures as roads, she was just telling me we were not on the road she thought we were and that meant that the Fortune Teller didn't know what was coming next.

That is, of course, if she was telling me the truth.

THIRTY-TWO

FRIDAY, NOVEMBER 20. I-17 BETWEEN PHOENIX AND FLAGSTAFF, ARIZONA

How had it never occurred to me that Brooke Jennings, the Fortune Teller, could get lost. That whole saying about a butterfly flapping its wings on one side of the world and a hurricane occurring on the other sounds a bit preposterous, but it makes a point. Small changes lead to big changes. Brooke's power lets her know what small changes could lead to big changes, but she had just told me that she was lost. That this wasn't the future she thought it was.

"You are not involved in what has happened to Wendy?" I asked, the energy gone from my voice.

"No," she said. "I swear it. Why would I do that?"

"Leverage," I said. "On me."

"I have leverage on you," she said, and the frankness of it was like a slap in the face. "I've never lied to you, Henry. I don't need to lie to you. All I want is my three days in Carterville. I... I hadn't expected this... this 'drift' in things."

"Drift?" I asked, not because I didn't get what she was saying but because I had to say something.

"Yes, drift," she said. "This future is very similar to the one I thought we were in, but it's not the same."

"So the memoir you read was not the one I am writing," I said, and I was glad she couldn't see the smile forming on my face.

"I never told you I read your memoir," she said.

"It's obvious," I said.

She was silent for a few more breaths as my old truck surged up the steep hill, the engine whining in protest as I kept up as much speed as I could.

"Henry," she finally said. "I am sorry this is happening to your family. Please believe me."

I have to admit that she sounded sincere, but this was Brooke Jennings, the poster child for "the ends justify the means" and she wasn't to be trusted. She could be lying to me right now.

I bit that back and said, "Thank you. What do we do now?"

She chuckled and it was a scary sound and that was weirdly comforting because she sounded like the old Brooke. "Oh come on. You know what the next play is and you most definitely don't want to and probably won't do it."

And I did know. I could turn around, head towards Florence, beg the warden to let me take her for a few days, and give her enough time in the zone of influence so she could see what was going on with Wendy.

But that would take too long and rushing a thing like that would give her too many opportunities to get away.

"You are right," I said. "I won't do that."

"I don't know what else I can do then," she said.

It was my turn to be silent as I mulled it over. Brooke and her power weren't available to help me, and in most any other case I would be content with that. But this was my family.

My brain made a leap and I said, "You remember more futures than the one you thought we were in." It wasn't a question. It had to be true. Like that butterfly in the story, many small choices make big changes, and it wasn't enough to be familiar with just one path through. To do as well as she had in prison, she had to have memorized a lot of possibilities, a lot of futures.

"Yes," she said, the simplicity of her answer surprising.

"Then remember this one," I said. "And then call me back."

I snapped the phone shut, focused on driving, and hoped that Annabelle was able to pull off what we needed.

———

Carterville powers run the gamut, from seeing the future, to telepathy, levitation, controlling another's will, and every odd thing in between.

Brooke isn't the only one on the psychic spectrum—there are several others. Trent Bashir is a famous animal communicator. He's done it long enough and effectively enough that I believe it. He knows what your dog or cat wants. Lisa Cummings always knows what the weather will be, but that seems to be the extent of it. And Steve Thompson has been banned from buying lotto tickets, but I don't think his power goes much further, otherwise he'd have a fat stock portfolio.

The only other person, that we know of, that can see the future is Carl George, but his power isn't as clean as Brooke's. He gets hints of the future, but he often sees them disconnected or out of order and, if he spends too much time in Carterville, he gets lost in what he sees and earns his not-so-kind nickname of "Crazy Carl."

That is what I asked Annabelle to do. Get Carl in the zone of influence and see what he can find out. I also asked Annabelle to get Ortega working on the Lilly problem from the law enforcement side, but subtly. No uniforms. No sirens.

Tracking cell phones would be helpful here, but it hadn't been nearly long enough for a judge to give us a warrant.

The reliable psychic Brooke was out, and Carl was in to pinch hit. At least I hoped he was. Annabelle hadn't texted back, which could just mean she was busy or driving.

And yes, I wrote earlier that I wanted to live my life without always reaching for the future. But that was before my family was on the line.

As I was passing Cordes Junction, I texted my son, Tom, to make sure he was okay. Thankfully he responded right away. I didn't tell him what was going on. He was an adult now and probably deserved to know, but I couldn't justify burdening him with the worry. This would resolve one way or another soon enough.

I was driving down a steep curving road into the Verde Valley when my phone rang from an unknown caller.

I tapped the phone and said, "Hello." I kept my tone neutral, this likely had nothing to do with Wendy and Lilly.

"Henry," Smitty said, his nasally voice instantly recognizable. "Don't hang up. We really need to talk."

I ground my teeth together, holding in unkind words and anger and said as casually as I could, "What about?"

If he was behind what was going on with Wendy and Lilly, then I was expecting him to make some kind of demand, even if it was veiled. If he wasn't behind it, I sure as hell didn't want to tell him anything about it.

He sighed and he sounded like some over-dramatic teenager. "Well… first off, I guess I owe you an apology," he said. "We've always had our differences, and well… I took things too far."

I was once again wishing this conversation wasn't on the phone. Was Smitty trying to apologize? This didn't sound genuine, and I couldn't imagine that it was, but it didn't sound like the start of a ransom demand. Whatever this was, I didn't have time for it.

"Just get to it, Smitty," I said. "I'm in the middle of something and I don't have time for any of your fake apologies. You don't regret what you did, you only regret that you got caught."

"So we're being honest?" he asked, his voice taking on a predatorial tone.

As the road wound downhill, the lights of the Verde Valley glittered in the dark. It's a bunch of small communities that fill this large valley, south of Sedona and Flagstaff.

"Yes," I said.

"Very well then," he said with a sniff. "I very much do regret getting caught, that is true. Your exile has been a delight to me until recently. It seems my father has somehow risen from the dead and is causing me trouble."

"Risen from the dead?" I asked, the phrasing of it catching my attention. It sounded rather Christian to me and Smitty was a man that only had faith in himself, although I did know from those months of research that his mother was devoutly religious and he went to church with her as a child.

"Yes," he said. "Texting. Calling. Breaking into my home."

"Well good for the both of you," I said, letting my anger fuel sarcasm in my voice. "I hope you have a tearful reunion and live happily ever after. I don't see what this has to do with me, and I don't have—"

"Please," Smitty said, cutting me off. "Just let me get this out."

I sighed. "Make it quick."

"I knew your old man, of course," he said. "So proud to be a Carter in Carterville, so happy that his second child was a boy and could carry on the legacy. So—"

I tapped the phone and hung up on Smitty. I had too much on my mind to be dragged down his twisted version of memory lane, no matter the reason.

With Smitty gone and the hum of the tires the loudest sound, something began to tickle at my mind. Something that made my stomach twist into a Gordian Knot. The idea made me sick, but it also gave me hope.

Something was off about all of this today. Wendy missing. Lilly acting strange. Ian's boyish exuberance missing from the calls with Lilly.

It wasn't quite formed, this thought, but it was on the tip of my tongue so I told my phone to call Lilly.

"Hello," she said, her voice quiet.

"Where is Ian?" I asked.

"What?" she said.

"You had me on speakerphone for the last two calls and I didn't hear him," I said. "Where is Ian?"

"He… he's on a play date," she said. "Why?"

That made sense. A boy like that needed all the play dates he could get, but that didn't explain the rest of her strangeness. As the road started to level off and I entered the Verde Valley, it clicked.

"Let me talk to your mother," I said. The faux nature of Lilly's behavior only had one explanation. Or, at least, only one explanation given my circumstances.

"Uncle Henry," she said, sounding distressed. "She's… I told you, she didn't come home this morning."

"Just put her on," I said.

"Are you okay?" she asked, and I felt the chill of doubt and the heat of shame. Maybe my gut was wrong. Maybe this wasn't what I thought it was.

A call from Smitty came in, but I sent it to voicemail.

"Here's what I think happened," I said, keeping my voice calm. "I might be wrong. I might be paranoid. But I think your mother is fine. She's there. She's listening. Her phone is just turned off. Brooke Jennings put you up to this because I needed to be in a particularly agitated state when Smitty called so that I would act like I didn't care about what he wanted.

"Annabelle is probably in on it too. She knew what was going on so she acted serious on the call with me but did nothing that I asked her to do. You all put me through this so I would be an ass with Smitty, and he wouldn't suspect that I was behind the return of his father."

There was silence on the other end and my stomach knotted further. Was I wrong? Was I just being paranoid? Working with Brooke will do that to you, without a doubt.

I heard some rustling and then Wendy came on. "I'm sorry, Henry," she said.

I felt this burst of emotion and my eyes teared up. "Thank God," I said. "I'm just glad you are okay."

"I'm fine," Wendy said. "She… Brooke… you have to stop her, Henry. I don't know how it's even possible, but you have to stop her."

"I'm sorry you got pulled into this," I said. "I know you didn't want to be a part of it."

"There's more to talk about," she said. "But when you get back. We'll talk then, okay?"

"Yeah," I said. "You guys are okay. That's what matters. I'll be there in an hour."

They were okay, but that wasn't all that mattered. Brooke had manipulated my family to put me in the proper state to deal with Smitty. Totally Brooke, not hard to see it now that I could, but Wendy was right. Brooke had to be stopped. Somehow, someway, she had to be stopped.

THIRTY-THREE

FRIDAY, NOVEMBER 20. I-17 BETWEEN PHOENIX AND FLAGSTAFF, ARIZONA

I really miss life before cell phones, when you could have a moment and the world would leave you alone, when you could just drive. I was on the phone more on my trip back up to Flagstaff, way too much.

The weather turned, clouds hiding the San Francisco Peaks, and a few errant snowflakes fell as I crested the Mogollon Rim and found myself back amongst the tall ponderosa pines.

I had just hung up with Annabelle and she confirmed everything. Today had been an act initiated by Brooke just so that I wouldn't be eager and blow it when Smitty called.

Annabelle had played it by ear in her call to me, but Lilly had one of Brooke's scripts, which is why, at least in part, she sounded so strange.

I didn't bother calling or texting Brooke to confront her about her lying to me. It wouldn't do any good. She didn't care what I, or anyone else, went through so she could get to the future she wanted.

What really twisted my mind as I drove, as the snowflakes swirled and the trees appeared as ghostly sentinels in my headlights, was that me finding it out the way I did was also part of Brooke's plan.

Lilly needed to be wooden in her delivery so I would see through it before I started calling every law enforcement agency in the area to help with the kidnapping of my sister and my niece.

But this doesn't feel like a victory of any sort. This feels like utter and complete defeat. The Fortune Teller knows all and sees all. There is no fighting her. There is no escaping from her machinations until she is done with you.

This is where my head was at when Smitty called again. My phone didn't recognize him, of course, since his number wasn't in my contacts, but I have an eye for detail and recognized the last four digits.

I put him on speaker. "What do you want?" I asked.

There was a moment of silence. "What's wrong, Henry? Did your puppy just die?"

"I suggest that you remember you called me," I said. "I suggest that you act at least a little civil or I'll block this number too."

"I'll just get another phone," he said, his nasally voice grating my nerves. "But I hear you."

"And leave my father out of this," I said. "One word about my family and I'll throw my phone out the window and change my goddamn number."

Smitty was silent. I was in a foul, dark mood, and I

couldn't help but think that this must be the exact mood I needed to be in for this call or Brooke wouldn't have dragged me through everything I had just been through.

I glanced at the flip phone still on the passenger's seat, half expecting a text from her confirming it, but it was silent.

Being Brooke's puppet was this weird echo-chamber-like experience of constant second-guessing and disorientation.

"I'll just get to the point then," he said and then went silent, but I didn't say anything so after a couple breaths he continued. "I need you to go to Carterville and find out what the hell is going on."

I felt a surge of emotion, a mixture of relief and dread with a side of schadenfreude and I didn't trust my voice. I reached out and hung up on Smitty, again.

What was the proper reaction to your sworn enemy offering to undo the terrible thing he had done to you? Relief? Doubt? Cautious optimism?

The latter is what I would like to be feeling but what Brooke just put me through left me deeply pessimistic. I was her pawn, we all were.

Smitty called right back, but I had had the moment I needed so I picked up.

"Don't lie to me, Smitty," I said. "I am in no mood." Vigorous disbelief seemed to be the safest bet.

"I'm not lying," he said. "I am ready to release you from your promise if you promise to find out what is going on."

I barked a brief, ugly laugh. "I'm not promising you anything, ever again, Smitty. And that's a promise."

"Nice," he said. "Your last promise to me is never to promise me something. Very nice. I guess if you don't want to go back to Carterville, the town that bears your name, the town that is desperate for you to return to your elected position, I guess we are done then."

"It's been a year, Smitty," I said. "Maybe I've changed. Maybe I don't want to go back."

It was Smitty's turn to bark out a laugh, and it was truly an ugly, condescending thing. "If that was true you would have already hung up on me again."

"Why would you ever release me from my promise?" I asked. "Let's face it, your sentence is going to be commuted one of these days—once you've promised enough powerful people enough favors—but if you release me from my promise and we were both back there together…"

I didn't finish the sentence because it was obvious. We would resume our little feud fueled by the last couple of years.

Well, I think there was a chance if I kept up the meditation and didn't bottle it all in, that I could let the feud go, that I could just do my job enforcing the law which Smitty would likely be busy breaking, but maybe it would look the same.

But wasn't all of this Brooke madness about "saving" Carterville, from the "Destroyers," from Smitty and me? Was this awareness really enough to defuse that? Brooke had said it was, but my mood was so dark, I couldn't see it.

Smitty's sigh oozed out of my phone. I must really hate him if his sigh drives me nuts like that. "I hear you, Henry," he said. I don't know where this "I hear you" thing had come from. This wasn't an idiom I had heard Smitty say before. "But maybe I have changed too," he added.

I laughed, not just a bark this time, but it was an ugly, ungraceful expulsion of stress and tension.

"I'm sure I deserved that," he said, but I could hear the whine in his voice.

"You tried to kill me," I said.

He sighed again. "I realize that. I… I'm sorry about that. I really am."

My mouth hung open as I drove down I-17 through the pine trees. Had Winston "Smitty" Smith just apologized to me?

"And what about William Reilly?" I asked. "And Patty? What about all the locals you addicted to your power intentionally. What about all the ruin that you left in your wake since the meteor hit?"

I wasn't thinking about the conspiracy or how I needed to agree to Smitty at some point so I could go home. I was furious and I let it out.

"I just want to go home, Henry," he said, his voice quiet. "Surely that is something you can relate to."

"It is," I said, the words tight and clipped.

"My father…" he began with a sniff. "He was the asshole of the century. I have spent my life trying to dig out from the pit he put me in."

He didn't mention my father again and my own struggle to live up to my father's demands, his vision for me and Carterville, but it was implied.

"I let my power go to my head," he continued. "I did. I see that. I…" He sighed again and it still got on my nerves but not as much. It seemed too good to be true, but there seemed to be some sincerity here, some regret. "I just want to go home. I know there will be conditions. The governor will have to apply some, I did confess to attempted murder, after all, but don't you want to be there too, Chief? Don't you want to be the one watching me, watching out for the town, making sure I don't get lost again?"

I'm not dumb. I knew he was calling me "Chief" instead of "Henry" to get what he wanted. I knew that Smitty wasn't instantly reformed, but I had never heard him speak like this before and it seemed like Smitty had changed, at least a little.

"I'm listening," I said. "What do you want?"

THIRTY-FOUR
FRIDAY, NOVEMBER 20. FLAGSTAFF, ARIZONA

I HAVE TO TELL SMITTY WHAT I HAVE DONE. I HAVE TO CONFESS. After he releases me from my promise, I need to tell him that I am behind the return of his father.

What I had planned doesn't make sense anymore. If there is a chance that Smitty will change, then I can't let this thing be a secret, be something I am constantly worried about him discovering. It will be a rot between us, and the two of us both being back in Carterville is going to be bad enough as it is.

But I am afraid. It might cause him to backslide. It might fester and his immediate goal on return will be revenge.

"You need to tell him *before* he releases you from your promise," Wendy said.

We were sitting in the living room of Lilly's house drinking wine. Ian was asleep and Lilly had gone to bed an hour ago. There had been a lot to talk about with everything that happened today, and now that it was late and quiet and I was beyond tired. I had just told Wendy about my conversation with Smitty, including me agreeing to come see him in the morning.

"That's crazy," I said, feeling my stomach tighten up yet again.

She bit her lip and nodded. She sat on Lilly's over-stuffed brown couch, wrapped in a fluffy blue robe, her feet tucked underneath her and a shorty wine glass in her hand with half an inch of red wine. "But you have to," she said.

If anyone else had told me that I would have laughed it off, but sometimes it's the job of a big sister to be your conscience when you need it.

"Why?" I asked. I had my own thoughts, but I wanted to hear hers.

"If there's a chance that Smitty has learned something from all of this," she began. "If there's even a small chance, resuming your relationship with him because of this big lie you told him, it will just go to hell from there. You know it will."

"But Brooke, she—" I cut myself off and cursed under my breath. I didn't want to be one of those people.

I once met a woman that had taken the Sedona mumbo-jumbo a bit too seriously. She consulted her little pendulum before deciding simple things, like which dish to order at the restaurant. She even explained that it wasn't like she was speaking to the divine or anything but that the pendulum reacted to unconscious movements of her hand as she held it and that was a way to get clear messages from her subconscious.

To each their own, but that was not my kind of thing. But Brooke? Someone who actually saw the future? It was getting hard not to lean on that even though I had been trying to resist it.

I nodded, mostly to myself. "Who cares what Brooke knows," I said. "But there's a big chance that Smitty won't take it well, that he hasn't changed enough, that he won't release me from my promise."

Wendy gave me one of those appraising, big sister looks, her eyes narrowed, and her lips pursed. "Would that be the worst thing in the world, Henry? Surely the last year has proven that you can exist outside of Carterville."

"It has," I said. "But…"

She shook her head. "No buts. You have to accept that you can survive outside of Carterville. If you go to Smitty needing him to give you something, to give you the thing you want most, the thing you can't live without, you will walk away resenting him even more, even if he gives you exactly what you want. If Smitty has really changed, if you two really talk…" She shrugged, yawned, and gave me a tired smile. "That might actually change things for the better."

"I'll think about it," I said.

"Think quick," she said. "You are off to see him in the morning."

I nodded.

She sighed, put her wine glass on the coffee table, and unfolded herself, clearly getting ready to go to bed.

"I meant what I said about Brooke, though," she said. "You have to stop her."

We had discussed that earlier after Ian had gone to bed and Lilly was still up. It was complicated. Brooke had, it seemed, saved Ian's life and that made Wendy and Lilly take her request concerning me and today seriously.

It was a simple thing. A letter from Brooke to Lilly that had quoted, verbatim, a conversation she had had with her mother that very morning and then a warning "Don't go to the park today."

This is the way of Brooke, the way she hooks you and then reels you in. Because of the quote of a private conversation that had to be written before the conversation was had, Lilly listened. Even though Ian threw a fit, she didn't take him to the park as promised. About the time they were supposed to be there, a drunk driver hopped the curve and ran into the swing set Ian is currently obsessed with.

So, yeah, they went along with Brooke's plan regarding me. It freaked Wendy out. How do you counteract a power like that? She was able to see past what it had done for her and her family to what Brooke could do in the wider world.

She had heard all my stories, of course, but this was her first direct contact with Brooke. It's hard not to be freaked out.

"But how do I stop her if I tell Smitty the truth and don't get back to Carterville?" I asked.

"How do you stop her if Smitty does release you from your promise and you can return to Carterville?" she asked, a quirky smile lighting up her tired face.

"Point taken," I said.

"Good night," she said.

I slowly rearranged the living room and made up the pull-out couch, Wendy's challenge and her questions echoing in my head. Was I strong enough to tell Smitty the truth before he released me from my promise?

How do I stop Brooke even if I can return to Carterville?

PART 5
FUTURE REALIZED

THIRTY-FIVE

SATURDAY, NOVEMBER 21. RED ROCK CORRECTIONAL CENTER, ELOY, ARIZONA

THE RED ROCK CORRECTIONAL CENTER IS A SERIES OF BLAND, windowless, off-white buildings deposited among the sandy agriculture fields of Eloy, Arizona. There's a low-slung brick building in front that you might mistake for a misplaced building from an office park except for the razor-wire topped fence surrounding all of it and the signs with the huge "Warning" on them along Arizona State Route 87.

Red Rock is a private, medium-security prison housing up to 2,000 adult men and is only about thirty miles from Florence where Brooke is.

Adjacent to Red Rock is La Palma Correctional Center, Saguaro Correctional Center, and an ICE facility. It seems Arizona likes to keep its criminals in the desert. Honestly, if you are not careful, you'll end up at the wrong prison, all three of these looking pretty much the same.

. . .

When I got out of my truck and stepped out into the warm fall afternoon, it felt like I'd been visiting too many prisons. And while I'll wax poetic about the beauty of the desert from my deck on Carter Hill, I like looking at the desert more than being in the desert.

Here you can see sandy soil, distant fields fallow in the fall, and some low, rocky mountains to the southeast.

All of this is south of Phoenix, not far from Tucson, north of the I-10.

I sighed and headed towards the red brick building. I didn't want to be here. I was tired and indecisive. After Wendy went to bed, in a fit of defiance, I turned off the flip phone Brooke had given me, convinced it was time to break that habit. But just like any addict, I was experiencing some withdrawal symptoms.

I felt for it in my back pocket, but it wasn't there. I shook my head. I wanted to go back. I wanted to get it out of the glovebox of my truck, see if Brooke left me any clues for what was to come.

But it didn't really matter, did it? Whatever I did today, Brooke had already prepared me for. This act of defiance was something she knew was coming long before I did, making it an act of compliance not defiance.

This is no way to live.

Don't get me wrong, I know how hard it can be to make the difficult choices in life, how much we might want someone like Brooke to help nudge us along, especially for the excruciating choices life brings us, but take my word for it, it's worse this way. Much worse.

As I walked towards the building, I was undecided on how to handle things with Smitty. I have too much pride to ask

Brooke and I just can't decide. Do I tell him that I am behind his current spate of daddy issues? Do I tell him before or after he releases me from my promise?

This really was no way to live.

As I walked towards the prison, I had a rush of empathy for Steve Lancaster, the tough-as-nails private security guy that was part of the whole "Destroyer" mess. Brooke had broken him, turned him into her lackey. At the time, I didn't have much compassion for how he ended up that way—he's in one of these prisons now—but today I had a good idea what it felt like to be him.

The other thought that occurred to me was that maybe Brooke had already broken me and I hadn't quite figured it out yet. Maybe the same had been true for Steve.

I stood staring at the innocuous red brick building when I was about ten yards away, my indecision manifesting in my stillness. This whole conspiracy to fool Smitty into releasing me from my promise, this hate that I had been confronted with by those I loved, this madness with Brooke…

It was too much. It just was. But that seems to be the way of life. It gives us too much and we either grow into it or are destroyed by it. Neither of those, growth or destruction, happen fast and it's not a linear path, but this is the way of it. Life challenges us, we rise to it or fall from it.

I took a deep breath, consciously chose growth, and walked in.

———

"You look like hell, Chief," Smitty said, a wolfish smile

animating his lean face, his blond hair too short for once to look scraggly.

Our meeting place was much more conventional than when I went to see Brooke. We were in a bland grey room designed for family visits with tables and chairs, barred windows, and buzzing fluorescent lights.

But what wasn't conventional was that it was just the two of us in this room. Normally such visits had plenty of other people. I wasn't sure if this was Smitty's doing or mine. I had called the warden and asked to see Smitty, but I hadn't specified this level of privacy.

"I feel like hell," I said, taking my cowboy hat off and sitting opposite Smitty. He was dressed in an orange jumpsuit, still thin and all angles, but something was different. Smitty was a few years shy of forty yet, but I was used to him looking older than his age, but here, even in this unflattering light, he looked much more his age.

"Looks like being away from Carterville has been good for you," I said.

He shrugged. "And imagine what I would look like if I was in Carterville and didn't spend my days healing others and taking their shit on."

My brow furrowed as I studied him. "This part of your plan?" I asked.

He shrugged again—it was a loose, imprecise gesture. "Less for sure, but I have debts to pay."

"I bet you do," I said. Brooke had used her power to manage her time in prison and Smitty had used the promise of his power to do the same.

We sat there for a few breaths, the silence awkward and thick. I was lost in my quandary, not sure how to proceed, no idea what was going through Smitty's head. We were enemies that now, it seemed, needed each other, except his need of me was an illusion. One I created with months of effort and lots of help.

"I don't really know how to do this," he said.

"Me neither," I said. "Bo's been teaching me how to meditate, so I don't let my hate drive me."

He nodded, his hazel eyes narrowing. "Maybe Bo should teach me," he said. "Is it working?"

It was my turn to shrug. "I'm not very good at it, but it does help. Some."

"And that hate that drives you," he said, nodding at me. "That about me?"

"In part," I said. I didn't feel the need to list the crimes he had committed against me and the people I loved. He knew them all.

"And Brooke," he added.

He didn't say it as a question, but I answered it anyway. "A large part."

He nodded. "She's not done with us, you know," he said.

"Oh, believe me, I do," I said.

His eyes narrowed again. "She's been in contact."

It, again, wasn't a question but I answered, fingering the chunk of turquoise on my bolo tie. "Yes. Has she contacted you?"

He nodded, his eyes flitting away.

"The enemy of my enemy is my friend?" I asked.

"We are down to that, aren't we, Chief?" he said with a sigh.

"It seems to be the only way," I said.

We lapsed into uncompanionable silence again. We really

didn't know how to do this. There was too much bad blood between us for this to be easy.

"But we can't defeat her," he said, staring at his fingers and I noticed that his fingernails were a mess, ragged, like he had been chewing on them. This could not be an easy place for him. Just like Brooke, the world knew who he was and wanted something from him.

"What if we could?" I asked.

He looked up, his eyes sharp, looking more green. "You got a plan?"

I nodded. "No idea if it will work, but I have a plan."

"And you need me for this plan?" he asked.

"I need to be able to return home," I said. He was staring at me, and I heard Wendy's words echoing in my head, so I opted for the truth. "But I don't really need to for this plan, it would make it easier is all."

He licked his lips and looked me up and down. "I still want to find out what the hell is going on with my father rising from the dead."

"It's not your father," I said. I can't say the words slipped out. The decision had been made, but it hadn't been a conscious thing. It had floated up based on what Wendy said, my night of thinking more than sleeping, and Smitty seeming different in person.

"You've…" he began. "Wait. That was quick. How can you know that?"

"Look, Smitty," I said, feeling like the room was getting a little hot. "You are coming back to Carterville. I want to return, too. If I do return, if we are both there, I want things to be different between us. And that means I have to do the right thing and just hope that you will too."

His brow furrowed. "And if I don't?" he asked.

I shrugged. "I guess I'll be taking a lot more meditation lessons from Bo."

He laughed, it was a brief bark but sounded like a real laugh and I smiled for a moment. He gave me a nod and said, "So different, how?"

"I don't expect us to be friends," I said, and one of his eyebrows raised. "But I would hope we could find common ground. A Carterville that is all about Karen Winslow's ambitions is not a good thing."

"Hell no," he said.

"Just like a Carterville that is all about your ambitions is not a good thing," I said.

He pursed his lips but gave me a nod and said, "And a Carterville that is all about Henry Carter's old-fashioned view of an era long gone is not a good thing."

"Agreed," I said. "But our common ground is, literally, Carterville. Too much of any one of us is not a good thing. We need to start talking and stop plotting."

Emotions played on his face, brief visitations of guilt and then shame, but only for a moment. "I am sorry," he said. "Especially about Patty. She… she didn't deserve that."

He might have been lying. In my view Smitty was a high-level narcissist and I don't know that they can suddenly learn to have empathy, but it had been a hell of a year for him too, most of it spent behind bars.

"She didn't," I said. "And while I'm not ready to let you off the hook for that, I am ready to tell you about your father before you release me from your promise."

"Before?" he asked, his brow furrowed in confusion.

"Before," I said. "An act of trust. You are not going to like what you hear and how you deal with it will tell me something."

"What?" he asked.

"If you've changed," I said.

He bit his lower lip and then nodded. "I assure you I have."

"Then let's find out," I said.

———

AFTER ESCAPING THE PRISON AND WINSTON "SMITTY" SMITH, I tilted my head to the sun, taking off my cowboy hat and letting it begin to warm me after the cool of the prison. Not that it was cold in there or anything, but it felt dense and stilted, "cold" for a lack of a better word.

It's the nature of prisons. They are there to contain those that have broken our cultural agreements, our laws, our norms.

Prisons may not be thermally cool, but they are cool in other ways, the motion of society slowing down as those that have been convicted of breaking the law are held away from the rest of society.

I took a few breaths trying to inhale the light, not that I could, but it felt like something Bo would tell me to do. Smitty gave me his answer after I told him that I was behind the return of his father. He laughed. Hard. A full belly laugh with tears running down his cheeks. He laughed so hard he couldn't speak.

I had sat there, frozen, not sure what to do, feeling stupid and weak. I wanted to hit Smitty or run away, but I just sat there, a stone-faced guard looked in on us, his brow furrowing briefly before leaving.

When Smitty could finally speak, he said, "Get out, Henry. Just leave." There was a sneer in his voice and on his face.

I left.

The whole "Has Smitty Changed?" question was a ridiculous one, at least if you take the question at face value. Of course he changed. But what seems clear is that he hasn't changed enough to get me back to Carterville.

As I sucked in cool air, free air, and let the sun warm my face, I wasn't feeling regret, not yet, just mostly relief to be out of prison and away from Smitty. And a huge helping of embarrassment.

It's my own fault. After months of planning and careful execution, I gave Smitty the power of the truth and, once again, he used it against me.

Still hearing his laughter in my head, shame heated up my cheeks, I put my hat back on and walked towards my truck, breathing deep and trying to summon the memory of meditation to calm me down some.

This whole conspiracy never sat that well with me. In the heat of hate, I was enthusiastic about it, but part of me didn't like it. It was a lie, and I don't like to make my way in this world with lies.

I do, of course. I'm not perfect. Like most everyone, I first lie to myself and then, by extension, I lie to those I love. But I try not to, especially with the big things.

I wasn't upset with Wendy. She was right to say what she said. I was right to tell Smitty the truth. Doing the right thing sure as hell doesn't mean you will get what you want, it just means you'll have an easier time sleeping at night.

Although I don't think that's the case here. I'm sure I'll be replaying all of this, hearing Smitty's laughter, for a very long time until sleep finally comes.

My plan had been, before Wendy said what she did, was after Smitty had released me from my promise and I had spent time "investigating," to tell him much of the truth, that Elias Carter was behind it, that it was part of a plot of Elias's to return to Carterville himself. It got a little convoluted, but it basically came down to Elias wanting me to be in Carterville when he took the old Carter home from Wendy and me.

It was a story of bad blood and revenge, a twisted story of family gone wrong, something Smitty would likely buy. It would also put the blame on my uncle who had betrayed me.

Hate had changed me, and returning to being myself is way more important than returning to Carterville. At least that's what I was telling myself there outside the prison in Eloy, Arizona. Regret and doubts hadn't showed up yet, but they always do.

THIRTY-SIX

SUNDAY, NOVEMBER 22. FLAGSTAFF, ARIZONA

THE TEAM WAS ASSEMBLED AROUND LILLY'S LIVING ROOM IN Flagstaff. Annabelle Unger, Bo Larson, Martin Lester, Isabella Ortega, Frank and Lisa Paulson.

I was pacing, updating them all. Annabelle and the Paulsons were on the couch, Bo was leaning against a wall, Ortega was seated in a brown overstuffed chair that matched the couch and kind of swallowed her, and Martin was perched on an arm of the couch next to Annabelle.

Wendy and Lilly had taken Ian sledding. The snow we just got wasn't that great for sledding but enough to occupy a five-year-old for a little while. I had already told both of them everything.

I found the story hard to tell. I had asked a lot of them, I had asked them to compromise their morals in the name of getting me back to Carterville, and then I told the truth and wasted all of their efforts.

They were silent as I told the story of my trip to Eloy to

see Smitty. There were looks of surprise and concern, but they all let me get it out.

It felt weird, like my voice was too loud, and I kept wishing someone else would say something.

"What now?" Annabelle asked quietly when I was done.

"Now we give Brooke what she asked for," I said. "She held up her end of the bargain."

"She did not," Frank said, crossing his arms, his blue eyes intense. "She saw this coming. She didn't warn you. You owe her nothing." He rubbed at his shaved head like he missed the hair that was long gone.

"I have to agree," Lester said, rubbing at his mustache. "There ain't a thing you owe her. She had to see you confessing to Smitty, you know."

Annabelle leaned forward. "But you want to complete your end of the bargain," she said, her bright, purple-streaked red hair contained in an unusual ponytail.

"I do," I said.

Ortega had been watching me, those brown eyes tracking my every move. She wasn't in uniform and her long black hair wasn't pulled back into its usual ponytail and was spilling over her shoulders. She said, "But you don't want to discuss why because we have to assume Brooke is present for every conversation."

"Exactly," I said with a smile.

"Has she said anything?" Lisa asked, her willowy frame looking small next to Frank's bulk.

"I don't know," I said with a shrug. "I turned the burner phone off."

"Good," Bo said, pushing off from the wall and taking a step towards me, so he was right behind the couch. He had gotten a haircut so his curly blonde hair was not in front of his eyes for once and I could see the intensity there. "Every time you want to turn that phone on, meditate."

I chuckled and said, "Then I would be meditating all day."

Bo nodded approvingly. "Then so be it."

"So why are you tellin' us?" Annabelle asked. "If Carter's Six has disbanded—and if you told Smitty the truth, there is no reason for us to continue—why gather us together, why bring this to us? If we have to act like Brooke is in the room with us, what can we really say about what comes next?"

I nodded and started pacing again. "I can't enter the city limits of Carterville but I can get her there. I can have her repeat the promises she made to me in the zone of influence, but I can't take her to the station, lock her up for three days, and watch her like a hawk."

"We got that, Boss," Ortega said, nodding to Lester who nodded back.

"Are you sure?" I asked. "It's a hell of a risk."

"Is it?" Lester asked. "Don't she know everything anyway?" He looked around the room, his eyes unfocused like he was seeing a ghost or something. "Hear me now, Brooke Jennings. You screw us on this, and I'll end you. So best do whatever the hell it is you do so that I get hit by a bus or somethin' if you plan on doing wrong by us. And as we both know, if you are in Carterville, you won't see me comin'.'"

There was silence in the room after Lester's speech, and for him that was a very long speech. The quiet man doesn't often have much to say. And he was right, as we learned during the "Destroyer" mess, if Lester used his power of not being noticed, Brooke couldn't see him coming.

I stood there staring at him, it was quite the leap he just

made, but once he had, it was obvious. If we had to assume Brooke was in the room, then we could talk to her directly.

"We all have powers, baby-girl," Annabelle said, looking around the room at the empty spaces like Lester just had. "You do more than ease your way through your sentence, and we'll all use them against you, so best you send a bunch of busses if you are plannin' anything."

There was an odd moment there, the air almost electric as everyone looked around for Brooke as if she was somehow visiting with us. I did it too and felt silly about not figuring it out and just talking to her like she was here.

And maybe that's a good thing. I would have just thrown obscenities at her most of the time.

It was like we just realized that there was a ghost here among us, an ephemeral presence we couldn't detect, couldn't make leave, but knew was there and listening.

What really creeped me out was knowing that Brooke's awareness had been with me for years. How much of my life had she seen, how many embarrassing moments, how many completely normal human moments that I would be embar-rassed for her witness?

I had another insight on Brooke, another layer of the onion on what it must be like to be her. This seeing others at their best and worst, seeing it unvarnished and unedited, had to change her. In my job, I've gotten a pretty good taste of that, and it has changed me, made me more cynical, more jaded, but what would the much bigger dose she has had done to her? And how common must human pain be to her if she's seen not only this future but many, many others?

Does this reality even feel real to her anymore?

"No tricks, Brooke," I said, joining Lester and Annabelle in talking to the empty space. "Play the hand you have been dealt, the hand you dealt yourself. I'm sure you can set things in motion, do things we can't even imagine to upend our plan, extend your time in Carterville, but don't. Just don't."

It didn't seem like enough and I felt as awkward as a kid getting up in front of class for the first time and speaking.

There was more stilted silence, no one else choosing to talk to Brooke, and then we got down to business and planned how to get her back to Carterville.

THIRTY-SEVEN

MONDAY, DECEMBER 14. JUST OUTSIDE CARTERVILLE, ARIZONA

I was as nervous as a long-tailed cat in a room full of rocking chairs as Isabella Ortega turned off 89 onto Carterville Road.

I was in the backseat with Brooke Jennings, still in her burgundy jumpsuit, her hands cuffed together, her blonde with brown roots hair longer and duller than when I had seen her a few months ago.

Ortega was in uniform and Martin Lester was in the passenger's seat dressed in jeans and a sweater as grey as his mustache.

It had been a long drive from Florence with very little talking. Neither Ortega or Lester are big talkers in the first place, and I had nothing to say to Brooke. I was afraid my plan would leak out, like I might just blurt it or something, so I didn't say any more than I needed to.

My request to take Brooke away for a few days had met with some resistance, and took some time to work out, which was surprising. I had begun to think that anything Brooke wanted happened without resistance, this reality so manipulated by her that everything just fell at her feet.

That was a silly thought, of course. She had landed herself in jail, after all, that being the only way she could find to get Smitty and me out of Carterville.

Even though I knew Brooke wasn't all powerful, as evidenced by the jumpsuit and the cuffs, hope had left me. Brooke had to have seen what was coming, and despite her "no paradox" assurances, I just couldn't believe she would let it happen. I was as broken as Steve Lancaster, only in a different way. I was still fighting, I just didn't believe it could work.

And I wasn't saying any of this. I didn't want Brooke to know what I was thinking.

Brooke looked at me and gave me a little smile that was somehow half shy, half come-hither.

"Oh hell," I said, I couldn't help it. It didn't matter that I wasn't talking, I was writing all of this in my diary, right here, and I didn't have to speak my mind for her to know what I was thinking because she had already read it.

"That's right," she said, her smile widening.

"So you know what's coming?" I asked.

"Of course, Henry," she said.

"Then why are we here?" I asked.

"I'll let you figure that one out," she said. "I know you will." She looked away at the juniper trees passing by outside the Carterville PD SUV we were riding in.

I saw Ortega eyeing me in the rearview, an unasked question on her round face. After so much silence, she wanted to know what was going on, but instead of imagining that

Brooke was in the vehicle with us, she really was. I don't write every damn thought down so there was some slim bit of privacy—or at least that's what I tell myself.

"We can only be here because you want to be here," I said. It wasn't like it was hard to figure out.

She glanced at me for a moment before looking back at the road, the small smile on her face more shy this time.

"Or maybe 'want' is too strong a word," I added. She didn't look at me, but she nodded her head once. "You 'saved' Carterville, which landed you in jail, and now you are trying to…" I really had no idea what she was trying to do.

She sighed and turned so she was looking at me. "I'm trying to save myself. That's all. End of story. I know you don't believe me, and I don't blame you for not believing me, but Carterville has…"

She stopped and stared at me for a while, her face suddenly looking older, like she was more my age and not twenty, like her power had aged her. "I can't say much," she said with another sigh. "I really can't, but just know that there is a reason that meteor hit Carterville, that we all got powers, and that I needed to do something about Smitty and you."

I caught Ortega's eye in the review again. She was the one person in the SUV without power and she had a secret about why she wanted to be in Carterville that she hadn't told me yet. She quickly looked away. Maybe because that was a secret she really didn't want to share, maybe because she was driving.

"What reason?" I asked. I was feeling bitter that Smitty would soon be back in Carterville and I wouldn't.

"A good reason," she said, like I was some kind of child asking about something I couldn't possibly comprehend. And maybe that was true. Brooke saw the world very differently than the rest of us, and I'm sure some of those concepts were hard to communicate.

"Has all of this gone to plan?" I asked. It wasn't just my bitterness about not returning to Carterville, it was her making me think Wendy and Lilly had been abducted, not warning me about the deal she made with my uncle. I had been put through the ringer and I wasn't getting what I wanted but Brooke was.

A little childish? Absolutely. I reserve the right to be childish at times as long as I am adult enough to recognize it when it is happening and not let it go on too long.

She sighed again. I was getting very tired of that sound. "You know the answer to that question, too."

She turned back and looked at the rolling forest outside, the terrain getting more hilly as we got closer to Carter Hill. I did know the answer to that question. It was yes. A resounding yes.

Brooke had seen all of this, and while it might not be the optimal reality (refer again to the prison jumpsuit and hand-cuffs) it was the closest to the one she wanted that she could manage.

I turned away from her and stared out the window too. My thoughts dark, my energy leaching away.

———

I WAS BEYOND HOPE AS ORTEGA DROVE US TO THE CARTERVILLE city limits. I was also beyond despair. It is a very hard place to describe. I was broken, I knew that, but I couldn't feel anything. I was going through the motions, doing what I felt was the right thing to do, knowing that it was going to go Brooke's way no matter what.

Except I had no idea what Brooke's endgame was. I just couldn't figure it out, so my mind just gave up.

This wasn't like meditation, when the "jump" happens, and time has suddenly slipped past and you feel refreshed. This was, in many ways, the opposite. Time crawled and I felt like there was no energy in my limbs, like my life force was leaking out of me.

Everyone was silent and I didn't like the silence, but I couldn't do anything about it, just like I couldn't do anything about Brooke. I had my plan, my one card to play that I hadn't spoken about or written about, but why even bother with that? It couldn't possibly matter.

I was in the middle of an existential crisis, pure and simple. A wide and deep crisis brought on by years of manipulation by the young woman riding silently next to me.

I wanted to hate her, but I didn't have the energy for that. Hate is active and this malaise that had infected me felt like it was taking away my ability to act.

That card I had to play, that thing I hadn't written, spoken of, and tried not to think much about, I let it go. It didn't matter. Nothing I could do or say here would matter. My life was scripted, my fate decided, my future sealed.

After what happened with Brooke during the "Destroyer" mess, I pushed thoughts of her away, with vigor. So much so that when the "Blood of Carterville" events started to happen, I didn't even think of Brooke until the end.

What I was doing was beating away the existential crisis, but it was a bill that was overdue, and it hit me and it hit hard.

"You okay, Boss?" Ortega asked.

I wanted to tell her the truth, tell her "no" but she might think that there was some immediate threat and, besides, I didn't want to give Brooke the satisfaction of knowing just how broken I was.

Brooke didn't move, she didn't give me another half-shy, half-come-hither smile, but I knew she knew and that just made it worse.

"I'm fine," I said.

Ortega gave me an arched-eyebrow look in the rearview that communicated, quite clearly, that she knew I wasn't fine. Not at all.

My mind rushed through all of this, all that had happened since I met the Navajo grandmother at the Four Corners Monument. The months of effort. The enormous amount of help I had received. My team confronting me about how I was driven by hate. Bo teaching me how to meditate. Throwing it all away by being honest with Smitty hoping that led to a better future.

I fingered the bolo tie I was still wearing, the smooth chunk of turquoise mounted in silver with a coyote engraved on the back.

Coyote, the trickster. The Navajo grandmother had said, "Coyote may be a trickster but he is not cruel. Coyote may test you but he will make you stronger. Promise me you will find a place for Coyote in your heart and keep him close."

I had kept Coyote literally close to my heart, but had I adopted the lessons of Coyote? I was certainly being tested, but were tricks being played on me?

That certainly rang true. So many tricks. The one that stood out was me going to Elias Carter, my uncle and my father's twin, when he knew I was coming and was, in his mind, trying to trick me out of my family home.

Thinking of Uncle Elias's wrinkled face made me think of my father. He never got to be that old, but I could clearly see my father in my uncle's face. It was he who I wanted to see.

Long ago in these writings, I said that Smitty and I both had daddy issues, and while that is true, they are very different kinds of daddy issues. Smitty's father was never there, while mine was maybe too there, asking too much from me.

The fresh memories of my uncle's face brought memories of my father back stronger than they had been in years.

"Work hard, son," he had said. I was eleven and helping him upgrade the plumbing of the Carter family house. We were mostly under the house and it was dirty and claustrophobic. We were sitting in the sun outside the house taking a break. "Always work hard."

"Why?" I had asked. I was a kid. I didn't want to work hard, I wanted to play more like the rest of the kids.

"Because life is a gift and working hard is how we honor the gift we have been given," he said.

I opened my mouth to ask a question, but he shook his head. "Back under the house, boy. There's more work to do."

I'm not sure why that memory came back to me. My father spent years instilling a work ethic in me, starting at a much younger age than that.

He taught me that hard work was its own reward. That you did your best not because of what you might get out of it or accomplish but because it was essential to being a decent human being. Because your character mattered much more than your accomplishments.

I can't say that the existential crisis was gone, but I had to do my best here. I had to play the card that I had even if Brooke could counter it with a wave of her hand.

It didn't matter if it worked or not, it only mattered that I tried. That I did the best that I could do. That I worked hard. That I didn't give up.

THIRTY-EIGHT

MONDAY, DECEMBER 14. JUST OUTSIDE CARTERVILLE, ARIZONA

Now that we were here, I was eager to be done with this, to see what happened when I played my card, to move on to the next stage of this game that Brooke Jennings was playing.

I sighed when we passed into the zone of influence and Brooke let out a girlish giggle that was spine-tinglingly terrifying. Ortega had slowed down the SUV, apparently knowing exactly where the border was.

It felt like someone had just plugged me in, power now available to me. This didn't extinguish the existential crisis, but it did dampen it. After a year away with only one brief excursion into the zone, it felt heady to be back.

Up ahead a little red Prius was pulled off the road right next to the "Welcome to Carterville" sign.

"You didn't need to do that," Brooke said to me, nodding towards the car.

"Oh yes I did," I said. Carl George was in that car and he had a power similar to Brooke's that interfered with hers. I think it was like an infinite hall of mirrors kind of effect with them both here, both seeing the future, although their powers manifested differently.

Brooke gave me a wrinkled nose look and rubbed at her temples. When they were both in the zone, Brooke gets terrible headaches and Carl gets very confused.

As we pulled close, I could see a head of wild red and purple hair in the car with Carl. Annabelle was with him as planned in case he got too confused.

"And please stop the games," I said. "You knew he was going to be here." She looked at me and opened her mouth to speak, but I forged on. "Let's just get to whatever twist you have planned. I am ready to be done with you."

Her grey eyes narrowed, and she looked me up and down like she was reassessing me. "I hate to break it to you, Henry, but you don't get to decide when we are done. But your point is taken."

The SUV crunched on gravel as Ortega pulled us behind Carl's car. No one got out, we didn't need to. We were in the zone of influence and now was the time to play the card, to do my best, to work hard at this problem.

We weren't in Carterville, the border of town about twenty feet away, but I could feel my power turn to the promise I had made to Smitty. The joy of feeling it morphed into a squirming restlessness that would fit a boy in a theater who really needed to go to the bathroom but didn't want to miss any of the movie.

"So let's have the promises," I said. "And then you'll get your 72 hours locked in a cell with your power."

A sinisterly playful smile played across her lips. "And what would you like me to promise you, oh mighty Promise Keeper."

I smiled, or tried to smile—it was likely a grimace. My shoulders and neck were stiff and what I needed was my power to ease off trying to get me out of here, a lot of sleep, and way too many drinks.

I undid my safety belt, turned, faced her, and said, "Do you promise that you will use your power while here in the zone of influence only to help you make your way through the rest of your prison sentence?"

"Yes," she said.

"Do you promise you will let us take you back to prison after the 72 hours without resistance or interference?"

"Yes," she said with a small sigh.

"Do you promise to serve the rest of your prison term and not use your powers to manipulate the length of it?"

"Yes," she said, rolling her eyes just a bit.

"Do you promise that the only other use you will make of what you learn here in the next three days is to make sure Annie Smith is okay, that she is safe, that you'll do what you can to ease her time in prison, and that she won't know that you are doing it?"

"Yes," she said. "But best not write that one down in your little diary or she's sure to find out."

I could feel Ortega's stare, but I didn't look away from Brooke's grey eyes. I hadn't shared that part with the group. It felt too personal, it still did.

"Please repeat the promises," I said. "I need more than just a 'yes' from you."

Her eyes narrowed but she gave me a small nod and repeated every single promise verbatim. There was no changing of words beyond switching out "you" with "I", no wiggle room introduced, no games except for her singsong, condescending recitation.

I looked around, actually surprised that something hadn't happened. Something to interfere with her promises. There were no cars going by and we were a ways away from highway 89 so it was silent, too silent. I could hear our breathing and a whisper of a breeze from outside but that was about it.

It was time to play my card, but I felt reticent, I felt the darkness of the existential crisis coming close, pressing against me, stealing away my will.

A thought stole into my head. I had been focused on doing this for so long, but was I right to do it? What if it did work, what if I was able to stop Brooke, stop the Fortune Teller, was that even the right thing to do?

Right and wrong are not simple, not black and white, at least not in most cases. Brooke's power was a true super-power, and it seems like it could do a lot of good in the right hands.

But power is corrosive and constantly shuffling through futures trying to find the one you want can surely drive you mad. Scratch that. If you have that power long enough, it *will* drive you mad.

It was power, power that could be used for good, but it was too much power.

But I still had doubts, so I turned and whispered under my breath, "I promise I am doing the right thing here."

And, yes, this was a strange use of my power, but I honestly don't know the depths of it or all it can do. I kept it a secret for years because I didn't want people making promises to me they would be forced to keep or try to extract promises from me like Smitty did. And then, as soon as my power was known, I was gone.

But I had my power back, and it was time to use it, so I tried.

Nothing dramatic happened, and I couldn't tell if it had done anything, but at least I had tried. It was one small thing that I could do.

I realize that in some of my past stories I was dealing with dramatic events like chasing a murderer, dealing with a ticking time bomb, or having a battle of powers that, literally, killed me, and here I was just thinking a lot and whispering to myself.

Not very cinematic. I know it looks different, but it was a hell of an internal battle instead of an external one. In some ways I'd prefer the external madness. Dealing with your own demons is harder than dealing with the ones on the outside.

"Something wrong, Henry?" Brooke asked, a sly smile on her face. "If there's nothing else, can we just proceed and get me locked up and move on with this?"

I turned back to her and smiled. I wasn't confident in the outcome but I was confident in the attempt. It seemed my whispered use of my power hadn't done that much, but no matter.

"Not yet," I said, taking a deep breath. It was finally time to play my card. I felt the eyes of Ortega and Lester on me. They may have figured out what was coming but we hadn't spoken about it. "Do you promise that after these 72 hours you will never use your powers again?"

Brooke blinked and looked dazed, but how could that be? She had to see this coming, didn't she? Her mouth opened, but she didn't speak and then she looked around, like she had been expecting something to happen.

I could only see the side of her face, but there were emotions passing through. Fear. Surprise. Regret, maybe. Each one was just a ripple, but this wasn't what I had expected. I actually hadn't expected to get to do this.

She looked back at me, her face now placid, and said, "Yes."

Now it was my turn to have emotions flicker through my face. Surprise. Disbelief. More surprise. "I need you to say it," I said.

She nodded and took a deep breath, opened her mouth and then closed it. She looked back out at the forest. "Are you sure you want to do this, Henry?" she asked.

"Yes," I said.

"Challenges are coming to Carterville," she said. "I did as much as I could, but I couldn't stop it."

"Stop what?" I asked.

She turned and gave me a wan smile, ignored my question, and again asked me, "Are you sure?"

I didn't look at Ortega or Lester, I held Brooke's grey eyes. Despite her power, despite the good she could do with it, she had thrown away lives to get us to this future and that was reason enough to take her power away. "I am sure," I said.

She nodded, licked her lips, and slowly said, "I promise that after these 72 hours I will never use my powers again."

Lester let out a long sigh like he had been holding his breath, but I kept my eyes locked with Brooke's. A smile invaded her face, one of those smiles of hers that made my stomach twist, and she said with a shrug, "It's fine. I don't need my powers after these three days. But I can assure you, one day you will find good reason to release me from that promise."

"I will not," I said.

The smile turned condescending, and she said, "Oh yes you will. I know who you will become better than you do. Surely you understand that by now."

I felt hate boil up in me, dark and hot, and I wanted to slap that smile off her face, but I remembered the Navajo grandmother and fingered the bolo tie with Coyote the trickster etched on the back. I thought of my father and his insistence that work and doing the right thing was its own reward.

I held her gaze until the smile slowly melted off her face, took a deep breath, and while I held that chunk of copper-laced turquoise, I said, "I promise you, Brooke Jennings, right here and right now, that I will never release you from the promises you have made to me today."

Ortega gasped and Brooke recoiled like I had actually slapped her.

Earlier when I said that I had one card to play, I lied. I had two, but I dared not even hint at it.

Now we were both compelled by my power. Her power wasn't usable after these three days of limited use and I couldn't release her from the promises she made.

Brooke blinked again, rapidly, her shoulders fell, she let out a ragged sigh, her hands flying to her face, and then began weeping.

Her weeping quickly turned to crying and then escalated to a full-body expression. This wasn't the tears of someone who was just sad or just hurt or just grieving. I had never seen anyone cry this hard or this fully.

And then she was holding on to me, her face buried in my

chest. I had no idea what was going on, but I wrapped my arms around her and held her. She no longer seemed like the fairly psychotic woman we all thought of as the Fortune Teller, but like the adorable girl with a slight speech impediment that had followed her father around with wide eyes eight years ago right before the meteor hit.

She was letting something go, something deep and terrible and painful. It would have been inhumane of me to not comfort her, and I felt my lingering hate for her melt. I had contemplated many times how hard her power must have been on her, but seeing it expressed this way, I couldn't help feeling for her.

"It's okay, Brooke," I said, as if she were my child and I was comforting her. "I'm here. It's okay. You are not alone."

She nodded against my chest and her tears intensified.

Earlier I had said that Brooke broke me. Holding her I knew, without a doubt, that her powers had broken her long ago.

"I… I wasn't sure," she said between sobs. "That you would…"

"Make you a promise?" I asked, trying to understand.

She nodded, her head rubbing against my shirt that was now wet with her tears.

I caught Ortega's eye and nodded to the little red car. They both got the hint and quietly left Brooke and me alone and I just let her cry.

I don't know about you, but I find my life overwhelming most of the time. So much is always coming at me, there is always too much to do and not enough time for the things that seem to matter the most. But Brooke? Seeing all of these futures and trying to find a way through, a way where her actions could cause the changes she needed. That was more than anyone should have to handle.

This realization did not excuse her actions, the death and trauma she left in her wake, but it did make her much more human.

I saw the red car drive back towards 89, Carl George leaving the zone of influence so his powers would no longer interfere with Brooke's. The Fortune Teller had been neutralized and he didn't need to be here.

I held on to Brooke for a long, long time, until she finally stopped crying.

THIRTY-NINE

MONDAY, DECEMBER 14. JUST OUTSIDE CARTERVILLE, ARIZONA

I don't know what I expected to happen but having the most powerful person I knew cry in my arms for a very long time was not it.

When you think of power you don't think of vulnerability as if the former somehow erases the latter. It doesn't. Power can make you more vulnerable. It certainly can leave you with much more to lose.

And Brooke, had, essentially, just lost her superpower and was… crying.

This was confusing and I had enough time to think about it as I held her, the two of us sitting there in the back of the Carterville PD SUV, amongst the juniper, piñon forest, the "Welcome to Carterville" sign in sight, Carter Hill looming against the backdrop of the tree-covered San Francisco Peaks.

I had spent a lot of time trying to understand Brooke Jennings, but this new behavior reframed everything that came before it and the word that came to mind was "desperate." Brooke had been desperate to get to where we were, to do what she did, but why? I just took her power away so why was this a moment of grief and not shock or anger.

Well, shock wasn't really possible, was it? And if she had seen this, knew it was coming, did all that she needed to make it happen, she couldn't really be angry, could she? And that left grief.

But for what? Her lost powers? The damage she did?

"I grieve the life I didn't have," she said, her crying finally abating, her voice muffled as she was still clinging to me. "I grieve that I never had a normal life."

"You knew we would end up here all this time?" I asked.

She shook her head and pushed herself up into a sitting position. She was reaching towards me as I pulled a handkerchief out of my pocket. She used it to wipe her face and blow her nose, but didn't try to give it back. I wouldn't have taken it and she knew it.

"I wasn't lying to you before," she said. "When I said we were in a different future, so for once I wasn't sure. A few things happened that I wasn't expecting."

"Like what?" I asked, looking around again, still expecting something to happen that would change this, but we were alone.

"You visiting Annie," she said. "Smitty calling you during the trial."

"So you weren't sure," I said, "but this is what you wanted. You wanted me to block your powers."

Her grey eyes darkened like an approaching storm. "God, yes."

"And you wanted to land in jail?" I asked.

She nodded. "Plenty of ways around that. I wanted to be locked away from my powers, locked away from people."

Her lips formed an "O," like she had more to say but she blew her nose again and sat back and shook her head, tears continuing to flow, but quietly.

I let her have a moment. I glanced at the dash and saw that Ortega had left the keys in the ignition, so we weren't stranded, although I couldn't be the one that drove her into town because my promise to Smitty was still in play and I was banished from my home.

That thought darkened my mood despite the victory of defanging the monster that sat next to me. Sure, she was way more human now, but she was still a monster. She had done too many inexcusable things on her quest to be here now.

"There are many similar futures," I said, my brain finally parsing through what she had told me. Her endgame played out but there were some differences.

"God," she said, with a wet sigh. "So many. Too damn many. I spent weeks here seeing the futures, doing little more than eating, going to the bathroom. It was…"

She trailed off looking out at the trees. Maybe she was realizing she had signed up for three more days of this, that her time with her power wasn't quite over yet.

"Why did you let Lila die?" I asked. If there was one grievance I had against her, one thing that truly turned her into a monster, this was it. Lila was beloved, and while Brooke didn't kill her, she could have done so many things to prevent her death.

"I knew her too, you know," she said. "Just a little bit. Just enough to feel the kind of person she was. I regret it, but it was the only path I could find."

"To get here?" I asked.

She bit her lip and nodded. "Lots of ways to go after that, but, yes, that was the only way to get us here and Lila's death was the inflection point."

What do I do with that? Lila was the kind of person that lit up a room, that made everyone feel just a little bit happier. She didn't have a power, she came to Carterville after the meteor hit, so it wasn't anything like that, it was just who she was.

Her death was, and is, inexcusable, but I don't know what Brooke saw, I don't know what the loss of Lila bought except for us being here now.

She turned to me, her grey eyes intense and said, "There are a few more things you'll need from me, you know," she said.

"What?" I asked. "Why?"

She smiled and it wasn't the old terrifying smile of the monster that she was. It was softer, more human, but it still made my stomach tight. "Because, Henry Carter, I need you to survive. Please hear that. Take it in. I need you to live a very long and very healthy life and there will be a few points in the future where you will need me. You have to live because I don't want to ever be tempted to use these damn powers again."

I sat there blinking at her. Of course. I had locked her powers away with my power, but if I was dead then all the promises made to me were off. I knew this to be true. When I fought Mary's powers with mine, I was dead for a few minutes before Smitty brought me back. During that time, Ortega was able to drive into Carterville even though she had promised to stay away for the night.

"Shit," I said.

She nodded and said, "I know." She licked her lips and added, "I know you never thought I was on your side, like I was somehow doing all of this *to* you. But, in reality, I have always been looking out for you. I am still looking out for you."

I think she meant to comfort me, but I just wanted to rip the door open and run away and never look back. Think about it. I had just learned that I was the favorite pet of the monster I had been fighting.

"I can't forgive you for Lila," I said, my mind going back to her.

Brooke nodded sharply, her tears flowing freely again, and said, "That makes two of us."

The silence after that was thick and uncomfortable. The monster was defanged but I was still her pet and that didn't sit well with me.

A couple of minutes later, Ortega's red Mustang passed us and pulled up on the shoulder behind us. We still had a prisoner. We still had a job to do.

"Your seventy-two hours started as soon as Carl left," I said as I moved to get out of the car.

"Wait," she said, reaching for me, sounding like that twelve-year-old girl I had first met. "Where are you going? Just take me to the station, please. I want it to be you."

I looked at her, how could she not know? Was this part of her game or was this future that different than the one she thought we were in?

"Smitty," I said, not feeling the need to elaborate.

"He didn't release you from your promise?" she asked, her eyes wide behind her glasses.

I shook my head.

She looked around. "No," she said. "He should have by now. You… you need to go back. You need to be there… I…"

It was painful to watch, but I kind of got it. What would it feel like if you knew everything that was going to happen and suddenly the script you had been following was wrong.

"You have a good stay in Carterville, ma'am," I said with a tip of my hat, as if I was talking to some random tourist.

I opened the door, a cold wind whipping through the vehicle, and moved to get out and she said, "Phone. Check your phone."

I sighed and pulled my smartphone out of my back pocket. On it was an alert, a text from Smitty. My knees felt weak as I settled back into the seat and closed the door, unlocked my phone, and read his long text.

I've been thinking about what you did and I have to say that I am proud of you, Henry Carter. You really have changed. You are not the Boy Scout you once were. Let's grab a beer when we are both in town, my treat. I release you from your promise to never return to Carterville.

The whole thing ended in a smiley emoji and it was a damn good thing I was sitting down as I read it.

I looked at Brooke and there was confidence on her face again, the little girl banished.

"He…" I began. "He… released me from my promise. By text."

It felt strange, like something that shouldn't be done via text. And I wasn't honestly sure if it would work. Someone else could have gotten his phone and done it and that wouldn't be enough, would it?

It's not like I truly understood my power.

"I'm so relieved," Brooke said. "If that text hadn't been there…" She shook her head and whistled.

"What?" I asked.

"Sorry to change the subject, but you know," she began with a smile, "with all this writing you are doing and all the futures I have seen, we could…"

I just stared at her, my brain too overwhelmed to see what she was getting at.

"Stories, Henry," she said. "I could tell them to you and you could write them. 'The Alternate Histories of Carterville Arizona,' by Brooke Jennings and Henry Carter."

She was beaming more like the girl I used to know but with an edge to the small smile on her lips. Good God, how many gears did this person have?

"No," I said. "The first one, 'The Blood of Carterville,' will be out soon, but I'm not sure I want the rest of what I've written to be released." She opened her mouth to speak but I kept talking. "No, Brooke. I will not. You want to write them, then write them."

Her brow furrowed and she looked confused for a moment and then nodded her head.

"So why are you relieved that Smitty had texted?" I asked, trying to wind her back before the tangent.

"Futures," she said with a sigh like I was a slow student, and she was a bad teacher. "I look for signs as to what future I'm in. That was an important one. If Smitty hadn't…" She ended, just shaking her head.

"What?" I asked.

"You said you didn't want to know about the other futures," she said with a little smirk. Brooke may have shown me vulnerability and some humanity, but she was still Brooke.

I was going to protest but then realized it would just extend my interaction with Brooke and why would I do that if I could finally go home. "You're right," I said, opening up the door and stepping out.

"Where are you going?" she asked, back to being the scared child.

"I need to make sure this is real," I said.

FORTY

MONDAY, DECEMBER 14. JUST OUTSIDE CARTERVILLE, ARIZONA

Brooke had been right all those months ago when she gave me that blue beany. It was turning into a cold winter. As I strode up the road towards the "Welcome to Carterville" sign, I was wishing I had it, or something similar, on. Cowboy hats aren't the best in the winter. My ears were prickling at the cold.

I zipped my jacket shut and smiled as a few flakes of snow started flying through the air. Carterville was right there, right in front of me, but deep down, I didn't believe it was true, I didn't think Smitty had really released me from my promise to not return, or if he did, that a text wouldn't be enough.

Ortega was back with Brooke. I had decided to do this on foot, just in case. I didn't want to try to speed through like someone trying to run past the last moments of a yellow light, like I was stealing my way back into town. I wanted to do it on my own two feet. I wanted to really feel the town welcoming me or repelling me.

Last time I had done this, my power fighting back against me as I walked closer was clear, but the blustery weather was providing its own resistance and it was enough so I wasn't really sure.

I stopped at the sign. "Welcome to Carterville. Established 1881."

It was a sign worthy of a fancier, more exclusive town with the sign itself made of copper, the edges greening, the letters cut from bright stainless steel, all of it hanging on a frame of rough-hewn pine logs in a base of volcanic rock.

When I was here before, I said the sign was a promise. That it promised that what was beyond it was special. I also said I thought that the mayor and the town council had spent too much damn money on it.

I didn't think that anymore. Carterville was fancy in its own way, it was definitely exclusive, in some ways the most exclusive town around with all the power flowing through it.

I was strangely hesitant. Despite the cold and the wind and the flying snowflakes, I didn't feel the ants-in-the-pants feeling I had last time. Smitty had really released me from my promise and I could return to Carterville, yet I hesitated.

Why?

There were parts of my new life that I really loved. The camping, the long walks, more time with Wendy, Lilly, and Ian, the lack of job stress and everyone in town wanting something of me.

I had built a new life, and while that life had been focused on returning, there were some good things, some things worth preserving.

I was going to return to Carterville, but Brooke was right. I had changed. My time away forged me into a different person. I didn't know what my life would look like once I walked past that sign, returned to my home, put the uniform back on, but I knew it had to be different.

FORTY-ONE

WEDNESDAY, DECEMBER 16. THE
CARTERVILLE POLICE DEPARTMENT

THE CARTERVILLE POLICE DEPARTMENT IS, MOSTLY, ONE BIG
room with two cells on one side and a couple of bathrooms
on the other side. It's old linoleum and crappy fluorescent
lights, dinged metal desks and whiteboards on the wall right
off Main Street behind a bakery, the sweet, fatty smell of it
such a distraction these days after being gone for so long.

I could smell it even though it was late at night and the
town was dark and quiet around us.

As Brooke in her burgundy jumpsuit went docilely into
the cell after her late-night bathroom break, the bolt snicked
into place and I removed the key.

There was a metaphor here, one that was glaringly apparent. I had locked Brooke's power away with my power, and
she had gone willingly. I was glad, don't get me wrong, but it's
hard to come away from an interaction with the Fortune
Teller and feel like you won.

I was back in uniform and it felt… strange. It used to feel

strange when I was out of uniform but after a year away it was the other way around. My equipment belt felt heavy and the weight of my sidearm was noticeable and distracting.

Brooke's three days locked in a cell had gone smoothly so far, amazingly smoothly. I was nervous the whole time, afraid something terrible would happen and the world would turn upside down and everything that I thought I knew would turn out to be untrue.

This is the way of the Fortune Teller, of Brooke Jennings, so there was nothing more to do than to hold steady, watch her like a hawk, and pray for the moment when it was time to take her back to prison.

Ortega, Lester, and I watched her 24/7, each of us taking eight-hour shifts, but there wasn't much to watch. She lay under her blankets most of the time, rousing only to eat her meals, which Frank cooked for her, and to go to the bathroom.

She never asked for a notebook or anything. Whatever she was learning she was able to remember it, somehow. And she never asked for different clothing than her burgundy jumpsuit.

In retrospect, she was the quietest, most compliant prisoner I had ever had in one of my cells.

We didn't talk much, I had had my fill of her, but I hadn't asked her about the mine explosion and the size of it.

Midnight was approaching as was the end of my last shift alone with her and there was something on my mind. A loop that hadn't been closed.

As she settled on the cot and started to meticulously arrange the blankets, I asked, "You were burying it, weren't you?" I didn't bother making it clear what I was talking about, she knew, she had promised to tell me about the mine explosion "when we are both back."

"Yes," she said. "It needed to happen."

I didn't need to ask why, that was clear. Whatever was buried under our town, whatever was providing our powers, needed to stay buried. The saving grace of Carterville powers was that they were limited to Carterville.

"So what is it?" I asked.

Her eyebrows raised and she looked out the bars into the office like she wanted to be sure we were alone, although she knew we were. "What is what?" she asked with a playful grin on her face that just grated against my nerves.

"Please, Brooke," I said. "Aren't we past the games? You have surely seen futures where it was unearthed."

She took a deep breath and let out a noisy sigh. "Habits, I guess."

"What is it?" I asked. "What confers our powers? Is it really a meteor? Is there a timeline to the powers? Do they ever go away? Do they change?"

I felt the weight of my bolo tie and I wanted to ask her about the Kachina, about Coyote, I wanted to reframe this in the language of the Navajo grandmother, which, much to my surprise, was starting to feel right.

There was a mystical feel to what had happened to us, wasn't there? How could you look at Brooke, at her power, at what she has done with it and not think of Coyote the trickster? How could you look at what happened to Carterville when the meteor hit, this little town on a mountain sacred to the Navajo, and not be inclined to believe that someone or something is messing with us?

Brooke smiled, wide enough to make me wish I hadn't asked, and said, "In due time, Henry. All of that in due time."

I shook my head and let her go back to her future seeing, or whatever you call it. I had case files spread out on one of the metal desks where I could keep an eye on Brooke, and got back to catching up on all the cases I had missed.

Just as I settled, just as my shoulders started to relax, she said, "Remember, Henry. I'm on your side. I'm always on your side."

My shoulders became cement again, but I didn't look up, acting like I hadn't heard her, not that that would matter.

That was the last time I tried to have a real conversation with her before we hauled her back to prison.

FORTY-TWO

MONDAY, JANUARY 4. CARTERVILLE, ARIZONA

Besides the main room of the Carterville Police Department there is one extra room that is sized more like a closet, that is a combination office and armory.

It was early on a Monday morning, three weeks after my return that I walked in and found Officer Isabella Ortega already at work in the closet-like room, the scarred metal desk she was behind wide enough to fill most of the space, barely leaving room to get around it.

She jumped up. "Boss," she said. "Sorry. Let me get out of your way."

I smiled. She had gotten used to using the office, she had been acting chief of police for over a year, after all. And it had changed her. She wasn't quite so shy and was more confident.

"No," I said. "Please, sit."

I sat down in the chair across from her. Carterville was still Carterville and there had been quite a bit of drama since my return, but that's another story. When I took the step to cross into Carterville after receiving the text from Smitty that released me from my promise, I was dedicated to the change I felt in me.

Those moments are lovely bright sparks but turning those sparks into a fire and bringing them into reality is hard work. Jobs really can make you more than you thought you could ever be, but they also ask a lot of you and take away a lot from you.

The last three weeks had been a whirlwind of adjusting to the town that bore my name, being back on the job, all while trying to nurture that spark.

"What's up?" Ortega asked.

I had finally had some space over the weekend, and I guess the change showed.

"I don't want this office anymore," I said.

Ortega looked puzzled and it was understandable. My statement was not very clear.

"I've decided not to run for chief of police this year," I said. Wendy already knew and wholeheartedly approved, and while it felt like the right path forward, it made my stomach clench to actually say it aloud.

Ortega blinked several times, opened her mouth to speak, and closed it. It seemed she wanted a longer explanation and I owed her one.

I nodded and sighed. "Brooke is back in prison and behaving herself. Smitty is back up at his gaudy house on the hill under house arrest with his healings closely monitored. Thankfully the governor didn't actually commute his sentence, just changed the conditions of it. We have our weekly chats and I actually don't want to smack him every single time. I…"

I was having trouble finding the words. This had been hard enough with Wendy who wanted me to stop being a cop, but Ortega was different. She was someone I had been mentoring, someone that I loved spending time with, someone whose image of me I wanted to live up to.

"It's okay, Boss," she said with a shy smile, like the old Isabella. "Just tell me."

"I love this job," I said. "I love this town. But after all the time away… Well, you know, this job just doesn't leave enough time for much of anything else. After my time away, I want more."

Her brow furrowed and it was hard to read her.

"So I want you to stay in that desk," I said. "I'll serve my term, stay on the job until next year, but I would like you to keep doing the administrative work." I gave her my best boyish grin. "You are a hell of a lot better at it than I am."

She nodded and almost looked eager. The "by the book" Ortega really was good with the paperwork.

"I'll spend more time out there," I said, nodding towards the small town that surrounded us.

"And then?" she asked.

Now it was my time to look shy. "I'm hoping that you'll run for chief of police," I said. "I'll back you, campaign for you."

She looked like she was about to get up and then shook her head. "No, Boss. I can't… I won't do this job without you."

I nodded. "I thought you might say that. What if I stayed on part time, ten or twenty hours a week, on call when you need me?"

Her face darkened and she looked down. I think she didn't

want to disappoint me. "It's okay, Isabella," I said echoing the words she just said to me. "Just tell me."

She looked up, a smile playing on her lips for a moment and then her face hardening. "I don't want to be chief," she said.

I nodded and I couldn't keep the disappointment off my face. While I didn't want the job anymore, I had to make sure I handed it off to the right person and Ortega was the only choice.

"I was thinking of running for town council instead," I said. "Angela Isaacs is retiring. There's no pay, but it's only part time. Figured it'd be a better way to keep an eye on the mayor and Smitty and..." I trailed off. That dream was dead and it hit me hard. I loved Carterville, I wanted to be part of this town, but I needed more space in my life. I needed some freedom.

"I think you should do that," she said.

I looked up and she had a mischievous smile lighting up her round face. "But someone has to be chief," I said.

"Not you," she said. "And not me."

"Who?" I asked.

"Don't get me wrong," she said. "I love my job. Want to keep it. I just don't want the pressure. And I don't have a power. I'm not a Carterville native. Not sure they would accept me."

That was all moot and she was stalling so I crossed my arms and just stared at her.

"Martin," she said. "Martin Lester."

I had fired Lester during the Lila Chang incident. He had crossed some line he shouldn't have, and I really didn't have a choice. He had then exiled himself from Carterville in his grief, but that seemed to have changed. He came to town fairly often now, had even helped out on a recent incident.

"Martin..." I said, still processing. I fingered the copper-laced bolo tie that I was wearing with my uniform, thinking about Coyote the trickster and how the story of a disgraced and exiled cop coming back to be chief of police suited a trickster well.

"Everyone knows him," she said.

"The quiet man as chief," I said. "The criminals won't see him coming."

She nodded.

Lester had been born here, had been a cop in Carterville longer that I have, and what he did during that Chang case was understandable and decidedly human.

I nodded and asked, "You think he'll do it?"

"He's going to be by later today," she said. "You can ask him."

I chuckled and got up. "Nope. You're idea, Ortega. You ask him."

The chuckle turned into a laugh as I saw the surprised look on her face. I left before she could protest. I was still the chief, but hopefully not for that much longer.

EPILOGUE
TUESDAY, FEBRUARY 16. FOUR CORNERS MONUMENT

Isabella Ortega and I weren't at the Four Corners Monument to play the touristy version of twister where you can physically be in four states at once. We were there to see a certain Navajo elder, the woman that had sold me the bolo tie I still wore every day, keeping Coyote close to my heart.

Ortega had been mysterious about the unanswered question, about why she had been so eager to come to Carterville. Since I was back, she had taken a long and well-deserved vacation and had texted me, asking me to meet her here, meet her at the booth where I bought this bolo tie and started my return to Carterville.

Martin Lester was manning the station with Annabelle, the two of them covering for us. He was, officially, working part time for CPD and we finally had three officers on the payroll. No, Karen Winslow and the town council did not come up with the money, I did. The first Carterville book is out and doing well. I don't need the money like I used to so we redirected some of my salary to bring Lester on board.

Lester has agreed, with some reluctance at first, to run for chief. Annabelle has agreed to be his campaign manager and mine for town council. Not that it takes that much in a town of 282. You have to be seen, you have to talk to pretty much everybody, and that's what we did on the job anyway.

It was a winter Tuesday and the crowd was light, what sounded like a small German family currently playing Four Corners twister as I walked over towards the row of booths set up on the New Mexico side.

It had been eight months since I had been here, but it felt like everything had changed. Before I was forced to leave town, I never thought there would be a day when I didn't want to be a cop in Carterville. Exile will do that to you, and the years slowly piling up, too. I wanted meaning and purpose in my life, I still wanted to do hard things, but just a little bit less.

I hadn't spotted Ortega yet, but she must be here. I paused and pulled out my phone and looked at her text again. *Time to spill. Meet me where you learned about Coyote on Tuesday at noon.*

She had deflected when I brought up wanting to know why she was so eager to be in Carterville, and I guess I really have changed because I let it be. Everyone has secrets, everyone needs to keep part of themselves locked away. Well… maybe not everyone, but most everyone I know.

No one can share everything. These memoirs are partially diaries, and even here I can't share everything. There isn't room and the mundanity that rules much of our lives isn't worth sharing.

I scanned the booths and only a few were set up. This is

not tourist season. My eyes caught on a weathered-faced Navajo woman who was looking at her companions at the booth. There was giggling coming from the booth as a young woman with long black hair, her face turned from me, tickled a girl sitting next to her.

Of course.

I walked over, taking my time and watching the interaction. The aged eyes of the Navajo grandmother locked on to me as the other two continued to play, seemingly not aware of my presence.

"Welcome back, Promise Keeper," the grandmother said with a tilt of her head, her accent thick. "I see that you have kept your promise, held Coyote close and been rewarded."

I looked down. My jacket was unzipped just enough to see the turquoise of the bolo tie sticking out.

Ortega stopped tickling the girl, the one that had translated when I had been her before, and looked up at me. "Hey, Boss," she said with a grin.

Her hair was down and a bit disheveled, her brown eyes mischievous. She wasn't dressed in her uniform but jeans and a brown down jacket, both of which made her look even younger. But beyond that, there was something different about her. She was more relaxed, more at home, maybe.

I smiled. I couldn't help it. The Navajo grandmother was Ortega's grandmother making the twisted path of this whole thing even stranger, but it was fitting somehow.

This meant, almost certainly, that Brooke had had a hand in Ortega coming to Carterville, and that was one thing I couldn't be upset about.

"Ya-ta-hey, Grandmother," I said, with a tip of my cowboy hat. I wasn't sure if that was the right thing to call her, but it felt right. I took my hat off in deference, the cool wind playing with my thinning hair. "Hello, Isabella."

The grandmother gave me a smile that lit up her desert-like face and warmed my heart. She started speaking in rapid Navajo, the words sounding once again sacred to me, and I felt the whisper of power I had felt the last time I was here.

"When the girl, the white seer came to me," Ortega said, translating as the girl—maybe a niece—sat quietly and stared at me. "She told me things. She spoke of a tragedy coming, a mystery, one that would tear at my heart, one that would leave me wanting."

The grandmother paused, her brown eyes still looking young in her old face as she stared at me. "Do you respect our ways?" she asked me directly, her words slow. "The Beauty Way?"

"I do not understand them," I said. "But I respect them."

"And yet you live on Sacred Mountain," she said.

I paused, feeling the intensity of her gaze and the weight of her question. "I was born there, Grandmother," I said.

She nodded and spoke Navajo which Ortega translated. "And that gives you reason to stay. We all feel the earth most where we were born. The land is part of us, but you live on Sacred Mountain with many who do not respect what they do not know."

I nodded, not sure what else to say.

Ortega glanced from her grandmother to me and there was something there. Worry, maybe an apology.

The elder started speaking again and Ortega translated. "The sad day the white girl predicted has come. The mystery that eats at my heart is here. My time on Turtle Island has been long and soon I must join my ancestors, but I must know what happened first and why."

I caught Ortega's eye again and there was more than a little mischief there. This was why she hadn't explained things, this was why she had mysteriously summoned me here. Maybe this was part of the reason she came to Carterville.

"Will you help me, Promise Keeper?" the elder asked me directly. "Will you respect what you don't know and travel into the unknown? Will you find something precious for me? Something that has been taken?"

I looked at Ortega and she gave me a weak shrug. "You are a private investigator now," she said. "I have some more time off coming and I could help you."

I looked around the plaza. There was no one playing twister and only a few tourists. The wind stilled and I could feel the energy of the moment, the power of the elder staring at me, the whisper of the future calling to me.

I didn't even know what the mystery was, but I sure didn't feel qualified to investigate something on Navajo land. I had been around the Navajo all my life, but I didn't understand their ways. What I did understand was my ancestors had committed crimes against their ancestors and I knew that residual guilt about crimes colored our interactions to this day.

But I had also been asking for time away from Carterville, for other kinds of challenges in my life.

I unzipped my jacket a little more and felt the bolo tie at my neck, the copper-laced turquoise with a coyote howling at the moon etched on the back. Maybe Coyote the trickster wasn't done with me.

I looked into Grandmother's eyes and I felt something. Power, maybe? Connection, hopefully. Sadness and need, certainly.

This wasn't a Carterville mystery that needed to be solved and I was quite sure that Coyote would have more tricks to play, but that sounded just about right.

"What is lost, Grandmother?" I asked.

Her eyes narrowed and tears formed and she spoke in Navajo, this time the words slow and ponderous but still sounding sacred. Ortega translated. "My friend is missing. The white girl, the seer from Sacred Mountain, said that you are the only one that can find her, that you would come when my granddaughter called. That you would respect our ways even if you did not understand them. Will you find what is lost before it is too late?"

I swallowed hard. It was a missing person case. I had handled some of these over the years, of course, but it had always been limited by my jurisdiction, limited to Carterville.

But now? I could follow the leads wherever they took me and that appealed to me in a way that was surprising and made me feel uncomfortable at the same time. I shouldn't feel excitement over what is a tragedy to this woman.

And Brooke came to mind too. Knowing she had seen this too, seen this far ahead, made me nervous. I had defanged the monster with my power, but hers is a power that transcends time so there could be more coming from Brooke Jennings.

I caught Ortega's eyes as she glanced at her grandmother and gave me a quick nod.

This was a new adventure. This is what I had been asking for. And I could not refuse this woman of mystery and power.

"Yes, Grandmother," I said with a small bow of my head. "I

will help you. I will respect your ways and travel into the unknown to find what is lost."

———

I STARTED ALL OF THIS WITH SAYING HOW ARIZONA WASN'T ALL one thing, having both mountains and deserts and a lot more variety than you would think, and how its inhabitants were just as varied. Viewing Arizona as just a big desert is as erroneous as looking at any human as just one thing, good or bad.

At the beginning of all of this, that was much easier to say about those that I love but now I think I can say that about some of the people that have caused me pain.

Annie Smith is not all one thing, and neither was our relationship. Tumultuous, yes, but full of love as well as strife. She's bitter as hell and I can see that, but maybe her time in jail will soften her some, maybe she'll see the part she played in all of this. In any case, I have the Fortune Teller's assurances that she will be watched over.

Winston "Smitty" Smith is not all one thing. He's mostly looking out for himself, yes, but it seems like he just may have changed. Getting caught and going to jail seems to have softened him just a touch. My fear of his sentence being commuted didn't come to pass. He is back in Carterville, yes, but he is supervised, and while I wouldn't say I have hope he will change, I think it's a possibility. More importantly, I have changed. I don't think my hate will magically disappear when it comes to the two of us, but I'm working on it.

Brooke Jennings is not just one thing. She's not just the Fortune Teller, but she is also a victim of her powers, even more than most of us, a young woman that was nearly crushed by what happened to her. Coyote seemed to have bestowed the greatest power on her and she has paid a great price for that power, but that is over now, hopefully. She's not exactly free from her powers, she still has many futures in her head, but hopefully it's enough for her to heal some.

And, most importantly, I'm not one thing. I'm not just the overworked cop in a little town chock-full of mysteries and populated by people with powers. I am not just the Promise Keeper.

I don't know what's next for me and for that I am very, very grateful. The burner phone Brooke gave me is locked away in the Carterville PD armory and I have no intention of ever using it again.

I've returned to Carterville, I've set a new course in my life, one that lets me be in the town that I love so much, but one that doesn't keep me so tied down.

I'm a cop and a private detective now and I just got my first client, Isabella Ortega's grandmother, a Navajo elder, who wants me to find her missing friend.

I don't know much yet, but Ortega and I are headed to Las Vegas for the weekend, where this woman was last seen, to see if we can pick up the trail.

I'm done writing for now. It's time to head out into the unknown and see what the future has in store. It's time to dance with Coyote some more and see what new version of myself awaits.

THE FUTURE OF CARTERVILLE

As of this writing (February, 2025) and with the release of *Return to Carterville*, the *Carterville Mystery Series* is complete—well, as much as any series like this can ever be complete.

At this point the only thing unpublished is a short story which is slated for release in late 2025 as part of a holiday short story collection.

This is my "out of order" series, in that I wrote *The Blood of Carterville* first and was so fascinated with the town, the characters, and the conflicts, that I went back in time and wrote *Out of a Christmas Sky* and *Destroyer of Carterville* to fill in the history.

I then went forward and wrote *Faces of Carterville* and now *Return to Carterville*.

With *The Blood of Carterville* I did what a writer should do, I did one of the worst things I could think of to my protagonist, Henry Carter—I exiled him from the town that bore his name. Now with *Return to Carterville* and with Henry home I feel like I've left Henry in a good spot and can move on to tell other stories with other characters.

My characters feel very real to me and until I got Henry home it felt like I owed him something, and that would be a good end to his story. I think he has that now.

But, you might be thinking—or, at least, I hope you're thinking—there are so many more Carterville stories to tell and you would love to read them!

And, frankly, so would I. Carterville stories are a blast to write and there are so many more stories I could write. I'll give you just a few ideas:

- Since this is my "out of order" series, I'd really like to write an intertwined series from Henry's point of view that starts before *Out of a Christmas Sky* and end before *The Blood of Carterville*. This series would have different powers, different characters, and different conflicts.
- So far I've only written mysteries from the point of view of Henry Carter, but what about a book from Isabella Ortega's point of view when Henry is exiled? Or what about a different genre completely, say a romance, told from a different characters point of view where Henry and the gang are supporting characters?
- What about Henry's promise to find the missing friend of the Ortega's Navajo grandmother? That wouldn't be, strictly speaking, a "Carterville" story but it would be and adventure to be sure.

Lots of potential there, right?

You might be wondering at this point what you can do to get me to return to Carterville with my writing. There are a few things and they all come under the heading of "spreading the word." Things like:

- Give someone a copy and get them into the series
- Leave a review wherever you buy books online (a sentence or two is fine)
- Post on social media about the series
- Reach out to me directly at RobertJMcCarer.com/contact and let me know that you'd like more.
- And be sure to sign up for my newsletter at RobertJMcCarter.com/newsletter so you'll be the first to know when more Carterville is ready for you. Don't forget there's still a fun Christmas short story coming.

Until the next Carterville story is ready, if you'd like a different kind of mystery, check out my *Walter Anchor, Ghost Detective* series. That's right. A ghost who solves murders. The ebook of the first case, *Detecting Haley,* is free when you sign up for my newsletter and there is a huge omnibus edition of his cases called *Unfinished Business: The Cases of Walter Anchor, Ghost Detective.*

ACKNOWLEDGMENTS

Since this book is an ending of sorts for Carterville (at least for now) I guess I should widen my lens a little for this acknowledgment.

The idea for Carterville hit me one morning in Las Vegas in the Golden Nugget Hotel and Casino. I was there for a writer's workshop and the basics of Carterville just appeared in my strange brain while I was doing my morning exercises staring out at the Spring Mountains. So I guess the first thank you is to the group of writers I had been hanging out with and the boost it gave to my imagination.

The second acknowledgement has to be to Stephen King for his series of stories told in Maine. That definitely fed into this and I was following his lead and creating a quirky town with tons of storytelling potential that is close to my own home.

The next person to thank is my amazing and so very supportive wife, Aleia. It is not an exaggeration to say that none of these books would exist without her. It takes her support, encouragement, and patient ear when I read every single book and story to her as part of the editing process. I can't thank you enough for always supporting my writing.

While a writer's job is mostly to be alone in a room making things up, I have a team that helps me once the story is told, so big thanks to by beta readers on this book: Roni Hornstein, Peter Klein, and Eliot Schipper. And a huge thank you to Diana Cox my most capable proofreader for making me look good.

And, most importantly, thanks to you for reading. I hope you have enjoyed your time in Carterville as much as I have!

ABOUT THE AUTHOR

Robert J. McCarter is the author of more than fifteen novels and over one hundred and fifty short stories. He is a regular contributor to *Pulphouse Fiction Magazine* and his short fiction has also appeared in *The Saturday Evening Post, Andromeda Spaceways Inflight Magazine, Everyday Fiction,* and numerous anthologies.

Robert writes in a variety of genres from contemporary fantasy to science fiction and just about everything in between. His diverse background–including a career in software engineering, growing up on a ranch riding horses, and acting–colors the stories he tells.

He lives in the mountains of Arizona with his amazing wife and his ridiculously adorable dogs.

Find out more at:
RobertJMcCarter.com

BOOKS BY ROBERT J. MCCARTER

Carterville Mysteries

- **Out of a Christmas Sky**
- **Destroyer of Carterville**
- **The Blood of Carterville**
- **Faces of Carterville**
- **Return to Carterville**

Walter Anchor, Ghost Detective Stories

- **Case 1: Detecting Haley** (also part of *Life After: Stories of Life, Death, and the Places in Between*)
- **Case 2: The Ghost Bride's Gift**
- **Case 3: A Long Hard Fall**
- **Case 4: Death of a Dentist**
- **Case 5: A Hollywood Kind of a Murder**
- **Case 6: The Red Arrow Murders**
- **Unfinished Business: The Cases of Walter Anchor Ghost Detective**

For a complete list of Walter Anchor stories, go to RobertJMcCarter.com/WalterAnchor

Novels in the "Ghost's Memoir" world:

- Shuffled Off: A Ghost's Memoir, Book 1
- Drawing the Dead
- To Be a Fool: A Ghost's Memoir, Book 2

- Of Things Not Seen: A Ghost's Memoir, Book 3
- A Boy, a Girl, and a Ghost

For a complete list the "Ghost's Memoir" novels, go to ShuffledOff.com

The Woody and June versus the Apocalypse Series

Find out more at WoodyAndJune.com

The Neutrinoman and Lightningirl Series

Find out more at Neutrinoman.com

Other Novels:

- Seeing Forever
- Where the Past Belongs: An Angelica and Ash Time Travel Adventure

For a more information, go to RobertJMcCarter.com